"Brace for impact!"

The tail of the [obscured by barcode] air. Alarms sou[nded] the consoles. Zano[obscured]

Bolan gritted h[obscured] kicked her peda[obscured] ...tted into emergency war power. The helicopter bucked, tilted, lifted and yawed as it slewed across the sky. Bolan had been in this type of situation before. They were done. The flight was over. The Dauphin started to turn into its death spiral.

"We're going down!" Zanotto punched the transmit button. "Mayday! Mayday! This is Flight Z-1. We are going down at coordinates—"

Bolan reached over and twisted the radio bandwidth. Nothing happened. It was as if the knob had been set and then snapped off on the Shield tactical frequency. "We're cut off!" he shouted.

Smoke oozed through the air vents and the fire alarm was peeping and blinking plaintively.

Bolan watched Afghanistan hurtle toward them.

MACK BOLAN ®

The Executioner

The Executioner

Don Pendleton's

AMBUSH FORCE

A GOLD EAGLE BOOK FROM

W🦅RLDWIDE.

TORONTO • NEW YORK • LONDON
AMSTERDAM • PARIS • SYDNEY • HAMBURG
STOCKHOLM • ATHENS • TOKYO • MILAN
MADRID • WARSAW • BUDAPEST • AUCKLAND

First edition May 2008

ISBN-13: 978-0-373-64354-7
ISBN-10:   0-373-64354-3

Special thanks and acknowledgment to
Charles Rogers for his contribution to this work.

AMBUSH FORCE

Printed in U.S.A.

Men who take up arms against one another in public do not cease on this account to be moral beings, responsible to one another and to God.

—U.S. Army General Order No. 100, 1863

Men who betray their fellow soldiers will face judgment from their God. But, before that happens, they will face judgment from me.

—Mack Bolan

THE
MACK BOLAN
LEGEND

Nothing less than a war could have fashioned the destiny of the man called Mack Bolan. Bolan earned the Executioner title in the jungle hell of Vietnam.

But this soldier also wore another name—Sergeant Mercy. He was so tagged because of the compassion he showed to wounded comrades-in-arms and Vietnamese civilians.

Mack Bolan's second tour of duty ended prematurely when he was given emergency leave to return home and bury his family, victims of the Mob. Then he declared a one-man war against the Mafia.

He confronted the Families head-on from coast to coast, and soon a hope of victory began to appear. But Bolan had broken society's every rule. That same society started gunning for this elusive warrior—to no avail.

So Bolan was offered amnesty to work within the system against terrorism. This time, as an employee of Uncle Sam, Bolan became Colonel John Phoenix. With a command center at Stony Man Farm in Virginia, he and his new allies—Able Team and Phoenix Force—waged relentless war on a new adversary: the KGB.

But when his one true love, April Rose, died at the hands of the Soviet terror machine, Bolan severed all ties with Establishment authority.

Now, after a lengthy lone-wolf struggle and much soul-searching, the Executioner has agreed to enter an "arm's-length" alliance with his government once more, reserving the right to pursue personal missions in his Everlasting War.

1

Stony Man Farm, Virginia

Alpha squad had been slaughtered. Mack Bolan flipped through the file. The reinforced squad of U.S. Army Rangers had gone into the Jalkot Canyon area of Afghanistan, and to a man they had come back in body bags. They hadn't just been killed; they had been stripped and quite possibly tortured. The exact circumstances of their deaths were uncertain because their bodies had been decapitated, doused with kerosene and burned.

"This stinks to high hell, Bear."

Aaron "The Bear" Kurtzman nodded and sipped his coffee. "That's what everyone at the Joint Chiefs of Staff is thinking, but no one is willing to say."

Bolan ran his finger over a map of Afghanistan. "The Rangers were supposed to be intercepting a Taliban courier?"

"That was the mission profile. A simple grab and go. An informant gave the CIA the courier's route and a timetable. The weird thing is that according to intel, both the sector that got hit at and the adjacent one have been pacified."

Bolan peered at the map. "Looks like the courier's route was right along the sector border."

"Again, it's weird. As a matter of fact, both sectors are supposed to be models of the post-Taliban reconstruction of Afghanistan. In Sector G, they're growing saffron for the spice market, and in H Valley next door they're growing flowers for the European perfume industry. According to reports, they're paving roads, building schools and there's not a woman in a beekeeper suit in sight. Before they were pacified, both sectors were nothing but poppy fields ruled by Taliban-friendly warlords like medieval fiefs."

"Who's running the show?"

"German coalition forces cleared both sectors."

"Interesting."

"I don't need to tell you, Striker. The Bundeswehr doesn't mess around. They give both the U.S. and the UK a run for our military-professionalism money. They've quadrupled their patrols and have poured in men and matériel."

Bolan had worked with the German army. They were about as good as soldiers got.

Kurtzman pulled up a file on his computer. "Shield Security Services has some operators in the area providing private security for some of the local businessmen and foreign contractors."

That was interesting, as well. Shield was the top shelf of international private security and hired only the best.

"It still stinks. How did they sneak past the German patrols? This was way too professional for the Taliban," Bolan argued.

"Well, you've got to admit they've been getting slicker. They had decades of getting fat and sloppy, looting the country of its wealth, beating women with sticks and stoning men in soccer fields for minor religious infractions. The coalition may have come in and kicked their collective asses, but they aren't gone. The Taliban are lean, hungry, angry and learning their lessons the hard way."

That was all very true, but it still didn't answer Bolan's questions. "I'm not buying a random band of Taliban bumping into Rangers in the field and wiping them out. This was a planned ambush."

"So…" Kurtzman took a meditative sip of coffee. "Are you willing to tell the President what no one else will?"

"Yeah." Bolan nodded. "This was an inside job. The question is who."

Briefing room, Tent City, Kabul

THE MEN FROM DELTA FORCE were seething. Nearly all Delta Force commandos were chosen from the United States Army Ranger Regiment. The Rangers were the Army's elite. That made Delta Force the elite of the elite. Delta Force commandos remembered their days as Rangers and knew with great pride that the Ranger Regiment was where they had launched their careers as Special Forces soldiers.

Now an entire squad of Rangers had been killed, beheaded and burned. The assembled Delta team was going hunting for some payback.

"All right, ladies!" The black lieutenant looked like an NFL linebacker who had been shoved through a trash compactor. He barely cracked five-six but he weighed 180 if he weighed an ounce, and his Afro pushed the limits of U.S. military hairstyle acceptability. Lieutenant Richard Dirk was "Dick Dirk" to his friends and equals in rank and affectionately known as "the Diggler" behind his back. The vertically challenged Special Forces officer had amassed a sizable legend for neutralizing the designated enemies of Uncle Sam on three continents and was currently working on his fourth. His voice was out of all proportion to his size. "Listen up! We're going hunting tonight, and your Uncle Sam in his merciful compassion had been kind enough to send us an observer to make sure we don't screw up!"

Groans and muttered expletives greeted the lieutenant's announcement.

"So I would like you all to give a warm, Delta Force welcome to Mr. Matthew Cooper from the Justice Department!"

Mack Bolan walked into the tent.

A lanky blond commando named Sawyer drawled out his disgust with an accent straight out of the hills of Tennessee. "Christ, LT, who is this fucking cherry? I—" Sawyer leaned back in his seat as Bolan locked eyes with him. It took a lot to give a Delta Force commando pause, but whatever Sawyer saw behind Bolan's blue eyes stopped him midsentence. "Shit, dude, don't look at me like that."

That wasn't enough for Lieutenant Dirk. "You will shitcan that talk, Sawyer, or I will personally correct your cracker attitude for you! You read me?"

Sawyer recoiled before the wrath of his commanding officer. "Shit, LT! Yeah—I mean, yes, sir! I mean…." Sawyer regained some of his composure. "But what the hell, LT? Are we Commies now with political officers spying on our asses? What the hell is an asshole from the goddamn Department of Justice doing here? Makin' sure we don't commit no atrocities? I mean who sent him? The Supreme Court?"

Dirk seemed to grow and expand in rage and stature as he prepared to rain his wrath on Sawyer.

Bolan interrupted the dressing-down. "Permission to address your men, Lieutenant."

Lieutenant Dirk continued to glare bloody murder at Sawyer. "Oh, by all means. Please do."

"Who is the angry god of your universe?" Bolan addressed the tent at large.

Bolan had files on all the men present. A hulking Latino private in the back named Obradors shot up his hand. "Why, Mr. Cooper, we do dastardly deeds for the Diggler!"

Lieutenant Dirk rolled his eyes and mostly kept the benevolent smile off his face.

"Well," Bolan conceded, "the lieutenant is the Messiah, but who is God?"

Special Forces operator opinions flew around the tent.

"Jesus?"

"Santa Claus?"

"Anheuser-Busch?"

Bolan shook his head. "No, it's the big guy in the round room." The tent grew quiet as Bolan invoked the commander in chief. "He's taken a personal interest in your situation."

Jaws set nervously and brows furrowed. That might be extraordinarily good or horrifically bad news. It was generally considered best not to have the Man's attention at all except when he was handing out medals.

Bolan tapped the com-link clipped to his shirt. "Gentlemen, I am not here to observe you, usurp command or steal your thunder. I am here to deliver the thunder. The standard chain of command has been circumvented. We will not be going through the Pentagon or United Nations coalition command. I am here to make sure that fire support, extraction and real-time data are available as needed. Short of a nuclear strike, it is my job to make sure that you receive everything you need." Bolan shrugged. "If you require a tactical nuclear strike, I can't promise it, but I will ask the President of the United States for it directly. However, if my services aren't required..."

"Oh, hell no!" Sawyer grinned delightedly. "Your shit is sacred, brother."

"Fuckin' ay," Obradors agreed.

Bolan nodded to himself. The Delta Force commando team was leaning forward eagerly. Everyone loved divine intervention. "Captain Fairfax will brief you on the mission."

"You heard the man!" Dirk bawled. "Now I would like you all to turn your kind attention to our friend and leader, Captain Fairfax!"

The commandos whooped for their commanding officer. Fairfax had been in Somalia and earned his officer's stripes and the jagged scar along his jaw the hard way.

Lieutenant Dirk edged up to Bolan as the briefing began. "Do you mind if I ask you a question?"

"By all means, Lieutenant."

"No offense meant, but, uh, just who in the blue hell are you, anyway? Don't get me wrong. It's nice that the Man has taken an interest in our little situation, but why exactly are they sending me a Fed?"

"None taken, and I'm not a Fed."

Dirk cocked his head suspiciously. "Well, you work for the Justice Department, don't you?"

"No."

Lieutenant Dirk blinked. "No?"

"No."

"I was told you did."

"That was a misinterpretation."

"Well, we're going out tonight, me and you." The lieutenant's eyes went hard. "So why don't you illuminate my ignorant black ass?"

Bolan sighed. He had been a soldier, and there was nothing worse than strange, murky individuals suddenly popping up from stateside during an operation. It implied mission creep and goat screws of epic proportions. "I don't work for the Justice Department. I have a working relationship with the United States government, and when I choose to take action, I liaise with the President through the DOJ."

"A…working relationship, and when *you* choose to take action you talk with the Man?" That gave even Dirk pause.

"Yeah."

"Directly?"

"Sometimes," Bolan admitted.

"So…you're a spook?"

"No, though I've been spooky."

"Paramilitary?" Dirk tried.

The man was getting warmer. "I guess you could call me an operator of a sort."

"You're—" Dirk's nose wrinkled in suspicion "—a merc?"

"Naw." Bolan shook his head. "I don't get paid."

"You don't get paid?" Lieutenant Dirk regarded Bolan like a primatologist who has just encountered a gorilla with wings. "So you're a…volunteer, spookerator, with a direct line to the President who does this out of love?"

"Close," Bolan conceded. "And payback. I'm pretty big on payback."

Dirk suddenly grinned. "Well, hell, that's all you had to say! Count me in!"

Bolan looked at Lieutenant Dirk long and hard. "You want in all the way?"

The lieutenant cocked his head. "You mean join the all-volunteer spookerator love and payback club? Sorry, man, I appreciate the offer, but I'm Delta all the way."

"What if I said I might need you on a one-shot deal, and it involves the dead Rangers."

"I'd ask you to clarify that a little."

"I think it was an inside job."

"Inside job?" Dirk's face became a mask of stone. "That's some real messed-up shit you're implying there, Spooky."

"Problem is, I don't have any proof. To get it, and get payback, I'm going to have to go inside. I'm going to need someone like you to piggyback my way in, and frankly I don't mind admitting I'd like to have someone like you on my six."

"This is getting really goddamn deep and dark."

"Listen, if we come back from this op tonight alive, and you trust me after, I'd like to buy you a beer and talk about it more."

"Ooh!" Dirk grinned. "Beer."

Pandit Valley

"WHERE THE HELL IS Coop?" Dirk hissed. "I told him to keep his civilian ass on my—"

Bolan spoke quietly. "I'm right here."

"Jesus!" Dirk turned around. "I thought you were arranging satellite feed."

"I was."

"Well, don't sneak up on a brother like that!"

"I didn't. I've been here for five minutes."

"Man… So what have we got?"

"It's a series of caves. The local villagers say two years ago there were some earthmoving machines up in the hills. There's no known mining in the area, and satellite recon shows no new construction. Most likely, what we have is a tunnel complex, probably using the preexisting caves as a template. Thermal-imaging satellites show low-level heat signatures venting from several sources around the cave area, probably cook fires."

"Great." Lieutenant Dirk wasn't pleased. In his experience the only thing worse than urban warfare was tunnel fighting. "We're going to have to dig them out hole by hole."

"I'll have a map of the complex ready in another couple of minutes."

Dirk brightened. "Someone gave you a map of the place? Why didn't you say so?"

"No one gave me a map. Someone's making me one."

Dirk paused. "Someone's making you one?"

"Yeah, hold on." Bolan pressed the mike on his secure line. "How we doing, Strike Eagle?"

Jack Grimaldi, Stony Man Farm's premier pilot, came back across the line. "Striker, I am over the target area."

Gadgets Schwarz came across the radio. He was Able Team's technical whiz, and Bolan had asked him to come up with something that would give them the edge on the dug-in Taliban. Schwarz loved a challenge and as usual had come up aces. "Striker, we are ready to deploy."

"Deploy when ready, Strike Eagle."

Dirk cleared his throat. "So, uh, who is deploying?"

Bolan looked upward. "I have a couple of friends of mine up at about twenty thousand feet in an F-15E Strike Eagle."

"Oh?" Dirk contemplated that. "What are they deploying?"

"UAVs."

Dirk nodded. U.S. Special Forces were ever increasingly discovering the joys of working with Unmanned Aerial Vehicles. "So what are they going to do for us? Fly in the cave and blow everything up?"

"No, we want prisoners and we also want any papers, computer files, cell phones or intelligence we can get our hands on. So it would be best if we went in and took care of business ourselves, by hand."

Dirk frowned beneath his night-vision goggles. "Okay, so…"

"So the UAVs are carrying ground-penetrating radar units. GPR scans work best in solid rock formations that will resonate to the radar pulses. The good news is that those caves are mostly solid granite. We're deploying three UAVs. With any luck, within a few minutes we'll have a three-dimensional map of the complex."

Dirk stared up at the stars. "Aren't our little friends going to hear the buzz bombs as they come in?"

"The UAVs are gliders. Once they're near the target, they fold their wings, deploy steerable chutes and extend padded all-aspect legs. GPR works better in direct contact with the ground, so the legs act as the antennas."

"You know, I thought I had access to all the cool toys, but this is shit I ain't even heard of."

Bolan shrugged. "I happen to know the director of the Future Warrior Project in Massachusetts. I gave her a call, and my friends brought over a few working prototypes."

Dirk considered that and how quickly it had come about. "Jesus, you really can make the magic happen."

"I'm a helper," Bolan agreed. "I'm here to help."

Dirk snorted in bemusement, and then Bolan and Bravo troop waited long minutes. The commando spoke quietly. "The Man wants blood for blood, doesn't he?"

"From what I understand, favors are being called in. More than favors—the U.S. is giving markers to people we'd normally never get in bed with," Bolan said.

"Except that no one gets to ice eighteen Rangers and walk away," Dirk stated.

"No, the Rangers get payback. No one is walking away. The President wrote a blank check to get a line on these caves, and he wants to see people in bags for his money."

Schwarz's voice came across the link. "Striker, this is Strike Eagle. The Eaglets have landed. We have solid returns from One and Two. Eaglet Three must have landed wrong. We are mapping. You should be able to pull it up."

"Copy that, Strike Eagle." Bolan pulled out a small handheld device and watched as the screen filled with radar patterns. Bolan examined the screen. "We've got one main entrance that leads in and up about fifteen yards and opens up into a large chamber. By shape it's a natural cave, about thirty yards by forty. Two tunnels branch off, one straight back and another off to the left, each about ten yards. They're straight and level, cut by machines, and each leads to another chamber. The chambers are symmetrical, and again, man-made. One appears to be filled with a number of large, symmetrical objects. The two chambers both have a tunnel coming out of them and meet in a fifth chamber. Basically, the complex is a rough hexagon, each chamber connected by a tunnel."

Dirk stared at what appeared on the screen to be little more than blobs and streaks. "If you say so."

Bolan pulled out a stylus, traced the diagram and killed the flashes of the radar pulses behind it, leaving five circles each connected by a line. "That's your map. I'm sending it to the PDA of each man in the troop." Bolan pressed Send and a few seconds later each man in Bravo troop signaled he had the map.

"God…damn," Dirk opined.

"I told you the President was writing a blank check on this one."

"Then by all means, let's give the man his money's worth." Dirk spoke into his tactical radio. "All units. Start moving in."

Bolan and Bravo troop began moving through the rocks. Delta Force always had access to the best toys, and Bolan had been given the keys to the candy store. Each man in the reinforced squad was equipped with a SCAR rifle chambered for the Russian 7.62 mm round. It was ballistically comparable to the old Winchester .30-30, but Bolan had no complaints about that. Some people thought the U.S. .223 was too light and didn't have enough stopping power. Others thought the other major U.S. military small-arms round, the .308, was too heavy and had too much recoil. The 7.62 mm was the porridge the Russian Bear had chosen, and her soldiers had collectively wept when they'd abandoned it to try to emulate the Americans.

These rifles were firing heavy subsonic bullets and had suppressor tubes fitted over their muzzles.

Bravo troop was as silent as wolves running through fog.

Corporal Sawyer's voice came across the link. "I got two sentries by the entrance to the cave beneath camouflaged shelters."

"You got a line of fire?"

"Affirmative."

"Take 'em," Dirk ordered.

Bolan was close enough to Sawyer to hear the action of his automatic rifle click twice and two spent pieces of brass tinkle to the ground. At the cave mouth, nothing seemed to happen save that an arm flopped out from what appeared to be solid rock.

"Sentries down," Sawyer said.

"Move in," Dirk ordered. "By the numbers."

"Mind if I take point?"

"Oh, by all means, please." Dirk waved Bolan forward expansively. "I'm sure Sawyer would love the company."

Dirk spoke into his radio. "Sawyer, wait on Striker."

"Copy that."

Bolan moved forward to Sawyer's position. "Corporal."

"Nice to see you up front, Coop. In my experience, civilians tend to lead from the back."

Bolan scanned the entrance. From Sawyer's angle, the Executioner could see that the rocks overhanging the cave mouth were really awnings, blankets stiffened with clay and dirt and stretched across stick frames so that they looked like rock formations. It was an old trick and a good one.

"You ready to step into the funhouse, Sunshine?"

"After you."

They moved to the mouth of the cave. Beneath the camouflaged awning, two men in local dress lay facedown with a single bullet hole through their heads. "We're in, Bravo. Come ahead."

Bolan and Sawyer moved down the tunnel. Bolan ran a hand along the wall. It was rough and appeared to have been recently widened. It was wide enough to drive a jeep through. Bolan knelt and found tire tracks in dirt among the many footprints. "Bravo Leader, this is Striker. Be advised there has been vehicle traffic in the complex. At least jeep size."

"Copy that, Striker," Dirk replied. "We're coming in."

Dirk left a team outside watching their six, and the rest entered. Bolan and Sawyer crept down the tunnel. Both men held up their fists for "Halt" and crouched at the entrance to a large chamber. There were about fifty men in the cave, and several fires burned. Many were asleep. Others crouched in small circles drinking tea and talking or running rags over their rifles.

Sawyer shoved up his goggles. "Well, I count fifty, and the map says there are four more caves."

"Most of them are sleeping."

"Well, how you wanna wake 'em up?"

Bolan reached into his gear bag, pulled out four grenades and handed a pair of them to Sawyer.

Sawyer stared at them. "Frags?"

"Stingballs. Each one holds several dozen hard rubber buckshot pellets."

Sawyer scowled. "Okay, that will probably wake them up, but then—"

Bolan pulled out a couple of Claymores.

Sawyer frowned. "Claymores? I thought you said you wanted prisoners."

"Stingmores. These contain hundreds of rubber buckshot pellets."

Sawyer grinned. "I think I saw this in a movie."

The lieutenant came up, and Bolan related the plan to him. "Then we hit them with flash-bangs and stomp them," Bolan finished.

Dirk was grinning as he turned to the two commandos behind him. "You heard the man. They beat 'em, and then we light 'em up!"

Bolan pulled the pins on his grenade. "On your signal, Lieutenant."

"By all means, please."

Bolan and Dirk hurled the grenades strategically throughout the cavern.

"Wakey, wakey, eggs and bakey!" Sawyer called out happily.

The men around the campfires jerked and rose, grabbing for weapons. Bolan and Sawyer crouched low and lowered their helmets, and the stingball grenades detonated. Men howled out in Arabic and Pashto as the blunt 20 mm rubber spheres traveling at five hundred feet per second struck them. Everyone else was leaping out of their blankets and rising while others fell around them.

Bolan and Sawyer stuck the stingmore mines into the dirt and pumped the detonator switches. "Gooooood morning, Afghanistan!" Sawyer sang out.

More than one thousand rubber buckshot pellets blasted across the cavern in two intersecting arcs, and men blinking from sleep were scythed down before they knew what hit them. Bolan and Sawyer stayed crouched, plugging their ears with their thumbs and shutting and covering their eyes with their fingers. Orange light still pulsed through Bolan's eyelids, and thunder rolled through the cavern. The second salvo of flash-bangs detonated moments later, and then Bolan was up and in the cavern with Bravo troop swarming in behind him.

The devastation was almost total. Fifty men lay on the ground, beaten, blinded, deafened and disoriented.

Lieutenant Dirk roared, "A and B Teams! Secure the side tunnels! Everyone else secure prisoners!"

The two teams charged to the side tunnels and aimed overwhelming firepower down them. In the cavern, plastic zip restraints appeared like party favors and moaning, suspected Taliban where swiftly hog-tied.

Gunfire broke out in the right side tunnel. Sawyer bawled back into the cavern. "We got resistance here on the right, LT!"

Dirk shouted orders. "C Team! Reinforce B! D Team, you're with me! Pincer movement!"

Bolan took point with Sawyer. Both of them had M-203 grenade launchers mounted beneath their rifles. The Executioner nodded at him, and they both fired the weapons down the tunnel and leaned back as the grenades detonated in the chamber beyond. They charged down the corridor, followed by Dirk with A and D teams. The chamber was dimly lit and filled with open metal racks. Two men lay dead on the floor, while another man clutched his face and fired a pistol in the general direction of the entrance. Bolan's and Sawyer's bursts peppered the would-be pistolero. He fell into one of the metal racks, and a row of six of them fell like dominoes.

Sawyer stared at the rows of racks. There were scores of them. Possibly a hundred or more. "What? Are they building a treehouse?"

Bolan stared at them. The racks were actually frames consisting of eight hollow aluminum rectangles bolted together. Each was about eight feet long and contained a series of metal hoops within them. Bolan estimated the diameter of the hoops to be approximately 132 mm. "No, those are rocket racks. The hoops inside are the launch rails." Bolan peered at the dark entrance to the next tunnel and turned to Dirk. "I strongly suggest we don't throw anything explosive into the next room."

"Yeah, I hear you." Dirk spoke into his radio, "Obie, what've you got?"

Obradors came back from the other side of the complex. "Two hostiles down. The chamber appears to be some kind of machine shop. Multiple generators and lots of welding equipment. Looks like they've been making frames and mounts for something, as well as a bunch of threaded collars, and I mean a lot of them."

Bolan spoke across the link. "You got a diameter on those collars, Obie?"

"Yeah, uh, about five inches?"

Bolan frowned as his suspicions were confirmed. "Anything else?"

"Yeah, your map?" Obradors said.

"What about it?"

"It's shit. There ain't no fifth chamber."

"What do you mean?" Bolan probed.

"I mean there ain't no tunnel. The wall is blank."

Dirk looked at Bolan. "And?"

"And ground-penetrating radar doesn't lie. Tell B and C teams to hold position and don't touch anything. Especially the walls."

Dirk gave orders. Bolan jerked his head at the far tunnel. "Let's see what's behind door number three." Bolan moved down the tunnel with Sawyer right behind him. There was no one in the next chamber, but it wasn't empty.

"Shit," Sawyer pronounced. "Missiles."

Bolan stared at the pallets of weapons stacked in pyramids. "No, unguided artillery rockets, 132 mm. The Russians call them *Katyushas,* or 'Little Katys.'"

"Jesus, they must have a hundred of them in here."

Dirk had one of his men videotaping their find. "A lot of them seem to be missing their warheads."

"Yeah," Bolan agreed, "and Obie has a machine shop on the other side of the complex making 132 mm threaded collars."

"Shit," Sawyer said.

"Shit is right," Bolan said. "You notice anything else."

Sawyer looked around the room and stopped. "There's no tunnel. No fifth chamber. Just like Obie said."

Bolan clicked on his private link. "Strike Eagle, this is Striker. Give me another GPR pulse, and triangulate the position of the tunnel to chamber five from my position."

"Copy that, Striker," Schwarz responded. "Coming up."

Bolan took out his little computer and watched as the GPR pulses flashed across his screen. Up in the stratosphere, Schwarz was scribbling with his stylus. The pulses faded, and the map of the complex appeared. A dot appeared in the chamber where Bolan was standing.

"That dot is you, Striker." A straight line appeared on the little map that went from Bolan's position through the tunnel to the fifth chamber. "The tunnel entrance is exactly ten degrees east from your position."

"Copy that." Bolan walked up to what appeared to be a roughly dressed but blank stone wall.

Dirk played the tactical light on his weapon across the rock face. "So, there's like a secret knob or something?"

"No. The tunnel's been sealed off from the outside. There probably isn't even a door, just brick or concrete with a layer of clay and rock molded over it for camouflage."

Dirk scowled. "You said sealed from the outside?"

"Think about it. If we hadn't used GPR, what would have happened? We'd have come in, kicked ass, destroyed the rockets and then dropped the caverns with explosives and walked away happy, mission accomplished. We never would have known to look for a fifth chamber."

"Yeah—" Dirk nodded as he saw it "—and the Taliban could come back later when the coast was clear and dig it up."

"Right. You got some shaped charges?"

"I believe we do." Dirk turned to one of his men. "Penner! Coop here would like you to make him a door!"

The demolition man came forward and stared at the wall. "Okay, assuming concrete, assuming the same diameter as the other tunnels…" Penner mumbled to himself in demo-speak as he put together a breaching charge and then packed the plastique brick against the section of wall. He took a few steps back from his work and pressed his detonator box. "Fire in the hole!"

The detonation was anticlimactic. There was a thump and a pulse of fire around the edges of the charge, but the explosive had been shaped to blow inward against the wall. A two-foot section of the rock wall was gone to reveal that Bolan was right. The tunnel had been bricked up and then covered with a layer of clay and rock. Penner and another commando went at the sagging brick with entrenching tools. They cleared a four-foot entrance and stepped back.

Bolan shone his tactical light down the tunnel. It was exactly the same as the other, and the entrance to the fifth chamber opened into darkness at the end of it. "You better let me go first. This part may be booby-trapped."

Dirk nodded. "Be my guest."

Bolan crawled through the hole and slowly went down the tunnel. Dust filled the air from the blast. He went into the chamber and played his light across several pallets laden with crates. The crates had Cyrillic writing on them. Bolan didn't read Russian, but he didn't need to. Nor did he need to open any of the crates. He recognized the green circle with the three-lobed, red warning sign for chemical hazard, and he recognized the colored bar code and the serial numbers and letters beneath it.

Dirk came across the radio. "What do we have, Coop?"

"We've got cyclosarin nerve gas." Bolan ran his light across the piled pallets. "A lot of it."

2

Tent City, Kabul

Aaron Kurtzman was well pleased, and his face showed it across the video link. "Everyone is singing your praises, Striker. Delta Force is oozing goodwill, and Hal said the President wants to clone a hundred of you in assorted colors."

"Yeah." It hadn't been a bad op. Some very unpleasant adversaries had gone down, and something very ugly had been averted.

"You don't seem pleased. You don't think you got the right boys?"

"Oh, we got the right Taliban boys, but we didn't get the thugs who backed their play against the Rangers."

"You still believe someone betrayed the Rangers' location?"

"It was more than just a tip-off. The Taliban had intel on composition and numbers, and they had serious backup. Light-support weapons, at least, being used by people who knew what they were doing. Even in the most desperate of circumstances, Army Rangers should have been able to fight their way out of a Taliban ambush. Instead, they were cut to pieces. Even in the face of overwhelming numbers, a few should have been able to escape and evade. We have hundred percent casualties. That's unheard-of, Bear, but since they were mutilated, beheaded, burned and their bodies stacked like cordwood, it's a little difficult to determine exactly what happened. So everyone is screaming Taliban."

"Yeah, well, it's Afghanistan, Striker—people scream Taliban with good reason."

"Bear, someone sold that gas to the Taliban. You want to take out a reinforced squad of U.S. Army Rangers with hundred percent casualties? How about starting a firefight in a narrow canyon and then ending it with nerve gas."

Kurtzman was no longer smiling. "Yeah, nerve agents are nonpersistent. So when help finally arrived, they found spent shell casings and RPG hits and suspected nothing."

"And the bodies were burned to prevent any telltales of nerve-agent exposure to be found."

Kurtzman let out a long breath. "Well, that means you're right. Someone set up the Rangers, someone gave the Taliban nerve agents and someone with the expertise had to be present to deploy the gas correctly."

"That's right, and it happened on German army turf."

"Striker, the Germans haven't produced chemical weapons since World War II."

"The East Germans did."

"Those stockpiles were destroyed—" Kurtzman sighed unhappily "—supposedly. You're going to have a hard time penetrating the German army."

"I can't, and winding a black turban around my head and pretending to be Taliban isn't going to work, either." Bolan flipped through his file again. "You said the Shield protection agency has contractors working in the area?"

"For God's sake, what are you trying to say?"

"Nothing I can prove, and nothing anybody will want to hear. Hell, I'm probably wrong, and frankly I hope I am. But we won't know unless I go in and tear things open. What I am saying is eighteen Army Rangers are dead. And if the United States Army Rangers are after you, you'd better have a weapon of mass destruction, because that's the only way you're going to stop them. I think that's exactly what happened, and far as I can see there are three possible players. I can't join the Taliban, and I don't speak German."

Kurtzman's craggy brow furrowed. "So you're going to join Shield."

"They're independent contractors," Bolan said. "It's probably the only cover I can use to poke around."

"They've got a waiting list a mile long," Kurtzman argued. "They've got Special Forces guys from all over the world taking early retirement just to join up."

Bolan nodded. "I know, so I'm going to need a guy they would kill to have join them and then piggyback my way in."

Kurtzman perked an eyebrow. "You have someone in mind."

Bolan grinned. "Indeed I do."

BRIGADIER EUGENE TOLER PEERED at Lieutenant Dirk's fist somewhat apprehensively. He sighed, rolled his eyes and then shook his head at Bolan. "Mr. Cooper, are we sure this is absolutely necessary?"

Bolan didn't blame the English officer one bit. The lieutenant's fists, like a lot of things about him, were oversized for his frame. "I'm afraid so, sir."

Captain Fairfax stood to one side shaking his head. He had been in Special Forces for decades, and nothing had ever prepared him for the utter surrealty of this situation, much less the fact that he was about to lose his best officer.

Dirk took a deep breath, and his knuckles creaked and popped as he balled up the soup bones. He looked at his hand as if it didn't belong to him and then at the brigadier. "You ready, sir?"

"Well…right!" The brigadier squared his shoulders, thrust out his jaw, straightened the front of his battle dress uniform and, like English officers and gentlemen since time immemorial, found refuge in Shakespeare. "'Lay on, McDuff.'"

It was a beauty of a whistling right hook. Brigadier Toler was a big man, but his head whiplashed on his neck as he flew back across the folding table behind him. It wasn't an act. The folding table collapsed beneath him, and he, his computer, monitor and everything else on his desk hit the floor with a tremendous crash.

Dirk's voice boomed out at parade-ground volume. "You limey son of a bitch! Good men died because of you!"

"Goddamn it, Lieutenant!" Fairfax bawled. "What in the blue hell do you think you're doing?"

Toler pushed himself to a sitting position in the wreckage and matched Dirk and Fairfax decibel for decibel. "Mr. Pitt!"

Toler's aide-de-camp peeked his head in and stared in horror.

"Mr. Pitt!" The brigadier pointed a damning finger at Dirk. "Place that man under arrest!"

"Sir!" The bookish young man visibly braced himself. "Guards!"

"Lieutenant Dirk is an American officer and can only be confined or charged by a U.S. military order!" Fairfax snarled.

"That man serves under NATO Afghanistan Coalition Command, and by God, I'll see him tried and court-martialed under its bloody aegis!"

Bolan didn't feel the need to add anything. It was all rolling along very nicely.

Pitt's voice rose a panicked octave. "Guards…"

It was Fairfax's turn to be outraged. "You can't do this!"

"I can and will!" Toler thundered.

"Guards…"

British soldiers with the scarlet-peaked caps of the Royal Military Police came charging into the tent. Toler lurched to his feet. A magnificent shiner was inflating all around his left eye. "Guards! The American lieutenant has just struck a superior officer! Put him under close arrest!"

The MPs' faces went from surprise to bloodred rage. A Yank had taken a poke at one of their officers. Truncheons rattled out of their sheaths.

Fairfax took a step forward. "By God! If you think—"

Toler roared like a wounded lion. "If the captain opens his bleeding gob again, clap him in irons for obstruction!"

Dirk beckoned the brigadier in. "Oh, you want some more of this? You limey mother—"

The Redcaps dived into Dirk. Dirk disposed of one with a hip throw and staggered one with a right hand before he took a truncheon thrust to the guts and the other two RMPs dived into his legs. Pitt couldn't have weighed more than 115 pounds dripping wet, but the brigadier's aide hurled himself into the fray with the enthusiasm and fury of wounded national pride.

The fight went to the ground and became a wrestling match. Dirk was a Special Forces soldier in prime physical condition, but taking down soldiers was what the RMPs were trained to do and numbers and weight told their ugly tale. The Redcaps inexorably got the upper hand, as well as an arm and ankle lock. Then the truncheons began falling on Dirk like rain. They continued to fall until he stopped moving. The Redcaps snapped on the handcuffs and kept Dirk pinned while Brigadier Toler's aide stood. The young man was shaking with adrenaline reaction, and his broken nose hung on his face like a flattened squid. "Prisoner is secure, sir!"

"Very good, Mr. Pitt. Have him placed in the brig and confined in full restraints. Once he's properly shackled, fetch a medic around to have a look at him."

"Yes, sir!"

Captain Fairfax's face was ashen. "This is intolerable. That man is an American officer!"

"That man will require a lawyer." Toler's voice dropped to reptilian coldness. "As his commanding officer, I suggest it is your immediate duty to see to it."

U.S. military stockade, Kabul

BOLAN WALKED INTO THE CELL and handed Lieutenant Dirk a short, two-page document. "Here you go."

Dirk took the paper. The Redcaps hadn't been gentle. His face was lumped as though he'd been attacked by a swarm of Alaskan mosquitoes. He quickly read the first page and flipped to the second and looked at the signatures and seals. "Jesus, I really am eatin' the big chicken dinner."

Bolan smiled. "You want salt with that?"

Dirk rolled his eyes ruefully. The big chicken dinner was U.S. military slang for a bad-conduct discharge. Dirk had dodged the bullet. The fix had been put in, but not everyone was in on it. There had been a chance the court-martial could have gone wrong and Dirk could have gotten the full dishonorable discharge. That was something that followed a man around like a pet for the rest of his life. A dishonorable discharge was one of the few stigmas left in American life that was like the mark of Cain. The United States Military was an all-volunteer organization. A person had to want to join up. To be dishonorably discharged implied that you had dishonored your country and the service. Nearly every application for employment in the United States first asked if you had ever served in the United States armed forces and if you had been honorably or dishonorably discharged. Given a choice, it seemed as if most employers would rather hire a thief, a murderer or a pedophile before they would give a job to a man with a dishonorable discharge hanging over his head.

The good news was that despite Brigadier Toler's highly credible Old Testament thunder, the United States would not let its soldiers be tried by foreign military tribunals whether or not they had the NATO or United Nations stamp of approval. The court-martial had been one of the swiftest ones in recent history. The reasons for the lieutenant's actions were considered top secret. Mission information leading up to the incident had been redacted. His two Silver Stars for conspicuous bravery had been mentioned early and often, as was the fact that while Brigadier Toler may well have been a superior officer, he was but an officer in the service of the United Kingdom rather than the United States and not Lieutenant Dirk's commanding officer. Dirk had been uncomfortable with it, but the question of race had been brought up in relation to Dirk's brutal beating at the hands of the Royal Military Police.

Dirk had gotten the big chicken dinner.

Bad conduct didn't go on your employment record. While a bad conduct discharge also implied that a person had screwed up—screwed up royally, no doubt of that—at least the person hadn't dishonored the country. But one look at Dirk's face told Bolan the big chicken dinner did not taste good. Dirk had devoted his life to serving his fellow citizens, and he had just been handed his walking papers. He was no longer a Delta Force lieutenant. He was now citizen Richard Lincoln Dirk.

Dirk gave Bolan one last, long, hard look. "Full presidential pardon?"

"Full pardon, reinstatement and promotion to captain. Guaranteed."

"I don't suppose you can you get that for me in writing?"

"The President has expressed his willingness to do it in his office and invite your mother." Bolan handed Dirk a second piece of paper with the presidential seal on it. "But yeah, you can have it in writing."

"Damn…" Dirk looked at the signature on the presidential stationery. "You really can make the magic happen. I've seen a few sealed orders in the past two years, and that is the Man's John Hancock."

"Check the small print. Pardon, reinstatement and promotion posthumously should you die during the course of this mission. I insisted on that."

"That's mighty considerate of you."

Bolan shrugged. "You ready to get out of here?"

"Damn straight. I know a kebab place two blocks from here that treats soldiers right, and the girls upstairs treat 'em even better. The owner imports them from Germany, and if you want to meet mercs, that's where they hang out to get hired."

"It's on me."

"Goddamn right it is," Dirk agreed. "And get me a gun. I'm feelin' kind of naked here."

Bolan drew a 9 mm Beretta Model 92 from the back of his belt. "Hold on to this. It was the first thing I could lay my hands on. Give me twenty-four hours, and I can get you anything else you want on special order."

"You sweet man." Dirk took the pistol and checked the loads. "Let's party."

Lars Shishlik Haus

KEBABS AND BLONDES weren't the only advantages of the Shishlik Haus. A half German, half Afghan named Lars Obiada ran the establishment, and he could only be described as a war profiteer. Soldiers at war always had their paychecks in their pockets and very little to spend them on. They were always looking for women and liquor. Both were hard to come by in post-Taliban Afghanistan. Obiada provided both, as well as some of the best hashish available. He had lived in Germany for the first twenty years of his life and served in the Bundeswehr, so any German coalition soldier in Afghanistan got his first drink on the house. The Shishlik was always dripping with German soldiers on leave, as well as soldiers from other coalition countries.

The blondes and hash were upstairs, black-market goods and gambling were in the back and the opium den was in the basement. The smell of the best kebabs in Kabul hit you the second you walked through the front door, and the bar was only ten steps away.

Bolan and Dirk gave their handguns to the coat-check thug at the door and took a seat at the crowded bar. Angry German rap music vibrated the walls. The proprietor was a huge man, and his Teutonic Afghan ancestry made for an interesting mix of blond hair, black eyes and a biker's black mustache and beard. He threw his arms wide as he became aware of Dirk. "The Diggler!"

"My man, Lars!" Dirk grinned.

Obiada poured two shots of whiskey into a glass without being asked. "And for your friend?"

Bolan peered at the row of bottles behind the bar. All were German imports. "I'll take a liter of the Paulaner hefeweizen."

The proprietor filled a massive mug full of cloudy yellow beer, dropped in two lemon slices and slid it Bolan's way. "We have not seen Lieutenant Diggler in some time."

"That's citizen Diggler to you, Lars. Hell, I ain't even the Diggler no more. I'm just…Dick." Dirk sighed and took a massive swallow of whiskey. "That's who I am and what I got right now. Dick."

"How could such thing happen? You are good soldier."

"I ate the big chicken dinner." Dirk downed the rest of his drink with a grimace and slid the glass forward for another. "Can you believe that shit?"

"I had heard this, and could not believe." Obiada leaned his bulk in conspiratorially as he poured brandy. "Is it true you struck British major?"

"No, oh hell, no." Dirk grinned and spoke a little too loud. "I bitch-slapped a goddamn brigadier!"

Bolan noticed a pair of heads turn their way down the bar.

"You do everything in style." Obiada laughed and turned an eye on Bolan. "And who is friend?"

Bolan stuck out his hand. "Cooper."

The bartender pumped Bolan's hand with pleasure. "Cooper. You, too, were involved in the…altercation?"

Bolan played a card. "Let's just say it influenced me to not renew my contract."

Wheels moved behind Lars Obiada's eyes at the word *contract*. "I am sorry to hear. First round is on me."

"You're a gentleman and a scholar," Dirk pronounced.

"I am scholar of life. As for gentleman…" Obiada suddenly frowned. "I think you have attracted attention of gentlemen at end of bar."

A voice with a Welsh accent snarled over the music. "'Ey, you."

Dirk and Bolan ignored him.

"'Ey you! Blackie!"

Just about the entire bar turned. Dirk let out a long sigh and brought his hands to his chest. "Who? Me?"

"Yeah, you." A lanky man leaned forward and thrust out his

jaw. He and his companion wore the green beret of Her Majesty's Royal Marines. "Was that you I 'eard bragging about sucker punching our beloved brigadier, then?"

Dirk raised his hands and gestured at his bruised and battered face. "Listen, man, I already took my lumps from the RMPs and got busted out of the service. I'm a civilian now. You already won. Let it go. I'll buy your next round."

The other marine was a skinny little rat-faced man, but he had a mean look about him. "Colour Sergeant, I believe the word he used was 'bitch-slap,' and he smiled when he said it, didn't he, then?"

"Mmm." The colour sergeant rose, and his head nearly brushed the ceiling. "You know, Jonesy? I don't believe he's repentant, not in the least."

Bolan lowered his liter of beer. "Listen, fellas, we don't want any trouble."

"You don't want trouble, Yank? You'd better stay out of it, then, shouldn't you?"

"I'm afraid the man's with me."

"Really?" The skinny one smiled unpleasantly. "Who's pitchin' and who's catchin', then?"

Bolan smiled back. "I hear the queen does both."

The colour sergeant took a moment to do the math, and a beatific smile spread across his face. So far it had just been an exchange of pleasantries. Now? The stomping was on.

"Aw, now. Who's a clever dick?" The sergeant pointed a finger at Bolan. "It's 'im, isn't it, Jonesy? 'Ee's—"

Bolan shot-putted his beer. It wasn't a heavy blow, but it was a thick, cut-glass liter mug full to the brim, and the Executioner fired it forward, mouth first. The sergeant took the stein across the bridge of the nose, and beer and lemon juice filled his eyes. Dirk spun on his stool and snap-kicked him in the groin, which dropped him to his knees clutching his crotch in beer-blinded agony. Dirk stepped up onto the sergeant's shoulder to gain some altitude, and rat-face Jones took Dirk's heel through his teeth.

"I swear to God!" Dirk boomed. "If one more English ass-hole so much as—damn it!"

Four English sailors in full white middy shirts, trousers and hats came roaring forward.

Bolan stood and scooped up his bar stool. He raised it high and then pitched it low into the leading man's legs, sending him tumbling to the tiles. The man behind him tripped and fell over his fellow sailor. The third sailor did a credible hurdle over the mass of Englishmen littering the floor, but the second he touched down, he took Dirk's fist to the jaw and joined them. The fourth sailor took a step back and yelled for assistance to the room at large. "Tommy! Queue up!"

The UK was the second-largest supplier of coalition troops to the Afghanistan situation. There were a lot of Tommys at the Shishlik Haus at any given time. British soldiers, sailors and air-men rose from their tables.

Bolan upped the ante. "I need every dogface in this shit hole to stand tall!"

American soldiers came crawling out of the woodwork.

This brawl was going to clear the benches. The only thing missing was the piano player diving out the window. Everyone froze as Lars Obiada emptied half a magazine from a Stechkin machine pistol into the roof. "Sit down!"

The potential gladiators sat back down to their liquor and ke-babs. The remaining English sailor pointed a finger at Bolan. "This ain't over, mate."

Bolan ignored the sailor and took his seat as the bouncers ar-rived to clear the carnage.

"Not you two. You know my rule about brawls."

Dirk shrugged. "Wasn't a brawl, Lars. More like a friendly beat down between allies."

"No fighting."

"All right, we'll go."

"No, not out front. Go through back. This way."

Bolan and Dirk exchanged looks and followed Obiada

through a door behind the bar. A narrow passageway led them past the kitchen, and a turbaned goon stood in front of a heavy wooden door at the end of the hall. He gave Obiada a bow and opened it. The room was small and low, and several games of poker were in progress. A big man pulled in a pile of chips and looked up with a grin. His salt-and-pepper hair was buzzed short on the sides and slightly long on the top like a lot of Eastern European soldiers. It was clear he hadn't done any PT in a while, but he was built like a refrigerator and radiated strength. He wore the almost universal khaki load-bearing vest of a private contractor, but the pockets were empty at the moment save for the bulge of a cell phone. The big man pointed a thick finger at a row of flat screen TVs on the wall. One was showing FOX news, another an adult film and a third showed security camera feed where Shishlik Haus employees were carrying out British servicemen in various states of disrepair. The man spoke with a Slavic accent.

"I enjoyed floor show. Much better than belly dancers. Even better than taking money from these losers."

Two Italian airmen who sat bereft of chips gave the big man a sour look but wisely kept their thoughts to themselves. Bolan had the man pegged for a Pole. "GROM?"

"Good!" The man grinned. "Very good!"

GROM was the acronym for Poland's Grupa Reagowania Operacyjno-Manewrowego, or Operational Mobile Reaction Group. The acronym also formed the word *thunder* in Polish. Poland had been one of the first Eastern European nations to sign up for operations in both Afghanistan and Iraq, and their special forces had been the first people they sent. GROM was their best, and while somewhat inexperienced, their best had the reputation of not being bad, and they were busy soaking up operational lessons the hard way in the fiery crucibles of the Middle East and Asia.

The Pole turned to the Italians. "Why do you still sit here? What do you intend to wager with? Your pants?" He jerked his head toward the door. "Go!"

The two airmen stopped just short of running. The big man shook his head as they left and returned to business. "The lieutenant, we know something of. You—" the big Pole shrugged at Bolan "—I do not know, but if you are with Dirk, this speaks well of you."

"Thanks. GROM spells *badass* anyplace I've ever been."

The Pole smiled modestly. "You are too kind." He pulled a business card out of his vest. "My name is Dobrus, Dobrus Stanislawski. Why do not you and the lieutenant come by the office tomorrow?"

Bolan took the card. It read Dobrus Stanislawski, Security Consultant, Shield Security Services and gave a phone number, e-mail and address in Kabul. He handed it to Dirk.

The former Delta Force commando nodded. "We gonna get lunch out of this? I been in the stockade eatin' MREs for a week, and I didn't get my kebabs tonight."

Stanislawski waved a hand around the premises. "Take-out from here?"

"You got a date, sex machine."

3

"Dick Diggler, agent of Shield." Dirk clearly enjoyed the sound of it. "Think we'll get our own business cards?"

"We don't have the job yet."

"Dude, we're shoo-ins."

Bolan and Dirk climbed out of the cab with their hands never far from their concealed Berettas. Shield's Kabul office was part of the new construction going on in the capital. Prevailing conditions favored thick concrete walls and few windows. The walls were pockmarked with bullet strikes and the occasional deeper crater of an RPG hit. Shield provided private security for businessmen, politicians and foreign dignitaries in war-torn Afghanistan, and that made the office itself something of a target. Strategically placed concrete pylons on the surrounding sidewalk prevented anyone driving a car bomb from getting up a head of steam at the building. The few windows were all upstairs and were more like the firing slits of a medieval castle than ornamentation or sources of natural light.

Bolan pressed the button on the steel security door and stared up into a camera lens. The intercom crackled and a woman's voice spoke. "Mr. Dirk and Mr. Cooper?"

"That's us."

The intercom buzzed and the door unlocked. They had to pass through a switchback series of three Kevlar panels before reaching the foyer. A beautiful young Afghan woman in a gray business suit and skirt sat behind a teak desk with the Shield logo behind her. "Would you gentlemen care for coffee?"

Stanislawski came through a door behind her. "They have beer and take-out waiting for them upstairs. Follow me, boys."

Bolan and Dirk followed the big Pole through a hall. It opened into a fairly spacious gym area with treadmills and weight machines. Dirk muttered appreciatively under his breath. "Goddamn…"

Dirk had a good eye. A woman in gray sweats was walking sideways on a stair-stepper machine. Wavy brown hair fell around a glowing face sheened with a healthy sweat. Savage work in the gym had turned her hourglass figure into sculpture, but not so much that she had lost any of her curves. She had big blue eyes, and her lips, nose and chin were sensuously sculpted.

Stanislawski called out jovially. "Connie! How long have you been on that machine?"

The woman's eyes never wavered from some middle-distance point of concentration. "Forty-five minutes."

"You are sick, little girl."

A smile spread across her face. "I still have to do the other side. This old ass just turned forty-two."

Bolan was sure many a woman in her twenties would have killed to have Connie's rock-hard behind, but he kept that to himself for the moment. Stanislawski led them down another hall. The second they turned the corner, Dirk burst out eagerly. "Man! What's her story?"

"Connie is our pilot. She flew Black Hawk helicopters for United States Army. She passed U.S. Army Ranger training, but of course was not allowed in ground combat. However, she flew combat missions in Desert Storm. Won Silver Star for bravery. Besides pilot, sometimes woman is useful in security missions. She can put on burka and blend with population or pose as Western nanny or tutor in 'babysitting' situations when armed man would be awkward." Stanislawski raised a knowing eyebrow. "Very useful girl."

"Oh, I got some uses for her." Dirk grinned.

"Like others—" the Pole grinned back "—you will try." He took them to the elevator, and they went to the third floor. The office at the end of the hall had "executive suite" written all over it. Stanislawski opened the door, and Bolan came face-to-face with a legend.

"Hello, men!"

Former Marine sniper David Dinatale had earned the moniker "Deadshot Dave" doing some very black operations work in Central America during the 1980s. During the 1990s, a mercenary soldiers' magazine had done a story on him, giving him and his rifle the cover photo with the headline The Most Dangerous Man In Desert Storm. A framed copy of the cover shot hung on the wall behind him, as well as the United States Congressional Medal of Honor, pictures of him shaking hands with two presidents and a copy of his bestselling, semiautobiographical novel. Above all, in the place of honor, hung the battered Remington 700 sniper rifle with which he had done his damage and earned his accolades.

Like a lot of the world's most dangerous men, Dinatale didn't particularly look the part. He was a short, wiry man with sandy hair that was swiftly turning gray. He had a glowing tan and a generous smile that could sell toothpaste. Sitting in his shirtsleeves, he looked like a highly successful car salesman. However, there were certain signs of the operator about him. He sat in his leather chair with the lazy ease of a predator at rest and looked as if he could crank off a hundred push-ups without breaking a sweat. There was something very sniperlike around the eyes. He shot to his feet and stuck out his hand. "Thanks for coming around."

"Morning, Mr. Dinatale." Dirk stuck out his hand. "I must say this is an honor. I loved your book. It's required reading over at Delta."

"You keep up that kind of talk, and you're gonna get yourself a date to the prom."

He held out his hand to Bolan. "Cooper, is it?"

"Yes, sir, and it is an honor. You don't get to meet a legend every day."

"Jesus, you boys are butt-kissers!" Dinatale waggled his eyebrows. "But I like that in an employee! You taking notes there, Toe-jam, you Polack son of a bitch?"

Dobrus Stanislawski snorted.

Bolan smiled despite himself. Most snipers were quiet, introspective men. Dinatale was the exception that proved the rule, and he exuded the frat-boy charm of a lovable rogue. Bolan reminded himself that Deadshot Dave had forty confirmed kills, and those were just the ones that weren't classified. Dinatale waved a hand at the cardboard boxes of take-out kebabs and roasted rice. A bucket of Moosehead beers on ice sat next to them. "Well, let's tuck in and talk a little business."

Everyone took a seat and began tearing into the cubed lamb and rice. Stanislawski took beers out of the bucket, twisted off the caps and passed them around.

"Well, now, gentlemen, I'll tell you I've got a line of applicants stretched from here to Baghdad. I got Alaskan National Guardsmen who've never done anything but paint snow in Nome sending me love letters. The good news is this. Dirk? Delta Force says it all. I'd be a fool not to hire you. Short of Navy SEAL, you just don't get a better résumé in this line of business."

Dirk grabbed a fresh box of kebab. "SEALs are pussies."

Beer nearly spewed out of Dinatale's nose. "Well…like I said, Dirk. I've checked your bona fides, and save for a certain incident with a British brigadier, you're rock solid."

Dirk stiffened, but Dinatale dismissed the incident with a wave of his beer. "Hell, my one regret is that I'm going to go to my grave without ever having punched out a superior officer. That's one you've got on me. Man! How'd that feel?"

"Well, at the expense of shooting myself in the foot?" Dirk smiled and shook his head. "Fantastic."

Dinatale sighed in envy. "The good news is if you take the job I'm not your superior officer. I'm your boss. You don't have to kick my ass. You can quit any time you want."

"I appreciate that, Mr. Dinatale. I like your style."

"Thanks. So let me ask you a question."

"What's that, Mr. Dinatale?"

"Call me Dino—everyone does."

"Okay, Dino, shoot."

Dinatale's eyes went hard as he looked at Bolan. "Who's this civilian son of a bitch?"

Dirk didn't bat an eye. "He's the baddest asshole you're likely to meet today, and you already met me, so that's sayin' somethin'."

"Well, that is sweet," Dinatale admitted, but he kept his eyes unblinkingly on Bolan. Few human beings could do the hard-stare harder than a veteran sniper. "But who are you, cowboy?"

Bolan was a veteran sniper himself, and he didn't blink. "Short version, I'm a spook without a contract."

Dinatale broke the staring contest with a sigh and leaned back in his chair. "You got a single reference I can check?"

"Well…I done dastardly deeds with the Diggler," Bolan suggested hopefully.

Dinatale rolled his eyes in defeat. "I've heard a couple people say that recently, and I must admit it does give me something of a chubby." The CEO of Shield turned to Dirk. "So you're willing to vouch for this spook son of a bitch?"

"He's the only white man I currently like, present company included, of course."

"I'll buy that, but for the moment. On your good word, Dirk. But he's your responsibility. It's like he's on parole. Got it?"

"Trust must be earned," Dirk agreed.

"Truer words were never spoken." The former sniper measured the two of them. "I dig you, Diggler, and I want to dig him. I really want to."

"Give him time." Dirk cracked himself open another beer. "He grows on you."

Dinatale laughed. "Well, I'll look forward to it, then."

Dirk put on his poker face. "Forgive my impertinence, Dino, but we don't look forward to nothin' till we talk cash money."

"Fair enough. You're ex-Delta, Dirk. 'Nough said. I'll start you at a thousand dollars a day."

"God...damn."

"And since you're holding Cooper's parole, I'll start him at the same and give you both a thousand up front. Deal?"

"Oh, hell, yes."

Dinatale's eyes were on Bolan. "Coop?"

Bolan put a little eagerness in his voice. "Oh, I'm in."

"Good enough. We're negotiating a job right now. You may be getting your feet wet as early as tomorrow night. Meanwhile, what are you boys carrying?"

Dirk pulled out his Model 92. "Cooper got his hands on a couple of Army Berettas, but they ain't my first choice."

"Well, here at Shield we have a weapons-standardization policy."

Dirk's face soured. Delta Force personnel were used to being allowed to carry whatever they thought they required. "You gotta be shitting me."

"No, I'm not." Dinatale grinned. "But it isn't to please any bean counters back in the States or for the sake of uniformity."

"Then what are you talking about, Dino?"

Dinatale held up a happy finger. "Did you know Shield is the first private security group to have corporate sponsorship?"

Even Bolan hadn't heard that. "Really."

"Show 'em, Dob."

Stanislawski went to a painted steel panel in the wall and punched in a key code. The door slid open to reveal a walk-in arms closet. The Pole pulled out an automatic carbine with a grin. "Polish Mini-Beryl short assault weapon."

Dinatale smiled happily. "Dob's our resident gun bunny and armorer here in the Kabul office. He used to be GROM, and with Shield's reputation, he got the Zaklady Metalowe company of Poland to provide us with all the small arms and ammo we can use as long as every time the U.S. merc magazines, that French rag or the evening news runs a story on Shield our boys are festooned with Polish steel. Zaklady Metalowe manufactures almost all the small arms the Polish military uses and exports widely. They give us everything from pocket pistols to antitank rockets. It's really not a bad deal. It's good kit, and it's done well by us here in Afghanistan and in our sister operation in Iraq."

Bolan had used Polish weapons, as well as been on the wrong end of them. Zaklady Metalowe weapons were nothing if not reliable, and the Polish designers had brought their version of the venerable AK into the twenty-first century with all the latest electronic sights and modifications.

"Dob'll get you checked out on all our current issue equipment tomorrow. Speaking of which, where're you boys staying?"

Dirk scowled. "Well, I spent the last week in the stockade, and I'm still picking lice from the inn we stayed at last night."

"We actually have a suite of room downstairs and hold down a floor in an apartment block two buildings down. We like to keep our people together in case of emergencies, and quite frankly, once it's known around town you're Shield, you're as much of a target as the people we're paid to protect. We'll put you up here tonight."

"Thanks, Dino."

"No problem. Dob will draw two grand from petty cash to give you some walking-around money."

Bolan nodded. "Not a problem, and thanks."

"Good, all settled, then." Dinatale nodded to Stanislawski, who rose to show Bolan and Dirk out of the office.

4

The assault rifle racked open on a smoking empty chamber, and the last spent brass casing tinkled to the concrete floor of the Shield shooting range. Dirk unshouldered the weapon and blew on the smoke oozing from the action. The silhouette target downrange had been torn to shreds by his series of 5-round bursts. "Ain't bad. Ain't bad."

Bolan lowered his own smoking weapon and turned to Stanislawski. "We'll take them."

"Ha!" The Pole clenched a meaty fist. "Polish steel, the best!"

Bolan and Dirk had raided the Shield armory. Each man now had a .223-caliber Mini-Beryl automatic carbine to call his own. The carbines came equipped with EO Tech holographic optical sights. The stubby carbines were too short to mount grenade launchers, but both weapons had launching rings for Polish Dezamet rifle grenades machined onto their barrels. Grenades, whether hand, rifle, rocket propelled or otherwise, were issued on an as-needed basis at Shield. Everything else was available at a kid-in-the-candy-store level of need.

Dirk had selected a polymer framed WIST-94 automatic pistol. Bolan had gone for an all-steel MAG-95. He'd also picked up a little P-64 pocket automatic. The pistol was just about the size and shape of James Bond's famous Walther PPK, only chambered for the far more powerful 9 mm Makarov round. The little gun kicked like a mule and was inaccurate beyond spitting distance, but it was a lethal little surprise to pull from deep cover, and Bolan had learned long ago that drawing a second gun was faster than reloading.

Bolan laid his rifle down on the shooting bench. Stanislawski did good work. Both the optical and iron sights were dead-on. The basement level beneath the Shield offices was split between an underground parking lot and an indoor fifty-meter shooting range.

The Pole was eyeing Bolan shrewdly. "You are excellent shot."

"Fifty meters, a carbine with an optical sight." Bolan shrugged. "It isn't hard."

"No, but your every move upon range betrays you as marksman."

"Well, I'm no Deadshot Dave, but I try to keep my hand in."

Stanislawski laughed. "Who is?"

A woman's voice rang out across the range. "I'll give the son of a bitch a run for his money if he's man enough to bring a six-gun." Connie Zanotto walked up to the shooting bench, unzipped her range bag and pulled out a pair of revolvers.

Bolan peered at them. At first glance they looked like Smith & Wesson .38s but the grip angles were slightly wrong, as were the fixed sights.

Zanotto looked at Bolan challengingly. "You know, I told them I didn't want some Polish jamamatic. I told them I'd been using a four-inch Smith since I made pilot back in the eighties. So what does fat boy do?" She looked ruefully at Stanislawski.

"Zaklady Metalowe?" Bolan suggested.

"Yup, Gward .38." Zanotto twirled the Polish revolvers around her fingers like a gunfighter. "They work just fine. I swear, you work for Shield long enough and you end up with a hard-on for Polish steel."

"I already have a hard-on," Dirk admitted.

Zanotto favored the commando with a very appraising look. "Oh, I'm sure you do. I hear they call you the Diggler."

Dirk flinched at the nickname. "Don't believe everything you hear."

"I was kinda hoping what I heard was true."

Stanislawski shook his head. "The .38. Old-fashioned. Underpowered."

"You know, big man? I shot exactly two Iraqis back in the day, and they didn't complain. As a matter of fact, all they did was fall down. And revolvers? They don't jam."

Stanislawski shook his head derisively. "This is why women should not be in combat."

"This is why you never get laid."

The big Pole sighed heavily. "She always wins these conversations."

"Back to business. I had a talk with Dino this morning." Connie Zanotto took out a speed loader and slid six shells into one of her revolvers. "We got a job."

Bolan broke down his MAG and began cleaning it. "What kind of job?"

"Babysitting. Local political VIP. Her name is Zahari Ziaee. Her husband was a secular reformist in the Afghan parliament. The Taliban blew his head off. So Mrs. Ziaee decided to run for his seat."

Dirk frowned. "The Taliban must love that."

"Word is they have a real hard-on for her. She stands no chance of being elected, but by their code her temerity has to be punished, and she has to be made an example of to other women who might likewise be tempted. They've put out the word they want her and her daughters gang-raped and beheaded, but they'll settle for the whole family perishing in flames."

Stanislawski spit out onto the range. "Taliban. Animals."

"She has three kids," Zanotto continued. "Camila is sixteen, Daywa is ten and the little boy, Gul Mir, is five. Since she's a single woman with a teenage daughter, I'm going to be the one who stays close to the family. Cooper, you, Dirk, Boner and Frame will be doing roof and perimeter duty on the ranch."

Dirk perked an eyebrow. "Boner?"

"Bonaventura. Ex-Marine. He's a newbie with Shield, but he's solid."

"Where's the ranch?" Bolan asked.

"Actually, it's more of a camel farm. The Ziaee family does a pretty decent trade in livestock when they're not getting themselves killed in the name of democracy. It's about twenty klicks outside the city."

"Anything else we need to know?"

"Yeah, Mrs. Ziaee has some local muscle on location. Supposedly former Northern Alliance vets. Supposed to be real trigger-happy badasses. We have no read on how reliable they may be. I'll have a file on the entire situation worked up for you by noon. Meantime, I'd grab a nap if I were you. We expect to roll out of here by six."

Dirk slid his carbine into a leather gun case with the Shield logo on it. "Actually, now that Coop and I are fat with cash, I thought we might buy some threads."

"Well, most of the contractors around here buy over the Internet or through catalogs, but there's a decent men's store downtown." Zanotto scrawled an address on the corner of a bull's-eye target and tore it off. "Here, give this to the cabdriver, and come straight back."

"Yes, ma'am."

Zanotto put on her hearing protectors and a pair of shooting glasses and began methodically punching holes in the black at fifty meters.

Dirk waved his little scrap of paper. "Let's go shopping!"

"WHAT HAVE YOU GOT for me, Bear?" Bolan typed. He sat in an Internet café in downtown Kabul. He'd taken a workstation with his back to the wall, and Dirk stood guard. Information scrolled down the chat window.

"Dobrus Stanislawski achieved the rank of sergeant and then was accepted into GROM. He achieved the rank of *chorazy,* which is like a warrant officer but different. Sort of more than a sergeant but less than a lieutenant. He served in Iraq. GROM wanted him to reenlist but he went private, went to Afghanistan and Shield snapped him up. He was also on the Polish army's Olympic weight-lifting team."

So far Dob was living up to his profile. "What about the Zanotto woman?" Bolan typed.

"Constantina Zanotto achieved the rank of second lieutenant in the U.S. Army. One of the first women to pass the Ranger training school. Also one of the first women rated to fly a Black Hawk helicopter. She flew some pretty hairy missions in Iraq delivering and retrieving Rangers. She also won a few Miss Fitness competitions. Her shtick was to wear a camouflage bikini and combat boots. About ten years ago, she left the Army. She went to Hollywood, did some stunt work and got a few bit parts in some TV action shows. Then she got into celebrity bodyguard work. About five years ago, Shield decided they needed some qualified women on the payroll. I guess she missed the action and flying. She signed up. The other rumor I dug up is that she and Dinatale were an item for the first year or two."

Bolan filed that one away. "What about Mrs. Ziaee?"

"She's a marked woman, Striker. The Taliban hated her husband, but her? They consider her a personal affront to God. They want her head, literally. And another thing you should know. I've been researching Shield operations over the past two years. There's a reason every guy who ever served wants to sign up with them. They're the highest paying and most professional outfit of their type. They go to the worst trouble spots of the world and see a lot of action, but despite their reputation they've lost some high-profile clients in Afghanistan and Iraq."

Bolan frowned. "What are you trying to say?"

"I'm saying there's a pattern here. I can't put my finger on it, but I don't like it. And when Shield has lost men, it's always the newbies who get killed. I'm saying you better be careful."

Bolan checked his watch. "Dirk and I have to roll. I'll check back in when I can."

"Copy that."

Bolan rose. "Dirk, you ready to roll?"

"Yeah." Dirk finished his coffee. "So what's the good news?"

"There's a good chance me, you and Mrs. Ziaee are gonna get fed to the lions tonight."

Shorkot village

"CAMELS…" Dirk wrinkled his nose in disgust.

Bolan had been around the beasts on more than one occasion, and they were nothing if not fragrant. "You get used to it."

"What if I don't *want* to get used to it?"

The Ziaee summerhouse was typical old-world Afghan clay cube construction, though on a grander scale than most of the other homes dotting the hillsides. Roughly a hundred camels lowed and groaned behind a ramshackle enclosure that looked as if it had been made out of rope and driftwood. Goats and chickens ranged freely. Dusk was falling. Bolan powered up his night-vision monocular and scanned the hillsides. Camels grunted. Goats bleated. The chickens were roosting for the night. A few children still ran and played as the sky turned purple.

Dirk checked his own night-vision equipment. "Coop?"

"Yeah."

"I got a bad feeling."

When a former Delta Force commando got a bad feeling, it was a good idea to listen, and Bolan himself had been having bad feelings for the past hour. "Me, too."

"Remember what you said about us getting fed to the lions?"

"Yeah."

"In my experience, when the lions come they bring RPGs."

"Yeah, that's my experience, too."

Dirk reached behind a hay bale and pulled out a pair of Dezamet rifle grenades. "Here, have some lion insurance."

Bolan took the dual-purpose 40 mm weapon. "How'd you get a hold of these?"

"Stole 'em from Dob's stash."

"How'd you sneak them past him?" Bolan considered himself a past master at scrounging, but he was impressed. "Dob was with us the whole time."

"I shoved them down my pants." Dirk grinned from ear to ear. "And who's going to suspect they weren't just more of me?"

Bolan jerked his head toward the back door. "Stand tall. We got company."

Camila Ziaee came out bearing a silver tea service. Zahari Ziaee was a handsome woman. Her daughter Camila was nothing short of stunning. She was the kohl-eyed tawny beauty of every merchant sailor's fevered dream. She spoke in halting English. "The…gentlemen? Will take tea?"

"Oh, hell, yeah," Dirk replied eagerly.

"Dirk…"

"I mean, yes, please, Miss Ziaee." Dirk smiled angelically. "That would be lovely."

Camila blushed charmingly, placed the tray on the hay bale and poured steaming tea into tiny silver cups. Bolan nodded. "Thank you, Camila."

Camila Ziaee blushed brighter. "Welcome."

"Camila!" Mrs. Ziaee called out from the back door. "Miss Connie wishes you in the house!"

Bolan knew she was speaking English for his and Dirk's benefit.

Camila shot Bolan a tentative smile. "You defend us. Thank you." She left the tray and ran back to the house. Mrs. Ziaee waited until her daughter was ensconced and walked out.

Bolan scanned the perimeter. "Mrs. Ziaee, neither you or your daughter should be outside after dark."

"This is my home. I will not be a prisoner in it."

"I'm not saying you're a prisoner. You're a target." Bolan glanced around the rocky hills. "And any Taliban with a telescopic sight can reach out and touch you. Mr. Dirk and I will kill him, guaranteed, but unless we're very lucky the Taliban will get the first shot. Do you understand?"

Mrs. Ziaee had seen forty years of war and been widowed at

gunpoint. Hard lines of suffering had been etched onto her face. She looked into Bolan's eyes openly. "You are kind to my family. You are kind to our servants. You are a good man, Cooper. I was right to go to Shield."

Mrs. Ziaee refused to wear the burka, but part of her political strategy was to wear the full robe and apron ensemble of a respectable Afghan housewife when she wasn't wearing a Western women's business suit. Beneath the apron Bolan could see the bulge of a pistol. Bolan reached down to his ankle holster and drew his P-64 pocket pistol. "Give this to your daughter. It's loaded with a round in the chamber. The safety is off. All she has to do is squeeze the trigger. Tell her if they get past us to shoot any man who comes for her in the face."

Mrs. Ziaee's jaw set. "You think the Taliban will come tonight."

"Mr. Dirk has a bad feeling." Bolan glanced around the little valley. There were a million places to hide. "And I think they are already here. Stay with Connie."

Mrs. Ziaee took the pistol and drew her own Tokarev pistol from beneath her apron. "As you say, so shall it be done." Mrs. Ziaee went back into the house with a pistol in each hand.

"Don't look around or anything, but—" Dirk flicked off the safety of his carbine "—you're right. They're here."

Bolan clicked the tactical radio on his vest. "Boner, I think we got company."

Arcelio Bonaventura was concealed up on the roof. The former Marine marksman had a full-length Beryl rifle rather than a carbine, and it was equipped with a PCS-6 passive night-vision scope. "Coop, I don't see nada."

"Frame?"

Jimmy Frame was out front watching the dirt road that led to the house. Frame was formerly 101st Army Airborne. "Nothing on the road, Coop."

Connie Zanotto appeared at the door cradling a Glauberyt submachine gun with a laser designator mounted beneath the barrel. "What's going on, Cooper?"

"I think we're about to get hit."

"Anyone see anything?"

"Nope."

"So…" Zanotto considered this. "What? 'By the pricking of my thumbs something wicked this way comes'?"

Bolan smiled slightly. It seemed everyone in Afghanistan was quoting MacBeth these days. "Yeah, something like that."

Zanotto glanced around the ring of hills. Darkness was falling across the little valley like a blanket. "It's over a thousand yards for a sniper shot. Even Dino would have a problem with this one. What're you thinking, mortars?"

"No, they're not outside looking down. They're inside already."

"How?"

Bolan gazed at the lights of the village winking on a few hundred yards away. "This valley was owned by the Taliban until the boys from the Tenth Mountain Division kicked them out. I think some of them never left. They just melted back into the population. I'm thinking there's a Taliban cell here, and they've been reactivated."

"Yeah, so how are they going to come?"

"Hard and fast. Once the firefight starts, gunships can be here from Kabul in twenty minutes. They don't have time for a siege. I'm thinking a storm of RPGs and then they human-wave the place. With any luck, they take Mrs. Ziaee and her children alive, drag them to some cave and make a movie while they cut off their heads. Ours, too. On the other hand, they don't think we have any heavy weapons. A car bomb wouldn't be out of the question."

Zanotto looked at Bolan quizzically. "We don't have any heavy weapons."

Technically, she was right. Rifle grenades were light-support weapons, but Bolan wasn't going to contradict her or let her know they'd been filching Shield ordnance until it became necessary. "Yeah."

"Well, you're just full of good news, aren't you?" Zanotto motioned toward the front of the house. "What are you thinking? We load up the family wagon and bolt?"

Shield bought nothing but the best. The team had arrived in an International Armoring Corporation Ford Expedition. The SUV was armored to Threat Level V and would stop an armor-piercing 30.06 rifle round. A rocket-propelled grenade, on the other hand, would light it up like the Fourth of July.

"No, the village will be a shooting gallery. We'd get greased in the cross fire," Bolan argued.

"So, what's the plan?"

"We kill them as they come. I counted four vehicles in the village. Two pickups, an open jeep and a VW Bug. The minute they move, we know."

Boner spoke from the roof. "Connie?"

"What ya got, Boner?"

"I got headlights. In the village. I—"

Boner was interrupted by a dull thud and a puff of yellow flame from an alley on the edge of town.

"Shit!" Frame shouted aloud, no longer bothering with the radio. "Connie! Someone's fired some kind of—"

The roof lit up in a yellow halo of fire, and Boner screamed. A pair of headlights tore out of the village, followed by another and another. Bolan raised his rifle but kept his sights on the dark recesses between the closely packed mud houses, scanning for the grenadier. Dirk's carbine opened up, as well as Frame's from the front of the house. Tracers streamed toward the oncoming vehicles. The VW was leading the pack down the dirt road, and a pair of pickups bounced and jolted across the rocky terrain like outriders. The jeep followed behind, completing the diamond formation.

Connie Zanotto shouted in her radio. "Shield Home, this is Connie Z at Shorkot village! We are under heavy attack! Boner is down! Alert the military we are under Taliban attack!"

"RPGs!" Dirk shouted. "In the trucks!"

"Forget the trucks." Bolan slid his rifle grenade over the muzzle of his weapon and kept his eyes on the edge of town. "The car—take the car."

The VW was burning toward them at fifty miles per hour. Bolan could see only one occupant crouched behind the wheel, and he was pretty sure the driver had no intention of stopping.

"Copy that!" Dirk clicked his own grenade onto his carbine and flipped up the sight. Bullets ripped from the oncoming vehicles, seeking out the team. Dirk crouched immobile as stone, carbine leveled. He had only one shot, and he was waiting for it.

Zanotto's submachine began ripping long bursts at the oncoming vehicles. An RPG-7 rocket hissed from the back of one of the pickups in response, and the Ziaee family screamed within as the antitank weapon slammed into the side of the house. The ancient construction of the house was their best defense. Antitank weapons were designed to burn through the steel hulls of armored vehicles and incinerate the men within. Thick clay walls were as good a defense as any, save that they were brittle and successive hits would crumble them. Kalashnikov rifles crackled from the jeeps and trucks, and tracers streamed toward the house.

"Taking the shot!" Dirk boomed. The rifle grenade thumped away from his carbine at two hundred feet per second and spiraled between the oncoming VW's headlights.

The Bug blew sky-high.

Dirk had taken his shot at a hundred yards, but even from that distance Bolan squinted against the wash of heat from the blast wave. There was nothing left of the vehicle. Bolan figured there had to have been at least fifty kilograms of high explosive, but that was the least of his concerns. He was waiting for a shot of his own.

Zanotto's voice was an angry snarl. "Christ, Cooper! Why aren't you shooting?"

Bolan's eyes suddenly went to slits as he caught sight of his target. The grenade's report was drowned out by the sound of gunfire, but he caught the pale yellow flash from the village. Bolan squeezed his trigger, and the little carbine recoiled brutally against his shoulder as it hurled the grenade toward the village. He had no time to gauge its effect.

The enemy grenadier had fired first, and Frame shouted and his weapon light strobed from the front of the house. The two pickups had swerved around the smoking crater the Bug had left and were now at fifty yards and closing. Bolan swung his sights onto the lead vehicle. The Mini-Beryl buzz-sawed in Bolan's hands as he printed a burst into the driver's-side windshield of the right-hand truck. The glass pocked with bullet strikes, and suddenly went opaque with arterial spray. The front tires turned sharply as the driver fell against the wheel, and the men in back screamed as the pickup tipped and rolled down the hillside, scraping them into oblivion against the rocks.

Zanotto and Dirk put the cab of the second truck into a cross fire, and window glass cratered and spiderwebbed. The truck slowed as the dead driver's foot came off the gas. Bolan flicked his selector to semiauto and began quickly squeezing the trigger at the RPG team leaning over the cab. The rocketeer sagged and dropped his launch tube as Bolan's first shot took him in the forehead. The loader twisted as the Executioner's second shot took him in the collarbone, and he screamed and fell in back into the truck bed as Bolan's third took off his ear.

The trailing jeep lurched to a stop, and its gears ground as the driver rammed it into Reverse.

Bolan slammed a fresh magazine into his carbine and flicked his selector back to full-auto. "Forward! Go! Go! Go!"

Dirk and Zanotto rose, and the three of them charged forward onto the dirt road, spraying short bursts into the open jeep. The four men riding it jerked and shuddered as they took hits. One man bailed out the back and ran, but Dirk's burst hammered him between the shoulder blades and dropped him to the dirt. The other three men never managed to get out of their seats.

Zanotto dropped her spent submachine gun and filled each of her hands with a .38 as she stopped by the stalled truck. "Cab is clear!" She hopped into the truck bed and pointed both pistols downward. "Got a live one here!"

"Copy that." Bolan moved on to the jeep. The occupants had been shredded. "Clear."

Dirk stared down the hillside at the crumpled pickup. The men who had been in the back were little more than smears. No one had gotten out of the cab. "Clear."

Bolan reloaded. "Dirk, me and you are going to the village. Connie, take the prisoner, check on Frame and stick with the family until we get back."

"Copy that, Coop."

Bolan and Dirk broke into a trot. The Executioner could hear the villagers alternately shouting, screaming and crying behind their bolted doors. He kept his eye on the edge of town until he came to the grenadier's position. Bolan's countershot had hit the wall of the alley, and the whitewash was blackened and scored from shrapnel fragments. A few feet down the alley an AK-47 lay in a puddle. A few steps farther a bloody handprint smeared the wall.

Dirk scanned down the narrow alley with his night sight. "No sign of the asshole. Nice shot, though. Looks like you got a piece of him."

Bolan pulled the Kalashnikov out of the puddle and looked upon it long and hard.

"What?" Dirk shrugged in the gloom. "It's an AK. There's more AKs in Afghanistan these days than in goddamn Mother Russia."

Bolan took in the 10-round magazine, the strap-on rubber butt plate and the extra eight inches of the ringed 20 mm muzzle attachment. "Yeah, but technically this a PMK-DGN-60."

Dirk sighed. "And that means…?"

"It means it's an AK designed to throw rifle grenades. They came out in 1960. They're obsolete, but not unusual to find in hands of irregulars in Third World conflicts."

"And so…"

"Something, maybe nothing."

Dirk scowled. "Okay, now you're getting spooky on me. What's all the weirdness over an obsolete weapon?"

Bolan dropped the AK back in the puddle. Taking it back to Shield might not be a good idea. "They're manufactured in Poland."

5

Shield Headquarters, Kabul

"Behold the conquering heroes!" Deadshot Dave Dinatale was grinning from ear to ear. Bolan and Dirk both got the bonecrusher handshake before they took a seat in the office. "I hear you boys popped your VIP-protection cherries in style."

"Thanks, Dino. How's Frame?"

Dinatale frowned as he sat in his leather chair. "Yeah, well, Frame was next to the truck when it got hit by the second grenade. He took a faceful of glass. Goddamn miracle none of it hit him in the eyes. He looks like a horror movie right now, but Connie says he'll clean up okay."

"Good. He stood tall."

"So, uh—" Dinatale gave them a fatherly smile "—where'd you boys get rifle grenades?"

Dirk raised his hand. "Stole 'em from Toe-jam."

"No." Bolan raised his. "I stole them from Toe-jam."

Dinatale looked back and forth between them. "You sweet boys."

Bolan and Dirk shrugged in unison.

"Listen, I ain't mad. As a matter of fact, I'm glad you did it. I admire initiative, and if you hadn't, we would've lost both the team and the client."

"We lost Boner," Bolan said.

"Yeah, his family will be getting a fat check. Mrs. Ziaee also expressed the desire to compensate Boner's family, and the Ziaee clan has money."

Bolan watched the old sniper's face. He wasn't exactly all broken up about Bonaventura's demise, but then again Dinatale had been a soldier for thirty years and had undoubtedly buried more friends and buddies than he had fingers and toes, and Bonaventura was a newbie who'd died the first day on the job.

"The bad news is, boys, the Afghan army has taken over protection of Mrs. Ziaee and family until the election."

"Man…" Dirk sighed.

"I know, I know. It was a three-week gig, and you gentlemen were looking forward to fat twenty-one-thousand-dollar paychecks. Well, you showed up Friday and got the family extracted back to Kabul by Saturday dawn, so, what the hell, I admire your ingenuity. Let's just call it a three-day weekend. How's that?"

"More than fair, Dino," Bolan said. "It's three grand I didn't have in my pocket when I walked in here yesterday."

"Good, I'll have Miss Aarash do the paperwork. You have a bank account you want it wired to or some other kind of—?"

"Cash?" Dirk suggested.

Dino laughed aloud. "Jesus, you boys have been mercs for barely twenty-four hours, and you already have the pirate vibe. Fine, cash."

"Cool."

"I do need you both to write up an after-action report for me. Miss Aarash will check you both out a laptop you can keep in your room. Take today off and rest up, but I'd like it on my desk by tomorrow morning. Check your carbines back into the armory, but keep your sidearms and let Dob know if you intend to steal a flamethrower or something. He considers all Shield hardware his, and he gets anal about it."

"No problem, Dino," Dirk said.

"Yo, Dino…" Dirk smiled slyly. "That Miss Aarash, is she—?"

"She's mine."

"Got it."

"Well, that'll do, gentlemen. Get some rest. We've got big things coming up."

Bolan and Dirk checked their carbines back into the armory and left the Shield headquarters. Bolan walked two blocks down the street and stopped at a corner kiosk. He slid a couple of bucks to the vendor and took a copy of the *Wall Street Journal* and two glasses of *doh*. He handed one to Dirk, and the former Delta man grimaced as the yogurt whey, club soda and lemon juice passed his lips.

"Jesus, can't we get beer?"

"The nearest beer is at Shield or Shishlik Haus, and I don't want to have this conversation at either."

Dirk nodded and took another tentative sip of the salty, sour mixture. "You know, with a shot or two of vodka this shit could grow on me." He raised a suspicious eyebrow. "I notice you didn't lay any of your bright ideas about our mystery grenadier on Dino."

"No, I didn't."

"So you really think we got set up?" Dirk asked.

Bolan had been giving that a lot of hard thought. "Two hundred and forty meters is the maximum practical range for the grenade projector we found in the alley. Our grenadier fired twice. He dropped a grenade right on top of Boner and one on the truck, at dusk, using iron sights, and he was dead-on. Whoever he was, he was good, and he saw fit to stay back rather than go jihad in a truck bed."

"Afghanistan has been at war almost nonstop since 1979," Dirk countered. "There's a shitload of wily old mujahideen vets out there who could do it. I've met some of them. I bet you have, too, and like you said, ex-Warsaw Pact matériel is available and in use in just about every Third World conflict going."

"Granted." Bolan stared up the street toward Shield headquarters. "You seen Dob around today?"

"No." Dirk's brows lowered as he considered the smeared blood they'd found on the wall. "No, I haven't."

"And how did the grenadier know Boner was on the roof? We snuck him inside the house, and up top, he was concealed behind the vegetable trellis and the pigeon coop. He was our ace in the hole in case we got attacked, and the first shot of the fight took him out."

"Dunno. Maybe he got careless and someone in the village watching with optics saw him. Hell, maybe one of the Ziaee family servants dropped a dime on us. There were half a dozen of them underfoot."

"Yeah, maybe," Bolan said. Neither man was buying it.

"Okay, fine. You, me, Boner and Frame? We're cannon fodder, I'll buy it for the moment, what the hell, but do you really think Dinatale would whack Connie? Much less throw her to those Taliban animals? She's Shield inner circle."

"That's a good question. We don't know if this goes all the way to the top or not. Rumor has it Connie and old Deadshot were a hot item for a while. Now they're not. I'll need to do some research on that."

Dirk smirked. "No doubt."

Bolan ignored the innuendo. "Let me ask you this. How much do you think the Taliban would pay to have Mrs. Ziaee and her family's defenses spelled out and compromised?"

"Probably a million at least, maybe more. They got Saudi and other rich Arab financial backing—Jesus! You're saying Dinatale is selling Shield clients to the highest bidder?" Dirk was appalled at the implication. "You know somethin'? Never trust a goddamn sniper. They're cold-blooded sons of bitches. Every last one of them. I mean, it's like they live out of their limbic regions or something. They're reptiles, know what I'm sayin'?"

Bolan just smiled.

Dirk's shoulders sagged. "Oh, Christ."

"No worries. Me and the lizards? No offense taken."

"Man…"

"Listen, we've got to tread real light. This reads the same way the Rangers got it. Taliban suicide cannon fodder, but with some very thoughtful, professional backup. I don't think our boy Dino would whack Connie out of spite, but maybe she saw something she wasn't supposed to. Maybe she saw something she wasn't supposed to and doesn't even know it. Like you said, we're newbies. Her? She's inner circle. If they put her on the Ziaee job, then somehow she's become a liability."

"I hear you. So how you wanna play it?"

Bolan handed Dirk a folded newspaper. "Here."

Dirk felt the weight of the steel between the pages and quickly palmed the tiny P-64 pistol within. "I'm already packing. What do I need this popgun for?"

"Check the loads."

The ex-Delta Force commando popped the magazine and raised an eyebrow at the protruding, blue needle-points of the tungsten-steel penetrators. "Armor piercing?"

"Dob wears soft body armor 24/7. Dinatale was wearing it in his office every time we've been summoned. They know about the 9 mms we're carrying. That pistol there is a gift from CIA Station Kabul. Shield seems pretty anal about controlling their operatives' weapons, and if they really are in the business of sacrificing a few here and there, then we know why. They won't know you have that." Bolan tapped his leg against the kiosk stool, and his own pistol clinked in its ankle holster. "And they think Mrs. Ziaee still has the one I gave her."

"I hear that." Dirk tucked the pistol away. "Thanks."

"Don't thank me. If it comes down to these two popguns we'll be in a lot of trouble."

"I think we're already in a lot of trouble."

"How so?"

"I agree with you that there's something shitty going on in the house of Shield, and that sucks. Hell, I'd be in just for that. But if you can really tie Dino and Shield to a squad of slaughtered Rangers, then this thing is one hell of a whole lot bigger than selling out clients. Something bad is going down."

"I agree."

"And so?"

"So we need to be good little soldiers. Do dastardly deeds for Dino. Make ourselves invaluable and get ourselves invited to the big show. Then we burn it down."

"Jesus Christ." Dirk let out a long breath. "So this is the spooky-ass cloak-and-dagger bullshit a brother always hears about."

"Yeah." Bolan measured the man before him. "You want out?"

Dirk slowly shook his head. "No. No way. I'm in. All the way. To the end."

"Glad to hear it."

"So what's our next move?"

"Why don't you go back to the room and write up our after-action reports."

"Yeah?" Dirk's eyes narrowed. "And what're you gonna do?"

"I got a date with Connie."

Dirk blinked. "Dick."

Bolan nodded. "See you tomorrow…Richard."

The Irish Club

CONNIE ZANOTTO WAS RADIANT in a little black cocktail dress. She tucked into her prime rib and Yorkshire pudding while Bolan tossed back a pint of Murphy's stout and began work in earnest on his shepherd's pie. The Irish Club was the only officially licensed bar in Afghanistan. Places like the Shishlik Haus operated under the radar and by heavy bribery of local officials, but the Irish Club was a legitimate business. The owners had been forced to fix the street outside and help fund a local Muslim school before a mullah signed on and said they could operate. By law, it catered strictly to foreigners. Afghan citizens were not allowed inside as patrons, and Afghan bouncers manned the doors to keep them out. Afghan staff worked at the club, but they'd all been given Irish names to protect their identities. Soldiers with assault rifles prowled the streets outside it to prevent attacks by any morally outraged citizens.

Zanotto paused and gave Bolan an appraising look. "That was quick thinking up at the camel ranch."

"Thanks."

"Listen, I like your tactical sense. We've got some big jobs coming up. I was thinking of asking Dino to put you on my team."

"Love to." Bolan polished off his stout and motioned an Afghan waiter whose name tag said Liam for another. "I think we work well together."

"Well, surviving one ambush doesn't make this a love affair, but I have to admit I like your style."

"Tell me a little more about Dino."

Zanotto's face froze for the briefest of moments. "What do you want to know?"

"I'm not prying. I mean, the man's a legend. But you've worked for him, in a professional capacity, and I was—"

"Well, well, well." An English-accented voice spoke loud enough for the whole pub's benefit. "And 'ello, 'ello, 'ello! What have we here, old son?"

Bolan sighed. He felt a headache coming on.

What he had were Her Majesty's Royal Marines coming on.

Colour Sergeant Bourne rose from a booth across the club. A bandage was taped across his broken nose. Jonesy and a pair of fresh Royal Marines rose with him. The four British soldiers made a show of removing their green berets, tucking them under the left epaulets of their uniform and then rolling up their sleeves.

Connie Zanotto raised a wry eyebrow. "Friends of yours?"

Jonesy smiled to reveal his missing incisors. "Should've brought your spade friend, then, shouldn't you, Yank?"

Zanotto's nose wrinkled at the racist remark. "Nice."

Bourne leered at Zanotto. "Must admit I fancy the bird you brought, though."

Bolan shook his head. "Connie, you heard about the British brigadier that Dirk lit up, right?"

"Yeah…"

"Well, the Royal Marines are still a little bit upset about it. We had a disagreement about it at the Shishlik Haus, and I think they're upset about that, too."

"I see. You think you can take these guys?"

Bolan weighed the odds. It was four to one, and Royal Marines had a justified reputation for toughness. He could probably take them, but it would be more than just broken noses and a few missing teeth this time. "Yeah, but someone's probably going to get maimed."

"Right." Zanotto turned toward the advancing Englishmen. "Listen, boys! I don't want any trouble."

"Then shove off, slag!" Jonesy snarled.

Zanotto's eyes went to slits. "Hard words make for hard feelings."

Colour Sergeant Bourne stalked forward. "Listen, love, this is men's business, but if you want to get treated like one, then you'd better be ready to—"

Bolan had no idea how Zanotto had managed to hide a two-inch Polish .38 in her little black dress, but it appeared in her hand like a magic trick as she rose from the table and thrust out the pistol in a two-handed grip. "You know, why don't you boys just go on back to base?"

Bourne stared down the muzzle and thrust out his lantern jaw. "You don't have the bloody guts, love."

Jonesy stepped forward. "Right! You're gonna get some man tonight then, missy! Let's see you—"

Connie Zanotto shot Jonesy in the face.

Gray, high-pressure mist erupted from the revolver like a rocket contrail and enveloped the Royal Marine's head. She turned her body like a turret and shot Sergeant Bourne and the other two Royal Marines in as many heartbeats. Jonesy screamed and clawed at his eyes as the tear gas seared his sensitive optic tissues. Zanotto spun the revolver in her hand to present the wooden butt like a hammer and cracked it into Jonesy's skull. His brow split and he fell to his knees. She spun the pistol again and opened her hand. She slapped another Marine across the mouth, and the cylinder of the .38 sent teeth flying.

Bolan blurred into motion. Blood flew as his fist crashed into

Bourne's already broken nose and smashed it flat across his face. The big sergeant's knees buckled and he sat down hard on the carpet. Zanotto continued her magic dancing-revolver routine. The pistol spun back into the shooting position, but rather than pulling the trigger she dropped to one knee and rammed the barrel into the last Marine's bladder. As the man folded in two, she whipped the front sight up under his chin and clipped him into unconsciousness. She broke open her revolver and ejected the cylinder. She produced a speed loader from a fold in her skirt and reloaded the pistol with lead. "We're out of here."

Bolan dropped a pair of twenties on the table, grabbed Zanotto's hand and the two of them bolted through the kitchen and out the back. "Tear gas rounds?"

"I'm a single girl in Kabul. You'd be surprised at the kind of invitations I get, subtle and otherwise."

Bolan didn't doubt it. "Where can I take you, Connie?"

Zanotto breathed in the night air. "Oh, I wouldn't mind a nightcap at some swank joint."

"Well, I could take you to Lars Shishlik Haus but…"

"But it's probably full of our friends and allies from the United Kingdom?"

"Something like that," Bolan admitted. "The Safi Landmark Hotel is just up the street. They've got a bar. Want to go for a walk?"

"I've got a bottle of Jagermeister in the freezer back at my place," Zanotto countered. "Wanna do shots?"

Bolan grinned. "Let's run."

Shield suite, Kabul

"WITH ABLE ASSISTANCE from Cooper and Zanotto, attack was successfully driven off. After Action: One KIA, one WIA, one prisoner taken. One Shield vehicle lost."

Dirk frowned. All reports needed to end on an upbeat note. Dirk resumed typing.

"Two enemy vehicles destroyed. Two returned to village.

Damage to Ziaee house minimal. Client survival 100%." Dirk nodded to himself and pressed Send. One hundred percent client survival had a nice ring to it. It was pretty accurate overall. Cooper was just about the most able son of a bitch Dirk had ever met. He smiled to himself. Connie Zanotto was able as most women got, and he harbored a few private hopes of her being ready and willing if Cooper dropped the ball. He'd left his filching the rifle grenades out of the report, as well as any mention of the grenadier firing from hiding in the village. Besides—

Dirk's hand went to his holstered WIST-94 pistol as someone knocked on the door. "It's open!"

Dave Dinatale walked in grinning. "How's it hanging?"

"To the left." Dirk grinned back. "I'm just finishing my report."

"Fine. Listen, you got a minute?"

"I do dastardly deeds for Deadshot Dinatale. My time is your time, boss."

Dinatale grinned. "You keep sucking up like that, and you're going to end up vice president of this corporation."

"What if I told you that's my dreamiest of dreamy dreams?" Dirk smiled.

"You are without doubt the most qualified man who has ever applied for a job with Shield. So let me ask you a question."

"Shoot."

"What are you willing to do for me?" Dinatale asked.

Dirk cocked his head. "What do you mean?"

"I mean like where do your loyalties lie?"

Dirk considered his response. "Dino, I just ate the big chicken dinner. I can still taste it, and it makes me want to puke."

"I hear you."

"But by the same token, I don't harbor any ill will toward my Uncle Sam. Hell, I still love the guy."

Dinatale gave Dirk a sly look. "But…?"

"But short of giving direct aid and comfort to the enemy, I guess you could say that I am open to suggestion."

"I'm glad to hear that. Very glad to hear that. Let me ask you another question. What do you think about Cooper?"

"Coop?" Dirk knew next to nothing about Cooper or whoever the hell he was, so he simply fell back on the truth. "I have no idea who he is. He showed up on an op as an observer. No one was happy about it. Then the shit hit the fan, and he showed me he was one crackerjack operator. We're talking Johnny-on-the-spot. He saved my life. Then I saved his. We agreed to meet for drinks at the Shishlik Haus, and I guess Obiada let Dob know there were some likely lads at the bar. The rest is history."

"What else do you know about him?"

Dirk thought about the vibe he'd picked up from the big man with the scary blue eyes. "He's seen the elephant. That I know. I think he got trampled by it, and he survived and picked himself up. He said he's occasionally done jobs for the government. That tells me he doesn't get medical or dental and doesn't have a pension plan. He's too young to retire and too old to start over. He's got nothing to put on a résumé, and when he backed my play with the brigadier his name became mud. All I know is this—he saved my life, he backed my play and the man has a code. He's willing to die for whatever he's loyal to."

Dinatale spent long moments considering this. "Dirk?"

"Yeah, Dino?"

"This has been a fascinating conversation. I'd like you and Coop in my office tomorrow at ten, and we'll talk a little more."

"Looking forward to it."

"You have a good night, Dirk."

"And you, man."

Dirk was pretty sure the room was bugged so he kept his thoughts to himself, but his thoughts were about what Coop had said out on the street. *"So we need to be good little soldiers. Do dastardly deeds for Dino. Make ourselves invaluable and get ourselves invited to the big show. Then we burn it down."*

Dirk was pretty sure they'd just been invited to the show.

6

Bolan rolled over. Connie Zanotto made a sleepy noise and flopped her arm across his chest. His phone was vibrating. It was a nice one, and looked like the kind of phone any world traveler would want, but it didn't look particularly special. However, once its properties were known, it was a phone any gadget geek would give his mouse hand to own. It was the product of Akira Tokaido's ingenuity and was just short of being a supercomputer. A sweep of its antenna had told Bolan the previous night that Zanotto's apartment was bugged.

Bolan killed the volume and flipped the phone open. Aaron Kurtzman's face was grinning at him in real-time courtesy of an NSA satellite.

Kurtzman caught the squelch and began text-messaging. "The room is bugged?"

"Yes."

"How are you doing?"

Bolan typed back. "Fine. You were right. The Ziaee gig was a setup. Me, Dirk, Connie and two newbies were acceptable losses. Dinatale is serving up the occasional client to the wolves, and he doesn't mind losing a few flunkies doing it."

Kurtzman's craggy brows furrowed. "It fits the pattern. Mrs. Ziaee is the first woman to run for a major office since the fall of the Taliban. The Islamic fascist elements out there would pony up millions to see her go down. I've been doing research on past Shield operations. In the last three years, Shield has lost seven clients, and each time they've lost employees doing it. Two per year, until this year he's spiked with four. Each client would equal big money with the right people if he's selling their heads. You'd think that losing clients and operatives would damage his reputation, but he's the hottest thing going. I don't get it."

Bolan got it. "Mercs go where the money is, and Dino pays top dollar. They don't talk about it much, but mercs are also looking for the action. The two don't always go hand in hand. A lot of jobs are babysitting or glorified security guard. You work for Dinatale, and you get to see the elephant. As for his client base, this is the Middle East. They love sacrifice and defeat almost as much as they love victory, and Shield has the reputation of fighting and dying for their clients. You can't beg, borrow or steal a rep like that."

"Yeah, except old Dino seems to have earned that reputation by sacrificing his boys like lambs."

Bolan had been thinking about that. The world of mercenaries was a shadowy place with a well-earned reputation for loss and betrayal, but that was almost always the fault of the clients, the shifting governments of the Third World. For a merc leader to willingly get his men killed for profit was unheard-of in the modern day. If it was true, Deadshot Dinatale had broken the code.

Bolan considered the legend he was working for. Snipers had always been a breed apart and not entirely accepted or trusted by the rest of the military. Special Forces operators ran around blowing things up, kicking doors in the middle of the night, and they very often held the lives of the unsuspecting in their optics, but the sniper was a different case. The sniper always had a specific target, one high-value target that he went out and hunted like big game. The target was almost always behind enemy lines, and the hunt could take days. It took a very special kind of soldier. That kind of soldier always made other soldiers slightly nervous. It was a standing joke at the U.S. Army sniper school that sociopathic tendencies were considered an asset rather than a liability.

Dave Dinatale was currently Uncle Sam's favorite living sharpshooter. He was one of the most successful men in the world at his craft, and he had earned fame and a respectable measure of fortune. The question was what would turn a master rifleman into the sort of monster that would sell out his clients and his own men for money. There were generally two possible answers to that question.

Greed or madness.

But Bolan was not here for an explanation but rather for vengeance. "The question is how is Dinatale involved with the dead Rangers and why?"

Kurtzman had been bending his genius on that one. "Let's start off by assuming you're right. The whole thing was a trap from the get-go, and the Taliban courier, if there ever was one, was bait. The big fat question of the day is why would anyone want to start a shitstorm by slaughtering a squad of Rangers. The action happened on the border between two pacified areas. If something fishy is going on in those areas, you wouldn't want to draw attention to it. The obvious answer is the entire thing was a diversion."

Kurtzman's logic, as always, was flawless, but there were still some huge dangling questions. "A diversion for what?"

"That is the million-dollar question. Dinatale sells some clients to the Taliban? Fine, I'll buy it. Slaughtering the Rangers? On paper, they'd love to do it, but why attract that counterattack by you and Delta Force? That battle set the Taliban in that sector back five years. Where's the payoff? I'm examining all current U.S. military operations to see what might be worth the sacrifice for the Taliban, but so far I'm not seeing it. If Dinatale is aiding and abetting the Taliban, he sure has a funny way of doing it."

Bolan's instincts spoke to him. "He's not aiding and abetting the Taliban. He's using them."

"What do you mean?"

"We both agreed the Taliban couldn't have pulled off the massacre alone. What if they weren't even involved?"

"The Taliban wasn't involved?"

It was becoming clearer and clearer in Bolan's mind. "No, I don't think so."

"What are you saying?"

"The Taliban was just the scapegoat," Bolan typed.

"The Taliban—" Kurtzman was clearly incredulous "—a scapegoat?"

"Why not? This is Afghanistan. If it rains tomorrow, you could blame it on the Taliban and everyone would believe it. They're the bogeyman around here and with good reason."

Kurtzman saw where this was going. "You're saying Shield wiped out the Rangers."

"Wiped out is the key. The Taliban could conceivably wipe out a detachment of Rangers, but they would've taken horrific losses doing it. Even if they managed to drag off all their dead, we would have heard about it. Shield is made up of professional soldiers and has access to the latest weapons. Given a good ambush, they would stand a chance of pulling it off."

"Stand a chance?" Kurtzman cocked his head on the tiny screen. "You're still not satisfied, are you?"

"No, the Rangers were utterly wiped out. Even for Shield, that would be a tall order. They would have to pull in every man on the roster, and I doubt most of their employees would go for killing Americans. Only an inner, hard-core circle would be involved."

"So Shield had help."

Bolan was sure. "Had to have."

"Who?"

"Comes down to location. Who could move enough men and materials through a pacified area to wipe out a squad of Rangers and then be able to cover their tracks and disappear again? Who would be in position to pick the perfect ambush site? My first guess is the people holding down the area in the first place."

Kurtzman's jaw dropped. "You're saying the German army wiped out a squad of U.S. Army Rangers?"

"No, but possibly elements of it did in conjunction with Shield operatives, and they used nerve gas to make sure no one got away."

It was several moments before Aaron Kurtzman typed back. "That's the most horrific thing I've ever heard."

"It's worse than horrific, Bear. It's unthinkable. That's why everyone is thinking Taliban. They're the easy answer."

"You know the President isn't going to be pleased with your little theory."

Bolan was all too aware of that. "That's the problem. It's just a theory. I'm going to have to prove it."

Zanotto spoke sleepily from Bolan's side. "What are you doing?"

"Gotta go," Bolan typed. He clicked his phone shut. He grinned at Zanotto. "Cruising porn sites while I wait for you to wake up give me some sweet lay down by the fire."

Zanotto's eyes flared wide awake. "Really."

"Yeah." Bolan leered.

"Horn dog."

She suddenly yelped happily as Bolan rolled on top of her. "You have no idea."

Kabul Hotel Restaurant

"Man, I had a spooky-ass conversation with Dino last night." Dirk tore into his breakfast.

"What kind of conversation?" Bolan asked.

"Like the sell-your-soul-to-Satan kind of conversation. I signed us both up, by the way."

Bolan related the pertinent points of his text-message conversation with Kurtzman. Dirk's expression slowly went from shock to stone-cold rage. "Oh, these bastard's go down. Every last one of them."

"Keep that rifle grenade in your pants for the moment. So far, this is just a theory."

"Yeah, well, no one's proved Einstein's Theory of Relativity yet, but my ass still ain't floating up out of this seat."

"I believe you're thinking of Sir Isaac Newton's Theory of Gravitation."

"Fuck it. I still ain't floatin' and the goddamn Huns are gonna go down for this." Dirk tossed down his silverware again. "Nazi sons of bitches."

"Yeah, well, I applaud your enthusiasm, but we've got to prove this theory before we act." Bolan took Dirk's gaze and held it. "And I need you frosty for that."

"Oh, I'm frosty. I'm ice-cold. But I'm telling you what you just told me is the only thing that's made sense since we jumped into this gig. Question is why. What the hell are the little goose-stepping storm troopers getting out of all this?"

It was a good question. "Don't know. Shield is making money. The German investment in this is the key to everything. You said you signed us up with Satan. Is that a metaphor, or is something going on?"

"Ain't no metaphor. We got a meeting with the man in forty-five minutes. I think we're looking at a raise or a shallow grave before noon."

"You still got that popgun I gave you?"

Dirk tapped the napkin covering his crotch. "Wearing it like underwear."

Bolan motioned the waitress for more coffee. "I say we take that meeting."

Shield Headquarters

BOLAN GLANCED UP at the sound of rotors.

Dino Dinatale grinned. "Connie's here."

The top-floor windows of Dinatale's office shook just slightly as the helicopter touched down above. Moments later, Zanotto and Stanislawski came in followed by two men. One was big and lanky in a gray tropical wool and clearly a bodyguard. The other man was as fat as a sumo wrestler and was clad in a white suit and black shirt. Only God knew how many silkworms had ruptured themselves to clothe the man. His short blond hair was plastered to his baby-pink skull with sweat from the exertion of riding the elevator down from the roof. For the moment, Bolan kept his eyes on the Pole. He was walking stiffly and keeping his left hand in the pocket in the jacket. Bolan noted that in the past the big man was an arm swinger when he walked.

Dobrus Stanislawski was injured in the upper body.

Dinatale bounced around his desk and greeted their two guests warmly. He threw his arms around the fat man and gave him a hug. "Herr Von Bach! How are you?" He turned and poked the muscle in the ribs. "Klaus! You look fit."

Dirk shot Bolan a look.

The fat man pulled out a black silk pocket square and mopped his brow and spoke in a German accent as thick as a wall. "Dino, call me Toni. My friends do."

Bolan reached into his pocket and pressed a button on the side of his cell phone and the ring tone sounded. He made a show of looking embarrassed. "Shit!" Bolan took out the phone and pressed a button. The ring tone cut out, and at the same time it silently took a picture of their two guests. Bolan pressed another button in the side as he repocketed it, and the photo bounced off an orbiting NSA communication satellite and hurtled its way across the globe toward Stony Man Farm. Bolan shrugged sheepishly. "Sorry about that, Mr. Dinatale."

"No problem, Coop." Dinatale gestured at Bolan and Dirk. "Toni, these are our two new men and maybe the best Shield has ever had the privilege of hiring. Dirk, here, is ex-Delta Force. And Coop?" Dinatale grinned. "I still don't quite have his shit figured out yet, but he's just about the spookiest SOB you're ever going to meet."

"You would trust them with your life, Dino?" the fat man inquired.

"No, but I'm gonna trust them with yours."

An earthquake jiggled through the rolls of fat as the big man laughed. Klaus, on the other hand, gave both Bolan and Dirk a hard stare.

Dinatale caught the vibe. "Of course, Klaus will be in charge of your personal security, but, Toni? This is Kabul. You'll want some extra protection. Short of myself or Mr. Stanislawski, it just doesn't get any better than these two. They've been working for me for a week, and they've already whacked over a dozen Taliban assholes and saved our client. Perhaps you heard about the incident with Mrs. Ziaee."

The fat man wiped his brow again. Despite the gelatinous exterior and piggy little eyes nearly hidden by pouches of fat, the force of his personality was palpable as he looked at Bolan and Dirk. "*Ja,* indeed, I have heard. It is the talk of Kabul. Most impressive. I am grateful, Dino."

Dinatale turned to Bolan and Dirk. "You two are authorized to make security *suggestions* to Herr Von Bach and Herr Kleelander, but you will follow their instructions to the letter until you are otherwise instructed. Do you understand?"

"Got it." Dirk nodded.

Bolan shot a thumbs-up.

"Good. Both of you pack an overnight bag. I need you two ready to fly in an hour." Dinatale turned to Stanislawski. "Dob? Issue these gentlemen PM-84s. Get them shoulder rigs, and make sure they each have a jacket that will cover them. Mr. Von Bach wants Shield personnel low-profile on this one."

"You got it, Dino." The Pole turned stiffly toward the door. "Boys? With me."

Bolan and Dirk followed the big Pole to go arm up.

The Huns were definitely in play.

7

Bolan had to make it quick. Dinatale had said he wanted them ready in an hour. They'd gotten packed and ready in fifteen minutes and beaten everyone else up to the roof. Over the past three days, Bolan had discovered that just about every room in the Shield office was bugged. The roof was just about the only safe place at the moment to make a phone call. Dirk checked the loads in his submachine gun and watched the door.

"What do you have on the Germans, Bear?" Bolan queried.

"A lot. The photo you sent and the names pulled up everything. The fat man is Toner Von Bach, or 'Fat Toni.' In the late 1980s, he was minor drug muscle for the West German syndicates, mostly moving Turkish heroin. When the Berlin Wall fell in 1989, East Germany was the poor relative in almost everything, including organized crime. The system in East Germany was rather primitive. Criminals basically paid off the Communist Party to operate, and the Party sent a slice to Moscow. When the Communist Party apparatus was wiped out almost overnight, organized crime was fractured across all lines.

"Von Bach was slimmer and hungrier back then. He became one of the young lions of what you might call the West German criminal 'carpetbaggers' who moved east looking for new opportunities. They took over former East German criminal organizations. The boys in Berlin keep an iron fist around Turkish heroin and Colombian cocaine coming into Germany, but the East Germans still have their Russian contacts for Central Asian heroin and hashish. Von Bach has a big piece of that action. He's something of an outsider in the German syndicates, almost an independent, but a powerful one."

"Who's the goon?"

"That is Fat Toni's right-hand man. Klaus Kleelander, 'Iron Klaus.' He's a real piece of work." Kurtzman made a face as if he had tasted something unpleasant. "He's a former East German frontier trooper."

Bolan understood Kurtzman's disgust. Under the Communists, it was the frontier troops, or *Grenztruppen,* who had patrolled the border between East and West Germany. Formally, their mission was to stop spies and suppress Western border reconnaissance. In reality, their job consisted almost exclusively of capturing or killing any East German citizen who tried to escape to the West. They were even more reviled than the infamous East German secret police. Controlling the border had also put the *Grenztruppen* in the unique position of controlling the importation of black market Western goods moving eastward and charging exorbitant fees to aid and abet, as well as blackmail and extort from defectors heading west. It was hard to conceive of a military unit more suited to crime, and when the hated *Grenztruppen* were abolished with the fall of the Berlin Wall, organized crime was what many of them turned to as a second career. All *Grenztruppen* were crack shots, and their utter ruthlessness was well appreciated by the German crime syndicates who often used them as hit men, bodyguards and enforcers.

Iron Klaus Kleelander would have earned his nickname the hard way and would be a very dangerous man.

"Where are you and Dirk headed?" Kurtzman asked.

"Don't know. Connie's got the helicopter hot on the pad, and we're packed for an overnight trip. Dirk thinks we've passed the first hurdle of trust, and I agree with him. Dinatale never would have let us meet Von Bach and Klaus if he didn't think we were solid."

"It sounds like you're on the right track, but—"

"Heads up!" Dirk snapped his submachine gun back into its shoulder rig and pulled his Windbreaker over it. "Company coming!"

Bolan clicked his phone shut as Connie Zanotto came out wearing a tightly tailored blue flight suit with a .38 worn openly in a shoulder holster. "Well, you boys are real eager beavers, aren't you?"

She gave no sign of the evening they'd spent together, and Bolan took her cue. "So who's Chubbs?"

"Von Bach?" Zanotto pulled herself up into the cockpit of her helicopter. The Aerospatiale Dauphin 2 was a beautiful aircraft. Its graceful French lines, slightly humpbacked appearance and the custom light-gray paint job made it look like the dolphin it was named after. Bolan noted the rescue winch, the groin-mounted searchlight, the lugs for door gun installations and the cleats and sockets for weapons pylons along the sides.

The helicopter was a shark in dolphin's clothing.

Zanotto began flipping switches. "He's some kind of venture capitalist out of Berlin. I've flown him twice in the last year." She pulled on a pair of blue-mirrored aviator sunglasses, and the Turbomeca engine began to thrum and whine as she powered up.

Bolan turned as the two Germans and a third man came out onto the roof.

Zanotto gestured at the new guy and shouted over the engine noise. "Coop. Dirk. This is Marko. He's one of our German hires. He's going to help us liaison with our guests."

The man stuck out his hand and they shook all around. "Marko Poertner, Panzergrenadiers."

"Dirk, Delta."

"Coop." Bolan shrugged. "Spook."

Zanotto checked her watch and pulled herself up into the cockpit. "Let's load up. We've got a schedule to keep."

The Dauphin was currently set up for VIP transport rather than gunship or search and rescue. The cabin was decked out with three rows of plush leather bucket seats, each with its own headset, cup holder and sockets for laptops and other electronic gear. They clambered aboard, buckled in and put on headsets while Zanotto brought the rotors to liftoff speed.

"Good morning, gentlemen. There's a carafe of coffee in the back and croissants in the minifridge. We have an ETA of about half an hour. Enjoy the flight."

The helicopter lifted up into the skies over Kabul, and the frame whined as the retractable landing gear folded into the bird's belly. Zanotto dipped the nose, and they arrowed off in a southerly direction. Bolan poured coffee all around, and the Germans began inhaling croissants without much in the way of thanks or table manners.

The line between city and suburb was short and almost instantly turned into rugged countryside and hills dotted with villages. Afghanistan was a dusty, pale peach color, almost like Mars, and cratered and rocky like the moon, except most of the real estate was vertical rather horizontal. It was some of the most hostile terrain on Earth and had been ground zero for guerrilla warfare for centuries. The Germans muttered to one another in hushed tones, but Bolan's grasp of German was limited to a few useful words and phrases. Dirk sat silently, apparently watching mountains slide past beneath them.

The terrain flew by. Zanotto was flying low and fast, hugging valley floors and weaving around obstacles rather than flying over them. She was pushing the helicopter just short of nap-of-the-earth combat flying. It was an exhilarating ride. Bolan had to admit she was good, but one didn't get the job of flying Rangers into combat by having your name pulled out of a hat. Bolan wondered whether she was flying low and fast for the fun of it or they really didn't want their journey noted by anyone.

Dirk grinned and pointed out the window. "Hey! There's some of the boys!"

Bolan glanced past him. A column of trucks was winding its way down a narrow valley road. Armored vehicles took point and rearguard position. Von Bach and Kleelander peered down in vague interest and then resumed talking.

Dirk leaned into Bolan's ear. "Luchs."

The ex-lieutenant knew his armor. The Spahpanzer Luchs armored reconnaissance vehicles ground along on their eight giant wheels. Their 20 mm cannon installations slowly rotated to scan the surrounding hillsides while the line of heavily loaded Mercedes-Benz trucks moved in convoy under their protection.

They were flying over German-coalition territory.

Zanotto's voice came through the headsets. "ETA five minutes to E Kamp, gentlemen."

Bolan caught sight of a military camp in the valley ahead. Jeeps, trucks and armored vehicles were parked in orderly rows. Barbed-wire fencing and earthworks formed the star-shaped perimeter of a firebase. Heavy machine guns and automatic grenade launchers were dug in to provide interlocking lanes of fire, and a platoon of 120 mm Soltam mortars in the middle of camp could provide counterbattery fire throughout 360 degrees. The blue-and-white flag of the United Nations fluttered from the flagpole, and beneath it hung the black, red and yellow tricolor of Germany.

Zanotto brought the Dauphin around in a tight orbit around the base. Bolan scanned the little town of tents below and figured the firebase was up to reinforced company strength. The design of the base and its weapon-heavy configuration told him they were close to Indian country, probably on the outskirts of territory held by coalition forces.

The helicopter dropped out of the sky like a stone but landed as light as a feather between a pair of Tiger 2 gunships. Zanotto's voice came through the headsets as they touched down. "Good luck, gentlemen, and thank you for flying with Shield. We hope you had a pleasant flight and hope to fly with you again soon."

Bolan and Dirk watched as Poertner and Kleelander assisted Von Bach with disembarking his vast bulk from the aircraft. Poertner clambered out, and Dirk suddenly began throwing

Bolan some furious hand signals while all three Germans' backs were turned. It was almost to fast for Bolan to interpret but he got the gist.

"Do you speak American Sign?"

A deaf person would have considered Bolan's signing abilities clumsy and infantile at best. Like a lot of his linguistic abilities, Bolan knew some useful words and phrases. However, he had memorized the American Sign alphabet. It would set a deaf person's teeth on edge, but much like Morse code he could slowly and painfully spell out a message letter by letter. The ability had saved his life before.

Bolan signed back a single word. "Alphabet."

Dirk rolled his eyes, and his right hand flew through letters like a bird as he scooped up his gear bag with his left. "Don't trust Marko."

Bolan nodded. It seemed Dirk spoke German and had spent the flight eavesdropping. He shouldered his bag and crouched as he jumped out onto the landing pad. He shot Zanotto a wink, and the pilot's lips pursed into a kiss and then split into a smile as the rotors above blurred.

Bolan leaned into Dirk's ear and spoke over the rotor noise. "I didn't know you spoke American Sign."

"My sister is deaf."

"Didn't know you spoke German."

"Army language school. If you volunteer and earn a proficient rating, it helps with pay raises and promotions, particularly in Special Forces. I rated in German and Spanish. I was thinking of going back for Arabic after this deployment, but then you came along and asked me to the prom."

Kleelander jerked his head in irritation, and Bolan and Dirk trotted to catch up with the Germans. Soldiers in disruptive-pattern camouflage came forward to meet them. A tall man with a shaved head strode among them and was clearly an officer. A jagged scar rent his temple, eyebrow and cheek. However, rather than drooping that side of his face, it had lifted it, making one eye look almost Asiatic, and lifted his eyebrow as if everything he saw was being questioned and found wanting. The left corner of his mouth was tweaked up into a perpetual smirk of evil.

A short, blond fire hydrant of a human who could've been Dirk's German twin was looking at Bolan and Dirk contemptuously. He nearly vibrated with nervous energy, and his close-cropped hair stood up out of his skull like nerve endings. Bolan, Dirk, Poertner and Kleelander formed a phalanx around Von Bach, but by the way Von Bach and the captain were smiling they apparently knew each other well. Bolan stood like a soldier on guard while pleasantries were exchanged.

The thick, violent-looking little German snarled at Bolan and Dirk. "You are in highly sensitive forward Bundeswehr position. Your cell phones and communication devices are required now. You will be issued tactical communications equipment as required."

Poertner nodded, but it didn't fill Bolan with confidence. He rolled his eyes and handed over his phone. Dirk held up his hands. "I'm clean, man. They took mine in the stockade."

Blondie and Dirk stared each other down. The German was obviously considering a strip search deep and hard, but whatever he read in Dirk's eyes made him think better of it. "Luncheon is being served presently in the mess. Your services are not currently required. Dismissed!"

It was interesting that they weren't being disarmed.

Dirk shrugged. "Dude, let's grind."

THE GRIND WAS GOOD. The Bundeswehr had a daily beer ration. It was one of the more appealing things about the German military. Most messes in enemy territory didn't serve beer and bratwurst for lunch. Bolan nodded at the cook for a second ladle of sauerkraut and he and Dirk grabbed a table to themselves. Dirk ran down what he'd picked up from the meet and greet on the landing field. "The scar-faced prick? That's Haupten Fir. *Haupten* is German for 'captain.' He's in command of the base."

Bolan almost smiled. "Captain Fear" seemed like an awfully

appropriate name for the scarred, skull-faced man who had welcomed them.

"The shouting, Nazi midget who never leaves his side? That's Stabsfeldwebel Ull Ulva. *Feldwebel* means 'sergeant,' but Ulva's rank is actually closer to chief warrant officer. He'll be the captain's chief ass-kicker and go-to guy around here. You've probably noticed that every kraut about, save for a few Panzergrenadiers running the armor and the helicopter pilots, is wearing a peaked cap with a flower badge on it. That flower is edelweiss, and it means these guys are Gebirgsjaeger, or German army mountain troops. These assholes are like our Tenth Mountain Brigade and just short of being a Special Forces unit unto themselves. I met some of these guys when I was stationed in Europe. Almost all of them are goddamn inbred cracker hillbillies recruited from the Bavarian Alps. Each one will rank as an expert rifleman by U.S. standards, each one is an expert skier and mountain climber and they'll all have the lung capacity of an elephant."

Bolan read the tea leaves. "So if you were going to cherry-pick some Germanic assholes to misbehave in Afghanistan…"

"Oh, these guys would be the shit," Dirk confirmed. "Most definitely."

The question of the day was what German thugs and German mountain troopers were doing cozying up in a forward firebase in Afghanistan. Some ideas came to mind. "The German coalition forces, they mostly have their areas held down pretty tight, don't they?"

"Yeah, except for some small skirmishes with some real minor warlords, their sector is pretty quiet. Quiet enough to loan men and matériel out for combined forces missions with other coalition members."

Bolan thought about their flight out to E Kamp. "I had us traveling in a south, southeast direction, and Connie had us on the money with about a half-hour flight time."

"Yeah." Dirk had done the math, as well. "We're near the border with Pakistan."

"Yeah," Bolan concluded.

They were in some of the most prime heroin real estate in the world.

Dirk sighed. "Well, sometimes one plus one actually equals two. Speaking of which, what do you think those assholes over there add to the equation?"

Bolan had noticed them. It would have been hard not to.

What appeared to be a horde of local hill bandits took up a pair of twenty-foot tables in a corner of the mess tent. They wore local Afghan homespun tunics, vests and pants and caps. In fact, their homespun looked a little too new, almost hot off the loom. Bolan noted they all wore combat boots and web gear, but the webbing was empty of weapons or munitions. The web gear looked fresh out of the box, except that much of it had powerful folds and wrinkles in it that use hadn't ironed out yet. That implied long storage.

The man at the head of the table was a monstrosity that would give Captain Fir a run for his money on the intimidation scale. He was built like a refrigerator. His filthy hair and beard stuck out of his head in all directions. The man's right eye was a crater of purple scar tissue he had seen fit neither to fill with a prosthetic nor cover with an eye patch. None of the men had guns, but all carried one or more bladed weapons. The big man carried a Russian-issue cossack saber that someone had ground down to a two-foot knife wrapped in local leather.

Bolan watched as they swilled beer, slopped pork sausages and roared at one another in ever louder and coarser tones. "I believe we are in a tent with godless men."

Dirk snorted. "So what are Ali Baba and his forty thieves doing in a mountain brigade mess?"

"I don't think they're local. See their web gear? And boots? It's all fresh out of the box."

"Yeah…" Dirk scanned the table full of drunken pirates. "Yeah, that gear ain't Russian, and it ain't local. Good eye. Though it does look Commie to me."

"It's ex-East German army."

"Shit…"

"Yeah. I'm thinking when it's hammer time, someone is going to load these boys for bear. You want to know how they add into the equation? Those men are the dogs of war. Deniable, expendable and if the money is right, easily replaceable. Not like our friends and allies, the mountain troopers, who've had hundreds of thousands of euros spent on their training."

"Much less cause an international incident if they were implicated in whatever nasty-ass shit these Huns got going down." Dirk took a rueful tug on his beer mug. "We're talking something serious. Know what I'm sayin'?"

"Oh, yeah." Bolan knew what Dirk was saying. "Serious enough to risk killing an entire squad of Rangers over."

"I grew up in Oakland. That's where the brothers live in the San Francisco Bay. I was in a gang. We fought over rock cocaine. Fought over who owned what street corner. But nothing ever got more serious than China White. You pushed H? You worked for the Chinese in San Francisco. You set up shop on your own? They'd send people across the Bay Bridge looking for your black ass. When Mexican brown started coming across the border in the '80s? Things got hairy real fast. That's when the Army and Uncle Sam started looking real good to me."

"That still leaves us with—"

The tent shook with an explosion within the compound. It was followed by a second and a third in rapid succession. Bolan's and Dirk's submachine guns cleared leather in unison. Cooks and German soldiers began running in all directions. Bolan's eyes narrowed. No one seemed terribly alarmed. The evacuation of the mess was as quick and orderly as a well-practiced fire drill. The Mongol horde in the corner drank on unconcernedly.

Dirk had noticed all this, as well. "So what do we do?"

"For the moment? Our job." Bolan deployed the folding stock of his weapon and charged out of the mess. The mortar platoon in the middle of camp had begun firing in counterbattery. Bolan watched the fall of shot as the bombs detonated into the neighboring hills. There was a smoking crater in the landing field, but none of the aircraft seemed damaged. A second crater smoldered near the perimeter, and closer to home one supply tent had been blasted to bits and a sea of blackened Bundeswehr equipment littered the compound in all directions. Pilots were already heating up the helicopters, and armed and ready soldiers were charging to the landing field to mount up.

Bolan charged past the guards in front of the command tent and skidded to a halt. Fir and Fat Toni were drinking schnapps and smoking cigars. "You all right, Herr Von Bach?"

"*Ja,* everything is good." The gangster smiled up at Bolan and Dirk benevolently. "Very good. Your reaction time was excellent and noted."

Fir gestured at a wall map. "The camp has been attacked by al Qaeda, and not for the first time. They are operating in the next valley. We are launching an immediate counteroffensive. Herr Von Bach and his companies have been instrumental in helping rebuild infrastructure in the neighboring areas and have business interests in the valley. He has contracted Shield to help provide security. You two and Marko will accompany Klaus and make sure those interests are secure. Do you understand?"

Yes would have been a pretty stupid answer, so Bolan stood to attention. "We're to obey Herr Kleelander's orders until we are told otherwise."

"Exactly so." Fir's skull-like smile spread across his face. "You understand perfectly."

8

The village was burning. Looking down from the NH-90 tactical transport helicopter, it appeared as if the fight had broken down into scattered small-unit actions in the streets and surrounding hillsides. Groups of weeping villagers, mostly old men, women and children knelt with their hands behind their heads under the bayonets of the Gebirgsjaeger. A pair of gunships rotated over the area in low combat orbits looking for prey. A bullet suddenly whined off the windscreen, and the door gunner rattled off a long burst into a pigeon coup. Feathers flew, and a man collapsed into view against the chicken wire.

Poertner yelled back from the copilot seat. "Hot LZ!"

"No shit," Dirk snarled back.

He shook his head at Bolan. "You know, I never thought I'd ever say it, but I want my Polish assault rifle back."

Dirk wasn't the only one. Bolan clicked down the folding foregrip on his PM-84. It wasn't a bad weapon, as submachine guns went. It was reliable, concealable, easy to control and plenty enough gun for most bodyguard work. However, the weapon was short-ranged, not particularly accurate and the low-power, Russian 9 mm rounds would not penetrate the body armor the German mountain troopers were wearing. They were nothing he and Dirk could shoot their way out of this valley with. It was a thoughtful weapon to issue to men whose loyalty wasn't quite proved yet, and it hadn't escaped Bolan's notice that they had been issued on Mr. Dinatale's order. "Yeah, me, too!" Bolan shrugged. "Don't suppose you happen to have any more grenades down your pants?"

"Not this time."

The helicopter dropped out of the sky, and Poertner yelled back and pointed to a lump of Afghan dwellings below. "We get out on that rooftop! There!"

The pilot didn't risk landing on the clay roof. He brought the chopper to a hover a yard above, and Bolan and Dirk leaped out and crouched to provide covering fire while Poertner and Kleelander joined them. Rifles tore at them from an alley across the way. Clay chips flew off the eaves, and Bolan leaped to one side and dropped. The men were firing from behind a Toyota Land Cruiser. Bolan rattled off a burst in return, but he knew his bullets wouldn't go through the car. Nevertheless, windshield glass cracked and spattered, and the gunmen dropped low.

Bolan counted four of them and shouted over the sounds of battle. "We need to take that position. Dirk—you and me. Marko, Klaus—covering fire."

Kleelander looked as if he had a choice remark in mind, but kept it to himself. He raised his rifle and began tearing bursts into the SUV. *"Schnell!"*

Bolan popped up, took two steps and jumped off the roof. The packed earth of the alley slammed him from heels to skull as he hit, but he bent his knees and popped back up into a run. Bolan shouldered his submachine gun and ran forward with the trigger held down on full-auto. Dirk's weapon snarled into life a second later. The bad guys crouched behind cover as they took fire from ground level and the Germans above. Bolan dropped his spent submachine as it racked open on an empty chamber and drew his pistol. "I go over. You go under."

Dust and gravel flew as Dirk went into a baseball slide. Bolan vaulted for the Toyota's hood as Dirk's weapon snarled between the tires. The four gunmen behind the vehicle screamed and jerked at the ankle-level assault. Two supersonic cracks blasted past Bolan's ear, and a pair of bullets hit the windscreen from behind. Bolan had no time for Kleelander's shooting, as he pulled a slide of his own across the hood and his 9 mm MAG began double tapping in his hand. Two of the men had fallen beneath Dirk's scything attack. The other two each took a twin shot to the face and fell. All four men were dead before Bolan's boots hit the ground. Dirk rose and reloaded.

Bolan slapped a fresh mag into his submachine gun and waved Kleelander and Poertner forward. "Clear!"

Dirk shot his weapon's bolt forward on a fresh round. "That covering fire was a little goddamn close, don't you think?"

Bolan's right ear was ringing from how close it was. "That's why I sent you low."

"You think it was on purpose?" Dirk asked.

There was no time to answer as Kleelander and Poertner trotted up. Kleelander pointed up the street to a house set into the hillside. A pair of light machine guns, Russian RPDs by the sound of them, were hammering out from the two front windows. Kleelander pointed. "There. We take that house. That is our responsibility."

Dirk looked at the thick-walled, fortified dwelling and the diminutive weapon in his hand. He clearly didn't relish the idea of another frontal charge. "Why?"

"There is an al Qaeda cell leader within the dwelling," Kleelander snarled.

Dirk jerked his head up at the circling gunships. "So light the fucker up."

Poertner scowled. "His name is Churagh-Ali Changaze. We wish to take the dwelling with minimum damage and capture him alive."

"Goat screw," Dirk stage-whispered.

"What?"

"Nothing."

Dirk turned to Bolan imploringly. "Man, do something."

Bolan jerked a thumb toward the machine guns defending the house. "We're going to need some backup."

"Gebirgsjaeger resources are tasked elsewhere," Kleelander barked.

"He wants us to charge that goddamn house, Coop."

Bolan ignored Dirk and pointed at another helicopter sweeping into the valley. "How about her?"

Kleelander scowled but began speaking into his tactical link. A second later, the gray Dauphin banked and arrowed toward their position. The cabin doors had been removed, and a door gunner was returning fire into the hillsides. The helicopter slewed to a halt, and fast ropes flew out from both sides. Zanotto tossed Bolan a thumbs-up as four men in khaki slid down and deployed. The helicopter rose up into the orbit of the gunships.

Jimmy Frame's face was a road map of staples, stitches and butterfly bandages, but the ex-Army Airborne man grinned as he ran up. "Hey, Coop!"

"Frame, why the hell aren't you in the hospital?"

"Dude! It's just stitches. Besides, if you and Dirk hadn't counterattacked on the Ziaee job, I'd be a lot more than ugly right now. Figured I owed you, so when Dino said he was sending men out ASAP I volunteered." He nodded at the three men behind him. "That's Fenner, he's Airborne like me. Nolan was an air commando and MacGoohan was a jarhead like Dino. Just call him Magoo."

Magoo was a big man with bulging biceps and a very un-Corps-like black handlebar mustache and ponytail. He looked more like a professional wrestler than a Marine.

Bolan nodded. "Nice to meet you guys. Frame?"

"Yeah, Coop?"

"You really came because you owe me?"

Frame shrugged sheepishly. "Yeah, well, you know, what the hell."

Bolan ran his eye over Frame's optically sighted Beryl rifle with the 40 mm Pallad grenade launcher mounted beneath. Bolan held out his submachine gun. "Then trade me."

Frame was appalled. "Oh, dude! You suck!"

Bolan shrugged. "Gimme."

"You suck," Frame reiterated. He reluctantly traded weapons and web gear.

Dirk watched the transaction with awe and then turned on the ex-Marine. "Yo! Magoo! Trade me rigs."

Magoo blinked once. "I don't owe you shit, Dirk."

"Man…"

Bolan eyed the thick, medieval-looking front door. "Klaus, who's in charge of the attack?"

Kleelander frowned. "Feldwebel Ulva. He is mopping up on the hillsides. Why do you ask this?"

"Get Ulva on the horn. Ask him if he has any GREMs."

Dirk grinned. "Damn skippy!"

Kleelander scowled mightily. "What is, GREM?"

"Ulva'll know, and tell him I'll need at least two and a rifle that can fire them."

Kleelander spoke suspiciously into his tactical radio. His eyes narrowed at the response. He nodded slowly and turned back to Bolan. "It comes."

They crouched and waited for the GREM. The battle was quickly becoming a mopping-up operation. A few pockets of gunmen resisted in the hillsides, but the machine guns in the helicopters kept them pinned while the German mountain troopers overran them. Most of the houses lower down the hill had been taken. More and more villagers were being yanked out of their homes and forced to kneel with the masses already huddled in the little square in front of the mosque.

A Gebirgsjaeger private came bounding up with three rifle grenades and an extra G-36 rifle. He snapped to attention and saluted sharply. "Soldat Steiner!"

Kleelander nodded, and Bolan relieved Private Steiner of the rifle and the GREMs. The Grenade Rifle Entry Munitions looked like regular rifle grenades save that they had a foot-long probe in the nose. When the probe hit the door, it detonated the explosive charge at "stand-off distance" so the explosion punched the door down rather than blowing it up or flying through to explode inside. It also meant that no member of an entry team had to disarm himself to swing a battering ram, and in case of a suspected ambush or booby trap, the door could be knocked down from a distance.

Bolan pointed at the private's ammo pouches. Steiner looked at Bolan uncertainly but unclipped his six-magazine chest pouch. Bolan took them and then handed his Beryl to Dirk. "Your Polish assault rifle back. As requested."

Dirk snatched the rifle happily and checked the loads. Everyone else shook their heads at the macabre round of musical armament. Bolan didn't care. He and Dirk were about to go through a door together, and once again they were mad, bad and dangerous to know at all ranges.

Kleelander stared frostily. "If you two are through."

Dirk shouldered his bandolier of magazines and grenades. "Locked and loaded, baby! Bring the shit on!"

Bolan pointed at the target. "Here's how we're going to play it. All the houses around here have rooftop doors. Me, Dirk and Magoo are gonna GREM right through the top. The second we're in—" Bolan handed one of the battering ram rifle grenades to Frame "—you, Nolan and Fenner are going through the front door."

"I am in command of this operation!" Kleelander snarled.

Bolan was ready for that. "I suggest you come through the top with us to secure Herr Von Bach's interests while Marko does the same with the front entry team."

Kleelander clearly wasn't pleased but appeared hard put to come up with a better suggestion. "Very well. I shall lead top team. Marko below."

"Done. Get Connie on the line. I want to get picked up and then fast rope down out of the machine gun's field of fire."

Kleelander turned away and got on the tactical link. Dirk leaned in as one of the gunships unleashed a ripple of rockets into a pocket of resistance higher up on the hill. "Once we get inside, I say we frag old Iron Klaus's monkey ass."

It wasn't the worst idea Bolan had heard. "We still need to figure out what's going on around here. If Fat Toni loses his right-hand man, that could throw a wrench in the works."

"Yeah, but I've seen the hard-ass stare he's been throwing your way all day. It ever occur to you maybe he's going to frag us once we're in? Those Grenztruppen sons of bitches are used to shooting their own."

It had. "Yeah, but I'm not quite ready to do him yet. We'll just have to watch each other's ass on this one."

"Yeah, man, I hear you, but I still say we put a cap in his ass and have one less thing to worry about."

"Hold that thought."

Kleelander pointed as Connie Zanotto came zooming in. "We do it! We do it now!"

"Marko! Your team! Covering fire!" Bolan tucked the two rifle grenades under his web belt as Poertner's section opened up on the front of the house. Dust flew everywhere in the rotor wash as the Dauphin dipped down to ten feet. Bolan grabbed a fast rope and hauled himself up into the helicopter. Green tracers streaked through the yellow murk of the dust cloud, seeking out man and machine. The rest of the team clambered in, and the Dauphin's rotors hammered the sky to pull them out of the machine gunner's arc of fire.

A pair of gunmen popped up on the roof.

"Connie!"

"I see 'em! Andy! Sweep the roof!"

Door gunner Andy leaned out on his chicken straps, and the smoking lines of tracers streamed onto the roof. One of the riflemen fell, and the other dived back down the roof hatch and yanked it closed with a rope.

Bolan clicked the GREM onto the end of his rifle as they slid over the house. He nodded at Andy. "Gimme a hand!"

Andy grabbed Bolan by the belt as he leaned out of the heli-copter. Bolan squeezed the trigger, and the rifle grenade lanced downward into the hatch ten yards below. Pale yellow fire flashed, and the wooden door snapped in two and flew downward in a shower of splinters.

Bolan grabbed a fast rope and stepped into space. "Go! Go! Go!"

Bolan, Dirk, Kleelander and MacGoohan slid down like spiders to the roof. Zanotto soared back into the sky. Bolan turned to face the other team's position up the street and knifed his hand down. "Go!"

Frame rose from cover, and the GREM thudded from the muzzle of his weapon. The front door cracked open with a shriek of timber and wrought iron. Bolan went down the hatch and took the steep clay steps three at a time. A gunman lay at the foot of the steps, struggling dazedly beneath the two slabs of broken door. He just managed to snake a pistol out of the pile of kindling as Bolan went airborne. He screamed, and the pistol squirted out of his hand as Bolan landed on him with both feet.

"Alive!" Kleelander roared from behind. "We want him alive!"

Bolan dropped to his heels as a line of bullets ripped up the wall inches from his face. He fired a burst back and drove the gunman back behind a doorway. The interior of the dwelling was dimly lit by smoking oil lamps. Bolan could hear the snarls of the machine guns in the floor below and the answering fire of Poertner's team. The shooter stuck his muzzle around the door and blindly ripped off another long burst.

"Frag him," Bolan shouted.

"Alive!" Kleelander roared.

"Dirk! Do it!"

The 40 mm Pallad launcher beneath Dirk's barrel boomed, and the 40 mm frag flew through the door. Bolan and Dirk both crouched back in the clay stairwell as shrapnel hissed and chipped against the clay walls and the shooter screamed. Mac-Goohan leapfrogged forward and covered the stairwell. Bolan moved to the door and found the man shredded and mewling.

Kleelander was screaming from the cover of the rooftop stairwell. "Alive!"

"Gonna murder that man…" Dirk murmured.

"Dirk, gimme another frag down the—"

"RPG!" MacGoohan shouted.

Bolan just had time to see the launcher pushed around the corner when the former Marine's paw slammed him back. The RPG thumped below, and MacGoohan flailed as the rocket-propelled grenade hit him in the face. The propellant charge had hurled the grenade from the tube, but the sensor required ten meters of flight before firing the rocket motor. It still flew with enough force to stave in the Marine's skull, and MacGoohan toppled backward like a tree with a football-shaped rocket grenade impaled in his face.

Kleelander gaped in horror. Even Dirk was appalled. "Aw…shit no, man—"

Bolan lunged and grabbed the grenade by its rocket motor. The rocket might not have fired, but once an RPG-7 grenade left the tube it was armed and the six-second self-destruct fuse was burning. Bolan heaved the gore-crusted missile free and flung it down the stairs. "Down!"

Bolan and Dirk hugged the floor while Kleelander cringed on the upper stair.

The house shook as the RPG detonated. The RPG-7 grenade was an antitank weapon, but even without an armored vehicle to slam into, its blast and fragmentation effect was impressive. Bolan bounced up with Dirk right behind him. Bolan squinted against the smoke and stink of high explosive filling the stairwell. He hit the ground floor to find one of the machine gunners down and the other dazedly trying to feed a fresh belt into his weapon. Bolan's burst cratered the side of the gunner's head and dropped him. Half a dozen lay dead or in various states of bloody disarray.

"Clear!" Bolan boomed. Frame and Fenner came through the front door guns ready with Poertner and Nolan behind. Kleelander came down the stairs a second later.

Bolan heard motion deeper in the house and moved to a doorway. "Klaus, any of these guys our men?"

Kleelander stared around in confusion. It occurred to Bolan very clearly that Kleelander was an assassin rather than a soldier. "Klaus!"

Kleelander seemed to snap awake. "*Nein!* He is not among these!"

Half a squad of men came pounding down the hallway screaming, firing and trying shoot their way out.

"Dirk!"

Dirk didn't need to be told as he raised his rifle.

"Alive!" Kleelander shouted. "A—"

Dirk's 40 mm thudded, and Bolan's team leaned or leaped out of line with the hallway. The frag detonated with a whip crack and men screamed. Bolan leaned back around the doorway. Two men were down, and four more were running back the way they had come.

Kleelander pointed furiously at a man wearing a camouflage vest and a green helmet. "That is him! That is Changaze!"

With the target identified, Bolan took the opportunity to put a burst into one of Changaze's gunmen. The killer faltered, and Changaze and his two remaining men ducked through an arch into a daylit area. Bolan maintained his position. Most old-style houses in the Middle East and Central Asia were a rectangle or cube built around a central courtyard. "Marko! Tell Connie I need her."

"What do you—?"

Bolan tore the tactical radio from Poertner's vest. "Connie! This is Coop! I need eyes on the courtyard! ASAP!"

"Copy that, Coop! Eyes on! ASAP!" Zanotto came back. Bolan could hear her rotors above. "Coop, I have four hostiles in the courtyard. One down. Two more behind a raised tree well. One by something like a cistern in the corner."

"Do you have a green helmet in sight?"

"Roger that, Coop. One hostile wearing a green lid. Positioned by the tree. Andy says he can take them from here."

"Alive!" Kleelander screamed. It was quickly becoming his mantra.

"Negative, Connie. Hold your fire."

Rifle fire popped from the courtyard. "Coop, we are taking ground fire."

"Connie, take a safe orbit but stay close. I'll need air support in a second." A plan began to form in Bolan's mind.

"Copy that, Coop."

"You will bring me Changaze alive!" Kleelander was trembling with rage. Bolan had usurped command, and every member of the team had accepted it without blinking. And despite his nickname, Iron Klaus Kleelander clearly didn't have the stones to try to take it back. He stabbed his finger at Bolan. "Alive!"

Kleelander spun on his heel and began furiously speaking German into his radio.

Dirk's rifle wasn't quite pointed at the big German. "He says that shit one more time…"

"Dirk…"

Dirk's eyes burned holes in Kleelander's back. "As for Changaze? Fuck him. I say we light him up. This one's for Magoo."

"No, we've got a job to do. We have to take him."

"Coop, there's three of them, we ain't wearing Kevlar, and then we gotta wrestle Changaze down? We go into that courtyard, we ain't coming back. I say we frag Klaus, commandeer Connie and her copter and bug the fuck out of here."

"No."

"Coop, we can't take him. Not like this."

Bolan gave some hard thought to the one clear glance he'd had at Churagh-Ali Changaze. The man was wearing black market U.S. Army Interceptor body armor and a Russian special forces helmet. With boron carbide ceramic plates protecting his torso and cold-forged titanium covering his dome, he was about as bulletproof as any warlord could hope to be.

They could take him.

"No, we can take him."

Dirk stared at Bolan as if he were insane. "You can't take him."

"I know, so you're going to take him."

Dirk was incredulous. "Oh, I'm going to take him?"

"Yeah, I'm going to set him up, and you're going to take him down."

"And this is going to happen how?"

"Like I said. I'll stand him up." Bolan shrugged. "Then you GREM him."

"GREM him?" The idea dawned on Dirk, and the man from Delta was clearly intrigued. "GREM him."

Bolan nodded. "You ever been bowling?"

"I been bowling."

"Then I'm going to stand him up, and when I do, you pick him up like a spare. I go low this time, you take him high."

Dirk stared at Bolan seriously. "You're the only white man I've ever loved."

"Just don't miss. My ass is going to be out in the breeze on this one. Here, trade me."

Dirk took the G-36 rifle and fixed the GREM onto the muzzle. "Oh, I won't miss."

Bolan took the Beryl and turned to the rest of the team. "Dirk and I are going to go fetch Changaze. Frame, if we don't make it, it's your call."

"Jesus, Coop."

"Any questions?"

Kleelander stood vibrating but said nothing.

Bolan got back on the radio. "Connie, give me a read on the courtyard."

Rifles popped in the interior as Zanotto took a peek. "Hostiles holding positions. One's on his cell to someone."

"On my signal, have Andy take the guy by the cistern. Then I need covering fire. He can't hit anybody else. I just need their heads down, and let him know I'll be hitting the courtyard a second later."

"Copy that, Coop. On your signal."

Bolan turned to Dirk. "Ready?"

Dirk nodded. "Let's do it."

Bolan clicked his radio. "Now, Connie!"

The door gun above began snarling on full-auto. Bolan ran forward firing. Tracers streaked down upon the courtyard like comets. Bolan hurdled dead men and went into a baseball slide. The covering fire above suddenly ceased. The cobbles were slick with blood, and he got a good body length of nearly frictionless travel before his boots came to a stop against the base of the stone tree well. The bolt of Bolan's Beryl rifle came to a stop with a conspicuous empty clack.

In the sudden silence Churagh-Ali Changaze and his AK-47 rose up to tell Bolan goodbye. His partner in crime rose beside him, equally intent.

Bolan slapped leather for his MAG pistol, but the killer had him dead to rights. With a clap of thunder and a flash of flame Changaze suddenly rose up and back like a man who'd hit the apogee of his bungee jump. He hurtled backward and slammed brutally into the courtyard wall. Changaze slid as limp as a boned fish to a sitting position. The man beside him was staggered from the GREM's side flash. He twisted and dropped beneath a long burst from Dirk's rifle.

The ex-Delta Force commando covered the courtyard from the doorway. "Coop! You okay?"

Bolan rose, pistol in hand. "Yeah, have Frame and his team sweep the rest of the house." He walked over to Changaze. The man sat wheezing while his eyes rolled around, glazed and out of focus. He had minor flash burns on his face and was bleeding from the nose. His right arm was clearly broken, but his armor had prevented his internal organs from turning into applesauce, and his helmet had kept his skull from cracking against the wall. He should enjoy being knocked silly while he had the chance.

Bolan suspected the rest of Changaze's life was going to be short and all downhill from here.

Kleelander came into the courtyard and stared about. He looked at Bolan and Changaze, apparently surprised to see that both were still alive. He thrust his hand at Bolan with renewed anger. "Your radio! Give it to me!"

Bolan considered refusing, but the time to take down Kleelander wasn't quite at hand. He tossed the tactical radio at the German's feet. "Tell Herr Von Bach the package is secure."

9

"Damn." Dirk shook his head as the villagers carried their loads down the hill to the waiting trucks. Gebirgsjaegers brought their loads down to the waiting trucks. "Well, you called it, Coop. All the way down the line, you called it, and you were right."

Bolan ran a rag over the G-36 rifle he'd refused to return to Steiner. He wasn't happy to be right. Three old Russian Ural military trucks had arrived just before sunset and disgorged the one-eyed Ali Baba and his forty thieves, and each man had an ex-East German AK-47 with a folding stock and a pistol. The big man also carried a tapered wooden club wrapped in ancient and stained leather. He pointed and waved with it as if it were his rod of command, and whenever or wherever he pointed his men scrambled to do his bidding and villagers dropped to their knees and averted their eyes. In the East, the bastinado was primarily used for beating the soles of a prisoner's feet. It was horrifically painful yet left no scars or signs of outward injury to the casual observer.

More importantly, it removed the victim's ability to run away.

The one-eyed man and Iron Klaus Kleelander had gone to work on Churagh-Ali Changaze. After less than five minutes of screaming, the two men had come out with well-satisfied looks on their faces. Just fifty yards up the hillside from Changaze's house, a pair of old army blankets loosely stitched to a wicker frame and smeared with clay and dirt had formed a perfect camouflage to the mouth of the cave.

Bolan had taken down enough drug dealers to recognize the kilo bags of heroin that were coming down the hillside.

Dirk perched his Beryl rifle on his hip. "It occur to you there ain't no Taliban in this valley?" He surveyed the cringing villagers doing the bidding of the Germans and their Afghan auxiliaries. Some, mostly captured fighters, were already hobbling from the big man's club. "Hell, they're probably praying for some guys in black turbans to come along and put a jihad on these assholes."

Bolan decided to take a chance. "Frame!"

Jimmy Frame was busy applying antibiotic cream to the railroad tracks of stitches crisscrossing his face. "Yeah, Coop?"

"That Frankenstein-faced son of bitch carrying the lumber, what's his story?"

"Dunno." Frame shrugged. "His name's Gulab-Sha. That's about all I know. I'm almost as much of a newbie as you, Coop."

Bolan glanced at the line of villagers piling kilos by the trucks. "You see that stuff?"

"You know, the way I see it, I'm getting paid not to see that stuff."

Dirk bristled. "That's what Magoo died for? A kilo of smack?"

Frame's face was all stitches, bruises and bandages, and his brown eyes stared back at Dirk out a sea of broken blood vessels, but they were all business. "Dirk, I got problems back home. I need this job. Don't screw this up. Don't even think about it."

Bolan raised a calming hand. "No one's screwing up anything, Frame. We were just…surprised. That's all."

Frame kept his eyes on Dirk. "Remember what I said." The ex-Airborne man turned on his heel and walked away.

Bolan sighed. Dirk was a crackerjack commando, but his investigative techniques needed a little polishing. "You think you can ease up a bit?"

"Okay, so I still ain't up to speed on all the secret-agent bullshit yet. I'm sorry, but you know we're in up to our eyeballs here, and don't tell me your people know where we are."

"Nope." Bolan wasn't going to lie. "They have no clue."

"So we're stuck in this valley with no way to get the word out.

You know, I tried to borrow Nolan's phone. He said no. He was polite about it, but he said no."

"Yeah." Bolan shook his head. "I know."

Dirk rolled his eyes. "Okay, so that wasn't cool, either."

"No, it wasn't. We came in as newbies and kicked ass twice, and Frame thought he owed us. I was busy sowing doubt in his mind until you got in his face. Asking Nolan for his phone isn't helping our cause, either. You want a phone? Steal one. Just remember if any communication gear goes AWOL, it's all eyes on us."

Dirk gazed down guiltily. "Sorry." He suddenly perked up. "We still have Connie. Connie still loves us."

"Connie loves me," Bolan corrected.

Deflated, Dirk fell silent for a moment. He and Bolan watched Gulab-Sha shove a flinching man to the ground in passing.

"So what do you think that asshole represents?" Dirk asked.

"Only one thing I can imagine."

"And what's that?"

Bolan had met the type before. "He's what goes bump in the night. He's the pacifier who's going to keep a lid on this valley, and any atrocity required has no German flag attached to it. When Ulva and his Huns leave, Genghis and his Mongols are going to make sure the peasants make their poppy quotas."

"Shield and the mountain troopers are going to trust that Cyclops son of a bitch?"

"He's their best option. The Gebirgsjaegers flattened the place, but they're still invaders. A bunch of blond, blue-eyed assholes start holding court, every old mujahideen with a tooth left in his head will be ready to start a guerrilla war. But this valley was being run by Churagh-Ali Changaze. Like you said, Changaze wasn't Taliban or al Qaeda, just a drug lord. Gulab-Sha? He's just more of what they're used to. Maybe a little more brutal, but one more local thug with enough AK-47s to enforce his will and the mountain brigade to back him up."

Dirk spit bitterly. "And us."

"Yeah, and us."

"We gotta get out of here. We gotta get this shit out there to someone who can do something."

"We gotta be cool, Dirk. We gotta—heads up."

Marko Poertner came by wearing the local homespun. He tossed a pile of laundry to Bolan. "You will put on these."

Bolan took the lump of clothes and started to go behind a wall.

Poertner pointed at the G-36 assault carbine. "You will surrender your rifle."

It wasn't an unreasonable request. If the Shield operators were taking camouflage, then the Heckler & Koch would stick out. "You bring me an AK and eight loaded magazines, and I'll be happy to."

Poertner met Bolan's eyes. The German blinked first. "Very well."

Bolan went behind the wall and stripped out of his khakis and put on the traditional Central Asian baggy trousers, long tunic and vest. He draped a *chawdor* blanket across his shoulders and tilted his woolen *pakol* cap at a jaunty angle.

Dirk wasn't pleased with his new duds. "This shit is not sexy."

Poertner returned with an East German rig, and Bolan traded him. He checked the loads and unfolded the steel stock. "So, what's happening?"

"We are staying put for a little while. Dino, Fir and Von Bach are all very pleased with you both. I predict you will receive bonuses. We all will, thanks to you." Poertner leaned in and spoke low. "However, were I you? I would be careful around Klaus. He bears no love for you."

Bolan nodded. "Thanks."

"It is nothing, as I say. You and Dirk's work today will put more money in every Shield man's pocket."

Bolan raised his head at the sound of rotors. A helicopter was flying over the valley and coming their way.

"Ah, good." Poertner nodded at the helicopter's approach. He'd been expecting it. "Dirk, Coop, you will excuse me."

The German trotted off to the landing area. The blue-painted civilian Huey wasn't Connie Zanotto, nor was it German military. It touched down in the dusty village square and six men and a willowy, good-looking blonde piled out awkwardly and crouched, clutching their caps against the rotor wash. They were dressed in the conspicuous Western foreigner garb of khaki pants and vests, only rather than being loaded down with weapons they carried cameras, video equipment and laptops and all wore press badges on lanyards around their necks. Ulva and a squad of soldiers went out to meet them.

"Christ on a crutch! Journalists?" Dirk shook his head. "These assholes actually want to document this mess?"

"You know, I think they do."

"What? Why?"

Bolan watched as the group shook hands all around and soldiers and journalists were paired off. "You see that? The journalists are being embedded. Each one is getting a trooper as a bodyguard."

"Yeah," Dirk agreed. "And they're all speaking German, too."

Ulva spoke at some length with the woman and one of the men. The sergeant pointed at various spots in the valley and then at the mosque and sites in the village.

Dirk squinted as he tried to read their lips. "What? The Nazi prick is bragging about his shit?"

Bolan had posed as a journalist a number of times and knew something about the profession. "No, he ain't bragging. See the blonde?"

Dirk leered. "Yeah, man. I kinda dig the librarian look."

"Well, she's the 'face' of this outfit."

"Face?"

"The correspondent. The face in front of the camera. The little guy? He's the technical director. They're setting up the shot."

"You're saying the press is in on this?"

"There's only two ways to beat the press. Buy them out, or keep them out completely."

Dirk watched as the technical director framed the sun setting between his thumbs and Ulva nodded approvingly. "This is some messed-up shit."

"Do me a favor."

"What's that?"

"I want you to go down there and stand around. Be out of the way. Look bored. But listen in on what's being said and what's going on. If they notice you and tell you to scram, don't argue, just do it. But pick up whatever you can."

"Yeah, okay, I got it. What are you going to do?"

"Like you said—" Bolan shrugged "—Connie still loves us. Maybe I can make a phone call."

"You think she'll let you use her phone?"

"No, but what she doesn't know won't hurt her."

"You said we shouldn't steal phones."

"I'm not going to steal it. She'll be asleep."

"How are you—?" Dirk stared heavenward for strength. "Aw, man! When do I get to do some James Bond, hot-blonde seduction shit?"

BOLAN LAY WITH ZANOTTO in a bedroll in the cabin of the Dauphin. She wasn't going to sleep anytime soon. Dating an aerobic superwoman had its advantages. Trying to outlast one was more problematic. The battle had raged most of the night. It was 4:00 a.m. and at the moment there was a mutual cease-fire.

Zanotto traced a finger across Bolan's chest. "Nice work, Coop."

Bolan stretched lazily and decided to change the conversation. "So who's this Gulab-Sha guy?"

Zanotto's nose wrinkled. "He's a real turd. Former secret police for the king of Afghanistan back in the day. Former scout for the Soviet army during the occupation. Former mujahideen when the war went against them. Former Taliban enforcer when the guys in the black turbans took over. Former Northern Alliance when coalition forces toppled them. Formerly human, as far as I'm concerned. Real slippery son of a bitch. All I can say is that in any dirty war cockroaches like him make themselves useful to whoever's winning."

"Yeah, that's what I figured." Bolan ran a hand through her hair. "So how did you feel about our mission today?"

Zanotto's smile faded slightly. "My mission was to deliver some reinforcements to save your ass. What was yours?"

"Replacing one scumbag with another."

Zanotto rolled out of Bolan's arms, reached over to the ice bucket and took a slurp out of the bottle of German sparkling wine. "Read a history book, Coop. That's pretty much what mercenaries do."

She had a point. She was also clearly very displeased with what was going on. Bolan could also tell that against her better instincts she wanted to talk. "Sorry, what happened today was just kind of…unexpected."

Zanotto stared out through the bullet-cracked cabin window toward the few scattered lights of the village still burning. "It always is…the first time."

"Working for Shield. It started off pretty righteous in the beginning. Didn't it?"

"It started off wild-ass fun. Dino gave me my own helicopter built to my specifications. When I wasn't flying in Iraq or Afghanistan, I had bodyguard details for the rich and famous. I spent more time in cocktail dresses than Kevlar, and during my time off, Dino took me around the world. I told him anyplace as long as it was sunny, and he took me to Bali, Acapulco, Australia…you name it, and Dino? Dino isn't a normal sniper. Dino likes to dance. Dino likes to party, and Dino knows how to treat a lady."

"But then somewhere along the way a line got crossed, didn't it?"

Zanotto's aquamarine eyes went hard. "You ask a lot of fucking questions, Coop."

Bolan decided to play some hardball. He let his own blue eyes blaze, and she flinched back before his sudden anger. "Yeah, well, I crossed a line today, lady. Those asshole krauts lined up the villagers at bayonet point and made them tote heroin, and I stood there like a good little Nazi and *Sieg Heil*ed. The film crews are here. I'm in it up to my eyeballs, and next week? I'm going to cash the bonus Dino gives me, and God help me, I'm going to ask him to send me out again. You're just going to have to forgive me if I have a moment of moral crisis here."

Zanotto stared at Bolan very steadily. "If you were the kind of man who didn't, then you wouldn't be here in my helicopter."

Bolan relaxed back, and Zanotto put her head on his chest. He took the bottle and tipped it back to finish it as she spooned into him.

He thought of Dinatale, Von Bach, Captain Fir, Gulab-Sha and their machine.

They were all going down.

Every last son of a bitch among them, and they had no idea what kind of lines Bolan was willing to cross to burn them down.

10

The sun was just starting to rise. Dirk hopped up on the wall next to Bolan, who was just finishing putting a razor edge on the East German AK bayonet. He tested the edge with his thumb, then spit on the sharpening stone and began work on the back edge with short circular strokes.

Dirk pulled out an Afro pick and began plucking the twelve steel tines through his hair.

Bolan nodded in admiration. "That 'fro is really starting to stand up."

Dirk examined his expanding hair critically in a signaling mirror and smiled in self-satisfaction. "Well, it ain't up to *Enter the Dragon* standards yet, but I admit it is coming along nicely."

"So what's on your mind?"

Dirk tucked the pick into the back of his hair like a samurai topknot. "Man, this shit's getting sicker by the second."

"Tell me about it."

"First off, Gulab-Sha is dirt. A—"

"Torturer and a turncoat who's worked every side of Afghanistan's sorrow for thirty years and keeps getting paid."

"So you heard about that. Fine, steal my thunder. Whatever."

"Tell me about the Germans."

Dirk grinned. "You know, I saw Connie's helicopter bouncing around on its landing gear last night."

Bolan sighed. "Just tell me about the Germans."

"Yeah, well, I did what you said. I went and leaned against a post while they had their preliminary photo shoot and bent my ear a little. They did a heroic little segment with Sergeant Ulva about how the Taliban had been driven from the valley. They showed all the weapons they'd collected and said they were slated for destruction. They filmed the heroin being piled on pallets, and then? Cut camera and out come a bunch of plastic bags full of flour or some such shit. Everyone clapped and smiled like righteous assholes while they doused it with kerosene and burned it. Butter wouldn't melt in these bastards' mouths, but meanwhile the H went onto the trucks and headed straight for Kabul."

"What about the guns they collected?" Bolan asked.

"They piled them in the cave and put them under guard. Along with every gun they found house to house in the village. The impression I got is that Sha is gonna do a little side business and sell them to some cronies."

Bolan began field-stripping his AK and going over it with a rag, a toothbrush and some German gun lube he'd managed to scrounge. "Then what?"

"Then Gerta Wilden did a beautiful little segment with the sun setting on the valley and talked about how the villagers here would now grow roses and saffron rather than heroin poppies and live in peace and prosperity. Then the interviews began." Dirk's eyes went cold. "That's when I almost greased every last one of them. But I remembered I had to be cool."

"What're you talking about?"

"Short version? Churagh-Ali Changaze and his assholes took over the valley about five years ago in a local power struggle. But the tribal headman of the village is an old guy named Behroz Daoud. His son is a kid named Babrak. The kid was fighting up in the hills during the battle, but he got captured. Anyway. They weren't compliant, so Gulab-Sha went to town on the old man. Beat his feet to jelly. I'd be surprised if he ever walks again. Made his son watch. When that wasn't enough, they dragged out the wives and daughters. The old man complied. They sat him down, tucked his bloody feet under his tunic and rolled cameras. I swear they must have gone through twenty takes to try and get one where he wasn't grimacing or crying. Then the director said the crying was good, and they made Daoud say how happy he was that the Germans had come and liberated them from the Taliban. Made him sound grateful about how now they were free. Made his son hug Ulva on film and offer him tea." Dirk spit. "Man, I've seen some shit in my day. But that was vile."

Bolan glanced up from brushing his bolt assembly. "So what else did you learn?"

"Well, it's like we suspected. Von Bach identifies heroin traffickers, mostly his competition, and then a Taliban or insurgent attack is staged. The mountain troopers come in and sweep out the unsuspecting local drug lord, declare a victory for the war on terror. Then they bring in some primate warlord like Sha who sets up shop, keeps a lid on things and does exclusive business with Fat Toni. A few Shield agents stick around to make sure the guys like Sha stay on the up and up."

"What about the journalists?" Bolan asked.

"Fat Toni owns them, lock, stock and barrel. The story plays very well in Germany. Gerta Wilden is starting to get famous. She was bragging to me last night how a big U.S. news network has sent out feelers about making her a foreign correspondent. The other news I got out of her is they have a tentative plan for a shoot next week."

Dinatale, Von Bach and Fir were moving fast. "Do we know where?"

"Not yet. Gerta said they arrived late yesterday and lost the light. So this morning they're going to be doing what she called 'happy village' shots. People working in the fields, eradicating poppies, kids going to school, digging a new well. The whole bit. It's enough to make you puke."

Bolan had to admire it. It was a remarkably tidy little setup. One of the better criminal machines he'd run up against in a while. Which also made it one of the most dangerous. The German syndicates were nothing if not efficient. Advancement was earned through ruthlessness and merit. The German army was one of the best-trained, best-equipped militaries in the world, and Shield was made up of veterans from the best the world had to offer.

Dirk nodded at the sun. "So, what'ya say we bug out of here?"

"How?"

"Well, you're the James Bond dude. Let's steal a helicopter. You can fly a helicopter, can't you? I thought all you superspies could."

Bolan regarded Dirk dryly and slid the bolt assembly back into his rifle.

Dirk held up his hands. "Sorry. I forgot. You're not a spy."

"Yeah, I can fly a helicopter," Bolan relented, "but I don't do it every day for a living."

"So?"

Bolan gazed down at the gleaming Tiger gunships as their German crews began morning maintenance. "So my chances of outflying those guys are slim, and beating them in a dogfight is none. Let's keep that as Plan Z."

"Yeah, but speaking of Z—" Dirk gave Bolan a sly look "—bet Connie could do it."

"Now you're thinking."

"And the Germans will be leaving soon for next week's gig."

Bolan slid in a loaded 30-round magazine. "Right."

"And you haven't told Frame or Connie yet that Dino put apples in our mouths and offered us up to the Taliban like Christmas dinner on the Ziaee job."

Bolan sighed proudly. "I can teach you no more."

Dirk folded his arms across his chest and leaned back against the house. "Okay, so why don't we run up the red flag and have these assholes fragged to hell and gone?"

"Run up a red flag to who?"

"Well…our guys?" Dirk suggested.

"You think the United States is going to launch an investigation into Federal Republic of Germany military matters?"

"They could start the goddamn ball rolling!"

"Yeah, the President would believe us, and he could whisper in the German chancellor's ear, and…" Bolan milled his hands encouragingly.

"And it'd go over like a French kiss at a family reunion," Dirk concluded.

"Yeah, and Dino? Fir? The fat man? They have contingency plans. They'll bug out and leave Gulab-Sha holding the bag. Not just holding the bag, but dead and anyone of import in an investigation slaughtered. There'd be a bit of a stink, but not enough for anyone to act on or take the word of some villagers against decorated veterans. That assumes any villagers would be left alive, and it would be chalked up to another Taliban atrocity."

Dirk nodded. "You're saying snitching ain't enough. We have to blow this wide open."

"Dirk, we're going to burn this down. To the ground."

Dirk gave Bolan an appraising look. "You've done this before."

The brutal fact was Bolan had. "The fact is good people are going to get hurt."

"Yeah, I know, and I can live with it." Dirk stared out across the valley. "But I'll tell you. It's hard to stay righteous in your world, dude."

"Dirk, that's why I picked you. You're our moral compass on this one."

Bolan lifted his chin toward the mouth of the alley. "Heads up."

Dobrus Stanislawski came walking down the lane.

"How the hell did he get here?" Dirk grimaced. "He wasn't on the choppers, and I didn't see him get off the trucks."

It was a good question. "Maybe he was here the whole time."

"God…damn it."

"We're dealing with pros here, Dirk. Keep it in mind."

The big Pole nodded approvingly at Bolan as he walked up. "Weapons maintenance. Good!"

"Yeah, so when am I going to get a real weapon to maintain?

I had a G-36 for about a minute, but these Germans are squirrelly about their ordnance."

"What do you wish?"

"Oh, I don't know. A rifle with a 40 mil and an optic sight? Say…something Polish?"

Stanislawski sighed benignly. "That can probably be arranged." He pulled a pewter flask from his vest. "A morning constitutional, gentlemen?"

Dirk reached for the flask eagerly. "I'll have a taste." He flicked back the cap and took a long pull. "Jesus…" He hacked and passed it to Bolan.

Bolan took a long pull and felt kerosene ignite in his throat. Poles were confirmed vodka hounds, and they liked it flavored. Stanislawski appeared to favor his vodka flavored with red-hot chili pepper flakes.

The Pole thumped the platelike mass of his right pectoral. "Puts hair on chest."

Dirk wiped away the tears from his eyes. "So what's up, big man?"

"Have job for you."

"Oh, yeah?"

"Yes, headman's son, Babrak, and friend. They are missing. We believe they fled into the hills last night. You two will hunt them down. Bring them back." The giant Pole shrugged. "Or kill them. Either is acceptable, but they are not to escape from this sector."

Bolan glanced at the gunships. "Wouldn't this be a better job for the mountain troops and a chopper or two?"

"Air resources are already tasked for today. Gebirgsjaegers have other tasks, as well." Stanislawski leered knowingly. "You two seem to have nothing better to do than chase girls and clean guns."

Dirk sighed. "Man…"

The Pole pointed at the rising sun. "They head west. Two teenage boys. On foot. With only six-hour head start. How difficult can it be?"

Bolan could think of few more difficult tasks than hunting Afghans in their homeland. Invading armies had been learning that since the days of Alexander the Great. They might be teenage boys, but they had grown up in this valley and would know the surrounding countryside like the backs of their hands. "Are they armed?"

"We believe there are hidden caches of weapons still in village. You should assume boys have rifles."

"I want that rifle with the optical sight."

"You shall have it. Go to supply tent. Take one day's food and two days' water. Tactical radios."

"I want night vision. Taking them after dark will be the best way."

Stanislawski nodded. "Very well. You shall be issued whatever you need. Bring boys back alive, or dead." The big Pole's eyes went to slits. "But I want to be sure. You understand?"

Bolan hopped off the wall. "We got it."

"Good, you shall leave immediately. Have it done by dawn tomorrow, and there will be bonus."

Bolan and Dirk trotted down through the village streets. "Dirk, let me ask you a question."

"Yeah?"

"Changaze's men. The casualties. When you were hanging around yesterday, did you notice if they shipped the bodies out on the trucks?"

"Naw, they got 'em stacked in a tent by the trucks. I think they're going to let the villagers bury their own and then burn the guys who were hired goons."

"Good enough."

"Why?"

Bolan broke off down a side street. "I'll meet you by the supply tent in fifteen minutes."

THE SUN WAS SETTING, and Dirk's anger had been simmering all day. As they came to the top of the rise it boiled over. "Christ, Coop! We're hunting kids!"

"I know." Bolan knelt by a footprint in the dust. Babrak and his friend were able outdoorsman, but the young men seemed more interested in speed than in covering their tracks. Their strategy lay in doing as much distance as possible and then using the night for cover. Unfortunately for them, the night was when men like Bolan and Dirk did their best work. Bolan scanned an arroyo through the optic of his Beryl rifle. "There."

Dirk scanned the broken terrain through the sight of his rifle and nodded as he spied the little rivulet of water trickling down the rock face. "Water."

"The boys are traveling light. Probably carrying nothing more than their rifles, a water skin and maybe a few rolls of flat bread. At the speed they've been moving, their water is probably gone."

Dirk glanced upward. Clouds were filling the sky. "No moon tonight. It's gonna be a dark one. They won't get far after the sun sets."

"They'll be holing up."

"So we wait."

"Yeah." Bolan squatted behind a rock and pulled out an MRE from his pack. He put the Meal Ready to Eat pouch and the heating element into the bag and poured in two fingers of water. Bolan slid the meal in the carton as the exothermic reaction began to heat the meal. The standard joke in the U.S. military was that the Meal Ready to Eat was the "three lies." It wasn't a meal. It wasn't ready, and you couldn't eat it.

Dirk looked up from boiling his own dinner. "What do you have?"

"BBQ pork rib."

"Oh, man! I got the penne with sausage. Trade me."

"No way."

Dirk scowled and rummaged through their pile of gear. "You got two packs of grilled beefsteak with mushroom gravy."

"Those are for the boys."

"Let 'em have the sausage!"

"Dirk, they're Muslims."

Dirk angrily shoved the MREs back in the bag. "The condemned getting a last meal? Nice."

"They're probably getting pretty hungry by now." Bolan tore open his MRE and began tucking into the ribs. Dirk sulked and shoved soggy pasta and mystery meat into his mouth. The sun disappeared behind the mountains in the east, and the temperature instantly began drastically falling. "They'll be lighting a fire soon."

"Good!" Dirk shoved aside his half-finished meal. "Let's collect the little bastards and call it a day."

Bolan pulled on his night-vision goggles and began scanning through his optics. He didn't have long to wait. "There."

Dirk scanned the rocks near the little rivulet. "I see it."

The boys were in a cave and had probably pulled as far back into it as they could and sheltered their fire. It would have been enough to shield them from the Taliban or bandits like Changaze, but the fire was still sending out light across spectrums invisible to the human eye. It reflected off the cave walls, and the night-vision equipment gathered up the stray light and amplified it thousands of times. In the green field of the NVG lenses, the entrance to the cave was softly glowing.

"Let's go get them."

Bolan and Dirk moved down into the arroyo. During the rainy season, the rivulet was probably a cataract, but even its gentle patter covered the sound of their approach. Bolan crouched fifty yards from the cave. No sentry had been posted. "These kids speak English?"

"From what I could pick up, there's a little school in the next valley over where they taught it. Being the headman's son, I'm sure Babrak probably attended, at least until Changaze took over and put everyone to work in the poppy fields."

Bolan decided on the direct approach. He walked up to the cave and shouted. "Babrak!"

Sounds of consternation echoed out of the cave and a second later an AK-47 rattled off a burst. *"Allah Akhbar!"*

"Great, they're going into martyr mode," Dirk said.

Bolan kept out of the line of sight of the cave. "Babrak, my name is Cooper. I'm with a man named Dirk."

The boy shouted back in anger. "You are the American mercenaries! You serve the Germans!"

"No, we're here investigating the Germans."

"Liar! You attacked our village!"

"I attacked only Changaze. I'm pretty sure you had no love for him. Let's talk."

"You wish to kill us to keep your filthy secrets!"

"That would take one grenade," Bolan countered, "which I happen to have right here in my hand."

Babrak searched for a response. "You... We are not afraid to die!"

"Neither am I. I'm coming in. I'm coming in unarmed. Kill me if you want, but my friend will blow up the cave in revenge and make it your tomb." Bolan unslung his rifle, unholstered his pistol and grabbed the MREs. "I'm going in."

"Okay." Dirk stared at Bolan frankly. "But we ain't selling these kids out."

"No, we aren't."

Dirk smiled slightly. "You got a plan."

"Yeah, but it's sketchy as hell. We'll take it one step at a time." Bolan cracked a light stick, and green light spilled all over him. "I'm coming in."

Bolan entered the cave. It quickly tapered to the point he was duckwalking. Smoke clung to the ceiling. He came to a tiny, banked fire pit and a pair of frightened young men with AK-47s. One was dressed in jeans and a plaid shirt beneath his sheepskin jacket and wore a gold earring. He was clearly Babrak. The other was in homespun straight out of the village.

Babrak eyed the packages in Bolan's hands. "What are those?"

"Food. You hungry?" Bolan knelt without waiting for an answer and got the MREs self-heating. They all squatted in an uncomfortable silence for about ten minutes, and then Bolan opened the MREs. The smell of beef and gravy filled the little pocket in the mountainside. According to Afghan custom, technically the cave was Babrak's and he should have been the one offering hospitality, but he and his friend were cold, filthy, exhausted and hungry, and all it took was one whiff to set them salivating.

Babrak summoned what resolve he had left. "You would poison us."

Bolan took a big, two-finger scoop out of one of the bags and chewed and swallowed it.

Babrak's friend snatched the other bag and began wolfing stew. Babrak looked vaguely betrayed but took the other MRE. Bolan nodded at the other kid. "Who's your friend?"

"He is Noorzay. We are friends since childhood."

He looked up from his food and nodded. "Noorzay."

"Nice to meet you. Listen, the Germans sent us to kill you."

Both young men stopped eating.

"I'm going to need to convince them that I did. Babrak, give me your earring."

"Why?"

Babrak and Noorzay gasped as Bolan produced a pair of human right ears. "I took them from the corpses of Changaze's men. I'm going to tell the Germans I took them from you."

Babrak nodded thoughtfully and gave up his earring. "I see."

Bolan looked at a small amulet Noorzay wore around his neck. The little tube of hammered silver and beadwork would contain a scrap of the Koran for luck. "I'll need that."

Noorzay's hand clutched the charm. "My mother gave this to me. For luck."

"Yeah, and I'm going to need all the luck I can get, and I hate to say it, but at dawn tomorrow I need both your mothers wailing in grief."

Noorzay nodded gravely and handed over the amulet.

"Babrak, tell me something I can tell your father so that he knows you're not dead."

Babrak considered. "Tell him I am sorry. I should have spent more time reading the Koran than surfing the Internet on the laptop he gave me."

"You have the Internet?"

Babrak puffed up with pride. "We are the only house in the village that does."

"Where's your laptop?"

Babrak pulled it out of his pack. "It is here."

"Give it to me."

The young man very reluctantly handed over his pride and joy. Bolan checked the battery and handed it back. "Leave your father a note, put it on a sticky so it will pop up when he opens it."

Babrak swiftly opened a window and wrote a few sentences. "There."

Bolan pointed westward. "The next two sectors are German held. I doubt you'll get through the patrols. If I were you, I'd stay in the hills close to your village. I'll see to it that some of your people leave food for you at night out in the fields. Where would be best?"

Noorzay piped up. "There is a rock formation near the east end of the fields. There is a dry streambed we can crawl along to reach it!"

"Good. Babrak, write it down."

Babrak shook his head as he typed. "Yes, but what are we to do?"

Bolan punched the stem of the earring into the lobe of one of the severed ears. "Wait."

The young man closed the laptop and handed it over. "But wait for what?"

"I'm not sure, but when it happens—" Bolan smiled tiredly "—you'll know. Then do whatever you have to do."

Babrak contemplated this. "I think I understand."

"I knew you would. My friend and I have to get back. Wait a day, and then make your way to the valley. Good luck."

"And to you, Mr. Cooper. And thank you."

"No problem. And Babrak?"

"Yes, Mr. Cooper?"

"Your village will be free."

The two young men bowed their heads in thanks.

Bolan emerged from the cave. Dirk shrugged in question. "So, you kill 'em?"

"Naw, just gave them a hot dinner and some good advice. They'll be back lurking around the village soon."

"So what story are we going to tell Toe-jam?"

Bolan held up the pair of bloody ears.

Dirk recoiled. "Jesus Christ!"

Bolan nodded. "We tell Toe-jam we killed them. I took their ears, and you're appalled."

11

Dobrus Stanislawski recoiled and crossed himself as Bolan tossed the ears on the table in the command tent. "Jesus Christ!"

"That's what I said." Dirk folded his arms across his chest in disgusted agreement. "That shit ain't right. Matt here has some sick-ass issues."

Bolan's face was impassive. He tossed Noorzay's amulet among the carnage. "Babrak and his little buddy are dead. Didn't you mention something about a bonus?"

The Pole openly reevaluated the man before him. "Yes. You are paid a thousand dollars a day?"

"That's right."

Stanislawski pulled out a fat roll of hundreds and began peeling them out as if he were dealing cards. "Last forty-eight hours? Double pay."

Dirk snatched his four thousand. "Damn, this shit ain't that sick. You lose any other sheep while we were away?"

The Pole laughed. "No, all has been quiet."

Dinatale spoke from behind them. "What about your VIP visitor, Toe-jam?"

"Yes." The big man grinned. "Boss is here."

Dinatale carried a cooler to the table and set it down with a thud. He flipped it open to reveal a case of Budweiser tall cans on ice. "The taste of home, gentlemen! You've done some yeoman's work here in this valley. Figured I'd show a little appreciation."

Dirk grabbed a tall boy. "Damn, Dino! When I got busted out

of Delta I didn't know I had a sign around my neck that said Will Work For Beer And The Benjamins, but hell, I guess I do."

Bolan took a beer and wiped it across his brow before opening it. "Thanks, Dino. I haven't seen the old red, white and blue label in a while."

"No problem. You guys deserve it." Dinatale peered at the table. "Christ, Cooper, ears? That's like Vietnam jungle shit. Old-timers at the PX don't even talk about that anymore."

Bolan put some steel into his voice. "Yeah, well, you know something, Dino? Babrak and his little friend weren't coming along quietly. They went all martyr on us. They stood zero chance, but they went to their maker as martyrs. And Dob didn't give us shit for insertion or extraction. You want us to foot it halfway across Afghanistan? Fine, but you're going to have to forgive me if I didn't carry those kids' carcasses on my back. Dirk wasn't into trophies, and Toe-jam said he wanted to be sure. So I just took care of it." Bolan let a little of the anger he already felt for Dinatale simmer to the surface. "And just between you and me, Dino? That was a real shitty job you sent us on."

Dinatale didn't blink before Bolan's gaze, but like Stanislawski a moment before, he was clearly giving the man before him a reevaluation. He nodded slowly. "I know. It was messed up. No doubt about it, but that's why I chose you two. There're guys who work for me, veterans, who couldn't have done it. You came through with flying colors. Fact is, the name over the door says Shield, but you and Dirk have been the tip of the spear on every mission I've sent you on. Outwardly, Shield is a protection agency, but as you've discovered sometimes we are proactive. You didn't like the mission? Good. That's real good, because if you had, you'd be a sociopath, and I only use them as cannon fodder when I use them at all."

Bolan finished his beer in a few bitter swallows. The can crumpled in his hand as he stared into the middle distance.

Dinatale smiled and shook his head. "Coop, I can almost hear what you're thinking, but listen. You and Dirk are just about the highest caliber operators Shield has ever seen. You want a home? You just might have one. You want high pay, lots of time off, full-ride medical and dental and a retirement plan you wouldn't believe, it's within your grasp. You get old or injured? Hell, your consulting services alone would be worth the price of admission. You and Dirk could end up executive partners, you keep this shit up."

"Yeah, Coop—" Dirk shook a handful of hundreds "—don't screw this up."

Dinatale kept his eyes on Bolan. "You down for this?"

Dirk waved his arms in agitation. "Of course he's down for this!"

Dinatale still kept his eyes on Bolan. "Dirk? I'm talking to Cooper."

"What am I? Chopped liver!"

"No, Dirk. You're a Delta Force officer. The best of the best." Dinatale's sniper stare continued to try to read Bolan. "But Coop has some skill sets you and I don't have. I want him, I want you both, but he's got to be all the way in or not at all." Dinatale cracked himself a beer. "So what do you say, Coop?"

Bolan shook his head wearily. "You know my answer."

"Yeah. I do." Dinatale nodded. "But I want you to say it out loud. For everybody's benefit."

Bolan took a long breath and let it out. "Dino?"

"Yeah, Coop?"

"I need a job."

Dinatale shook his head. "Everybody *needs* a job."

Bolan's shoulders sagged like a man who had just willingly sold his soul. "Mr. Dinatale, I want a job."

Dinatale poured the charm back on. "There was no malice in that, Coop. I ain't trying to ride you, bust your balls or establish who the alpha male is. I just needed to hear that you want in. All the way in."

"Yeah…I know."

"Oh, buck up, camper!" Dinatale popped Bolan a fresh beer. "You just joined the winning team!"

Bolan smiled grudgingly.

Dinatale held out the beer and jiggled it at Bolan tauntingly. "And you're whining? What's up with that?"

Bolan yanked the beer out of Dinatale's hand and appeared amused despite himself. "Fuck you, Dino."

"That's the spirit, soldier!"

Stanislawski scooped up the ears and the amulet gingerly. "Good work, gentlemen. Dino, I will see you all later."

"Take her easy, Toe-jam!" Dinatale took the Pole's seat at the table and grinned. "What say we drink some beer, men!"

"THAT DINO IS ONE charming bastard." Dirk stumbled just a little bit as they walked to their tent. "Gotta admit that."

Dirk was right. The three of them had spent most of the morning killing the case of tall boys and trading war stories. The early-morning beer-bust had been a hell of a lot of fun. For a little, wiry guy, Dinatale could hold his liquor, though he had pretended otherwise. Several times, and with the subtlety of a sniper, Dinatale had tried to catch Bolan in a lie. It had been a very well-orchestrated interrogation, with the ace sniper probing for things that could be double-checked. Alcohol was still the most powerful truth serum Bolan had ever encountered.

Coupled with camaraderie, shared danger and the fact that human beings generally wanted to talk, it was a highly potent mixture, and Dinatale knew how to use it. Bolan knew his cover would stand up to the scrutiny of most sources Dinatale could call upon. The question was, would it stand up to the sniper's hard-won instincts. Bolan had some hard-won instincts of his own.

Bolan had a bad feeling.

That feeling was intensified as a single, heartbroken voice rose in the Middle Eastern wail of grief. Bolan and Dirk glanced up the hill toward the village as the wail was joined by a second and a third and then a dozen, turning the sob of sorrow into a spine-chilling chorus of despair.

Dirk's shoulders twitched. "Man, that never fails to freak me out."

Dobrus Stanislawski had gone up the hill and shown the ears to all parties concerned.

Dirk prodded Bolan in the ribs. "You better watch your ass, dude. Some grief-stricken granny is going to go grab the family scimitar off the mantel and lop off something you care about."

"I know."

"Yeah? Well, you should've factored that shit in before you started tossing severed ears around."

Bolan stopped. "Dirk?"

"Yeah, Coop?"

"I'm making this up as I go along."

Dirk sobered up considerably. "I hear you."

"Chances are, we aren't getting out of this valley alive. I got a feeling Dino doesn't trust us, at least he doesn't trust me. You put Gulab-Sha, Shield and the mountain troopers still in the valley together, and we're outnumbered about eighty to two. Until Babrak and Noorzay sneak back and make contact, the villagers hate us, and I mean us, as in you and me. I don't think Dob spent a lot of time explaining how the brother wasn't involved in the ear-removal portion of the hunt."

"No, don't suppose he did. So what do you want to do?"

"We play some cards. I've got to talk to Connie before she hears I've been taking ears."

"And me?"

"You have to get a message to the headman, Behroz. You've got to let him know his son is alive and that he and his friend Noorzay will be ghosting the village within twenty-four hours."

"And how the hell am I supposed to do that?"

"I have Babrak's laptop. All the phones have been gathered up and destroyed, but as far as I can tell the phone lines to the valley haven't been cut. You have to get the laptop to Behroz. That's our ace in the hole if we need to make a clandestine communication, and we need the villagers back on our side ASAP."

"This gets spookier by the second."

"No, this isn't spook shit. This is exactly what you've trained all your life to do."

Dirk just stared. "And how's that?"

Bolan smiled and quoted the United States Army Special Forces motto. "*'De oppresso liber.'*"

"'To liberate the oppressed.'" Dirk gazed up toward the village. "Yeah, I feel you. I'll get the computer to the old man somehow." He looked back toward the makeshift airfield. "Looks like Connie's shining her chopper. Now's probably gonna be your best shot."

"All right, we'll meet up later." Bolan walked down toward the parked helicopters. Zanotto was wiping her windscreen and frowning at the chips and cracks of the bullet strikes from the past battle.

Bolan walked up and grabbed a rag. "Hey, baby!"

Zanotto raised an eyebrow. "You smell like beer."

"Budweiser, tall cans. Dino can be generous."

"Yes, he can. So what do you want, Coop?"

"You know what I want." Bolan leered.

The pilot blushed slightly. "Yeah, but I never met a man who volunteered for rotor-wiper duty who didn't want something else."

Bolan gazed on innocently. "What else could I want?"

"A favor."

Bolan sighed. "Am I that obvious?"

"I'm a woman who spent twenty years in the U.S. Army. I know when I'm being hit on, and I know when someone wants a favor."

"Okay, so I'm hitting on you, and I want a favor."

"Charming." Zanotto snorted. "You're a pig."

"Yeah, but I'm a charming pig. Admit it."

Zanotto clambered up onto the lip of the cabin door and squinted up into the starboard engine's air intake. "Okay, at the risk of giving away the entire farm, how may I be of service to you?"

Bolan grinned. "Nice."

"Just spill it."

"Can I borrow your phone?"

Zanotto's voice went from flirty to professional. "Coop, as you might expect, the operational situation is kind of sensitive at the moment. Engaged Shield contractors are to remain dark for the time being. Save for team leaders, all communications are to remain tactical in nature. You need to make a call? I suggest you go ask Dob."

"Yeah, but I'm not asking Dob. I'm asking you," Bolan said. "And we both know he'll say no, anyway."

"Probably with damn good reason, too."

"I'll keep it short, I promise."

Zanotto eyed Bolan suspiciously. "Straight up, Coop. Is your mother in the hospital or something?"

"No, but I'll tell you straight up. I got a few things on the fire back home, and I haven't been able to check in for days. I know I've got some people worrying about me and some stuff that could go south if I don't keep the ball rolling."

Zanotto was clearly conflicted.

"C'mon, Connie," Bolan cajoled. "Please…"

"Cooper…"

"Tell you what. You can stand here and listen if you want. I guarantee I won't say where I am or mention word one about the valley."

The pilot pulled her sat phone out of her flight vest and handed it down. "You know? Dino would describe this as a lapse in tactical judgment. I could lose my bonus over this."

Bolan flipped open the phone. "You're the best!"

"Yeah, yeah, just make it quick." She hopped down from her helicopter and stabbed an accusing finger at Bolan. "And you're paying for my minutes! I'm already over this month."

Bolan dialed the Farm. Shield headquarters and the apartments they kept for their operators were all bugged. Bolan suspected Zanotto's phone might be bugged, as well. He had to weigh that against the fact that Dinatale had already tried to send him to his death once and the valley was turning into a death trap.

In Virginia, the Farm instantly noted it was receiving a communication from an unknown and nonsecure source. It instantly bounced the signal to the NSA electronic warfare division, which began trying to track the signal's path. Bolan dialed an extension and got an automated operator that simply asked him to leave a message.

"Hey! This is Cooper. Pick up!" Bolan said.

The voice-recognition software instantly compared the sentence against a vocal catalog of Bolan's speech patterns and that sentence in particular. It gave the match a ninety-seven percent chance.

Kurtzman picked up a second later. "Striker! Where are you?"

Zanotto stood staring frostily at Bolan with her arms folded.

"Hey, Bear! Only got a minute." Bolan nodded encouragingly at the pilot. "Need to ask you a favor."

There was probably no nation on Earth with the telecommunications prowess to crack the Farm's electronic security. Kurtzman knew he was secure, but that didn't mean Bolan was secure on his end, and Kurtzman had caught the casual tone in Bolan's voice. "Shoot."

Bolan kept his eyes on Zanotto. "The Rangers who were slaughtered in the Jalkot Canyon. What did the Army forensics team determine about the weapons the attackers used?"

Zanotto's jaw dropped.

She froze as Bolan's 9 mm MAG blurred out of its holster. The safety came off with a click as he pointed it between the pilot's beautiful blue eyes.

Kurtzman pulled up the file on his end. "Not much. They found hundreds of bullets and shell casings, consistent with a firefight. The only thing it mentions specifically is Kalashnikovs and RPGs. Even some of the coalition forces use them, though."

The muzzle of Bolan's gun never wavered from Zanotto's face. "Bear, I need forensics tests on any remaining evidence the Army still has. I need to know if the small arms used against the Rangers were of Polish or East German manufacture."

The pilot turned pale.

"I'd check specifically against the Polish kbk AKMS and the East German MPi-KMS72," Bolan continued. "Those are the two models I've observed so far in my investigation. Most of the AKs in Afghanistan are Russian or Chinese. They're all basically the same, but the East German and Polish weapons will have been built in different factories on different machines and very likely built to higher tolerances. Someone who knows what they're doing should be able to compare spent bullets and brass and detect the difference."

"I'm on it."

Bolan could see Stanislawski ambling toward the airfield. "Gotta go."

"Striker! You've been dark for days! Where are you?"

"Don't know, try to track the signal on satellite. Gotta go." Bolan lowered his pistol and handed Zanotto back her phone. "Dob is walking over right now. You want to turn me in, now's your chance."

Zanotto's eyes blazed. "What the hell are you? Some kind of cop?"

"I don't know any American cops with any jurisdiction in Afghanistan except for MPs on U.S. bases."

"You said 'so far in my investigation,'" the pilot countered. "What is that supposed to mean?"

"I'm investigating the annihilation of a squad of U.S. Army Rangers. I could tell by the look on your face you've heard about it." Bolan let his voice grow cold. "You used to fly for the Rangers, didn't you?"

Zanotto's .38 cleared leather and the hammer cocked back under her thumb. "Fuck you, Cooper."

"Now, I'm pretty sure I have Dinatale on accessory to murder, torture and drug trafficking, but I'm not a cop. He has to go down for that, no doubt, but that's incidental. I came to Afghanistan about the Rangers, and my investigation led me here."

"And Dirk?"

"He's an ex-Ranger just like you, and he volunteered to get the battalion some payback."

The revolver wavered in the pilot's hand. "What do you want from me?"

Bolan let a little of the iron recede from his voice. "Nothing."

"Nothing?" She shook her head bitterly and holstered her pistol. "I'm a good Italian girl, Coop. Sicilian. I've seen *The Godfather,* and the 'Some day, and that day may never come, I will call upon you to do a service for me,' is coming and coming soon, you son of a bitch."

Bolan holstered his pistol. "I'm not going to ask you anything, Connie. But sometime, probably in the next forty-eight hours, you're going to have to make a choice."

"Damn you…"

"I'll help you. Where was Dob during the Ziaee fight?"

"What?" Zanotto blinked. "I don't know. Off on a job."

"Find out where if you can, but don't let Dino catch you."

"And why do I want to do that?"

"Because I think I fragged him in Shorkot village."

"What the—?"

"He was the grenadier. Dino sold the Ziaee family to the Taliban. He sold us all to the Taliban that night."

"That's bullshit! And—"

"And Frame got disfigured."

Zanotto's lip trembled.

"And Boner went home in a bag," Bolan finished. "And while you're at it, ask yourself if there's anything in the last six months that might make Dino decide that you're a liability."

Her face froze, and Bolan knew he'd hit a nerve. "I'd think about it if I were you, long and hard, and I'd be ready to fly with thirty seconds' notice."

"Goddamn it…"

"Are there any cell phones or radios around besides yours?"

"No, like I told you. This valley is dark. Unless you're a team leader, they've all been collected. Anything the villagers owned has been confiscated or destroyed."

"Dirk and I made contact with the headman's son. He and his friend are going to be lurking around the eastern edge of the poppy fields. Dirk is taking the kid's laptop to his father. As soon as we can, we'll tell the old man you're one of the good guys. If all else fails, go to the eastern edge of the valley and try to meet up with the kids. If the Gebirgsjaegers come back, all bets are probably off, but with Babrak and Noorzay, there's a chance you might get out of the valley."

"Jesus…" Tears brimmed in Zanotto's eyes. "How did it come to this?"

Bolan had seen things come to this before. "You took a job. You made fat cash, got to travel, got to fly, and then one mission… You crossed the line, but you're a good soldier, and you stuck by your buddies. Then you were in, and every line you crossed got a little easier and got you in a little deeper, until there was nowhere else to go."

Tears spilled as Bolan read the pilot her résumé.

"Connie, if you want out, I'm the only shot you have."

She ran a hand along the Dauphin's graceful line.

Bolan tilted his head toward the gunships. "I'd wait. Next time Dino sends you to Kabul, keep going. Don't stop until you get to Goa."

Zanotto pushed at the tears on her face angrily. "What? Where Interpol will be waiting."

"No. You don't turn me in, and we're square."

"You're going to take Dino down?"

Bolan nodded. "Oh, yeah."

Zanotto nodded back. "Then count me in."

12

"Behroz has the laptop." Dirk shook his head. "Poor bastard has hamburger for feet, and he was kneeling and thanking me."

Bolan drank tea by the village well and watched as the villagers went out into the fields under the guns of Gulab-Sha's men. "Anyone see you?"

"Naw, I was sneaky. Though I'll tell you, when I interrupted dinner, I thought for sure the whole family was going to go jihad on me with the kitchen cutlery. Probably figured I'd come for their ears, as well. Then I handed him the laptop. He took it like I was handing him a snake. I had to play goddamn charades just to get him to open it, but when the kid's message popped up, I was gold, baby!" Dirk grinned and pulled his pick from the back of his head and began happily teasing his hair ever higher. "So how'd you do with Connie?"

"She's on the team."

"Cool. I wasn't looking forward to trying to hoof it out of here."

"She also told me Dino had something going on, really big and really secret when the Rangers got hit. About half the Shield operatives on the payroll all went dark at the same time. Strangely enough, he gave her the weekend off. She didn't think much of it at the time, so she went to India and hit the beach. She didn't hear about the Rangers until she got back."

"Then what happened?" Dirk asked.

"She said Dino was acting weird, but she figured he was upset about the massacre like every other American in Afghanistan. But when she read up on it, she noticed it happened between two of the German sectors. She's Ranger all the way, so she asked Dino if any of his 'sources' might know anything about it or be able to help. She says he got real cold."

Dirk frowned. "And she couldn't put two and two together?"

"Dirk, I think a big part of her didn't want to. An unprovable suspicion is one thing—turning on your team is another. She was already up to her eyeballs in it, and if she was wrong she'd bring down Shield, betray all her friends and probably end up in jail."

"Yeah, I hear you." Dirk shook his head as he watched the villagers troop back up the hill. "We gotta act soon. I think once the Germans leave, Gulab-Sha and his boys are going to go to town on the village pogrom-style."

Bolan had the same feeling. The German soldiers were maintaining a very professional bearing and Sha and his men were keeping in line with them, but once the Gebirgsjaegers left, as long the poppies were cultivated and the quotas made, they wouldn't care too much about atrocities. Bolan had a pretty strong feeling Dinatale didn't care, either. "The weapons they confiscated from Changaze's men. They still in the cave?"

"Last time I checked, and if they ain't, then there's two dudes standing guard duty outside for no reason I can figure."

"Good, then—"

Stanislawski bawled, "Cooper!"

Dirk rolled his eyes and replaced his pick. "Duty calls."

Bolan ambled over. "What do you need, Dob?"

"It's your lucky day! Dino is sending Connie to pick up a few more Shield operatives and get minor repairs to helicopter. He says you can go back with her." The Pole grinned salaciously. "Think of it as forty-eight-hour pass."

Dirk waved his arms. "What about me?"

"Villagers have never seen black man. Dino wishes to keep you for intimidation purposes until valley is running nicely."

"Man…"

"Connie is already prepping chopper." Stanislawski glanced

at his watch meaningfully. "You had best grab your gear and get moving."

Bolan grinned at Dirk. "I am out of here."

Dirk's eyes went to disgusted slits. "You suck."

Stanislawski laughed. "Best get going."

Bolan loped to the tent he and Dirk shared and grabbed his gear bag. He noted it was heavier than when he'd left it. Bolan lifted the flap as he peered inside. Inside were three Polish rifle grenades, one armor piercing, one antipersonnel and one incendiary/smoke phosphorus round. The incendiary round had a yellow sticky note on it that read "Love Dirk."

The man from Delta Force had come through again.

Bolan shouldered his carbine and his pack and trotted toward the airfield. The gunships had left at dawn, along with one of the transports and about half the Germans.

Zanotto was shrugging into her flight vest. She gave Bolan a big smile and then muttered, "This isn't good."

"No, they're splitting up me and Dirk. I think there's a good chance Dino doesn't suspect Dirk, but I don't know how much that will protect him once things go south."

"Well, I've checked the chopper from tip to tail. If it's been booby-trapped or sabotaged, it was done by someone who knows helicopters a hell of a lot better than me." She sighed. "So what do we do?"

"We go."

"I could fake a malfunction."

Bolan gazed hard at the Eurocopter NHI NH90 transport parked in the other landing space. "That would send up a hell of a red flag, and there are still German mechanics around."

"All right." Zanotto smiled like a shark. "Then let's kick this pig and see what happens!"

"I'm with you, baby."

Zanotto climbed behind the stick as Dirk, Frame and Stanislawski ambled up to the airfield.

Dirk waved. "Bring back some beer! Dino's stash is gone, and

Dob's pepper shit rips me up!" Dirk's hand dropped in front of his chest and darted and weaved in a flurry of cramped American Sign. A lot of it Bolan couldn't read, but he got the gist of it. "Twenty-four…I don't hear…I'm gone."

If Bolan wasn't back in twenty-four hours, Dirk was going to hoof it out of the valley and get help or start the guerrilla campaign. Bolan would have preferred forty-eight hours, but he didn't have the time to respond in sign language. They were surrounded, and Bolan had the terrible feeling the death warrants had already been signed. If Gulab-Sha wanted to play hide-and-seek with Dirk up in the hills, then God help him. The problem was that once Dirk did his damage Sha would call on the German mountain brigade for assistance.

Then the game would be God help Dirk.

Bolan simply signed the letters *"O K"* and tapped his ankle where the P-64 pocket pistol was holstered against the Dauphin's fuselage. Dirk grinned and showed Bolan his middle finger.

The message "watch your ass" was understood.

"Bus is leaving!" Zanotto called.

Frame and Stanislawski waved them away as Bolan stashed his carbine and his bag and then climbed into the copilot seat. The twin turbines overhead whined up to speed.

Zanotto checked her dials and adjusted her headset. "Off we go!"

The helicopter lifted off in a maelstrom of peach-colored dust. Bolan waved as Dirk, Frame and Stanislawski squinted against the storm. The chopper spun on its axis, and the airframe whined as the landing gear retracted.

Bolan tapped his headset and held a finger up to his lips meaningfully.

Zanotto nodded. She understood the chopper might be bugged.

Zanotto brought the helicopter up to clear the peaks of the valley. Mazes of rock formations and twisting crevices and canyons unfolded beneath them. They were five minutes' flying out of the valley when Dinatale's voice crackled across the radio. "Z Flight, this is Dino. Come back."

"Dino, this is Connie. What's up?"

Bolan could almost hear Dinatale's eyes go sniper cold as he spoke. "You disappoint me, Connie."

Zanotto's phone had been bugged.

Her voice was cool and conversational. "You know, Dino? I knew there was a reason I dumped your sorry ass." She dropped the chopper low, hugging canyon floors and skimming the crags as she flew nap of the earth.

Dinatale laughed across the radio. "You are so predictable."

Black smoke and fire erupted from the side of a canyon.

"I've got missiles!" Zanotto yanked her stick over and plunged the helicopter down in a stomach-plunging evasive maneuver as multiple projectiles trailed smoke toward them. Her left forefinger stabbed toward her console. "Initiating countermeasures!"

Bolan roared, "Wait for it!" but he was too late. The infrared flares arced outward from both sides of the Dauphin and bloomed into incandescent light. Zanotto had been conned. Missiles weren't the problem yet. The weapons coming at them were rocket-propelled grenades. The two rocket grenades lumbered across the sky trailing smoke and fire at 120 yards per second. They were blunt, dumb and blind, but they still had their six-second self-destruct fuse, and a good operator could time the weapon to detonate close to a flying target.

The fuselage rattled like hail as bits of metal scored its sides. Zanotto was good, and she'd jinked them out of the radius of most of it. The problem was the infrared flares were a one-shot deal, and now the hammer was going to fall in the form of infrared homing surface-to-air missiles.

Bolan caught the flash of the launch in a crag behind them. "Missile on your six!"

"Shit!" Zanotto dived for the deck. Her opponent this time was a higher animal entirely. The infrared seeker in the missile guidance unit was fixated on the clouds of heat exhausting out of the Dauphin's twin engines, and Zanotto was out of scintillating flares that would light up in the seeker's lens like exploding suns and confuse it. And unlike the lumbering rockets, the missile was a cometlike streak swiftly accelerating to twice the speed of sound.

"Here it comes!" Bolan shouted.

Zanotto yanked on her stick. "Brace for impact!"

The tail of the Dauphin lifted straight up in the air as if it had been kicked in the rear by a giant boot. Alarms sounded and red lights flew across consoles. Zanotto snarled in rage. "We're hit!"

It was a pretty obvious statement, but Bolan gritted his teeth and held on. Zanotto kicked her pedals, yanked back on the collective and more alarms began peeping and telltales flashed as she throttled into emergency war power. The helicopter bucked, tilted, lifted and yawed as it slewed across the sky. Bolan had been in this situation before. They were done. The flight was over. Inexorably, the Dauphin started to turn into its death spiral.

"We're going down!" She punched the transmit button. "Mayday! Mayday! This is Flight Z-1! We are going down at coordinates—"

Dinatale's voice broke across the transmission. "Connie? Who the hell do you think is receiving?"

Bolan reached over and twisted the radio bandwidth. Nothing happened. It was if the knob had been set and then snapped off on the Shield tactical frequency. "We're cut off!"

"That's right, Coop," Dinatale gloated. "And Jesus, from here? You guys aren't just going down, you're on fire."

Smoke was oozing through the air vents, and the fire alarm was peeping and blinking plaintively. Zanotto put her heel through the communications console. "Fuck you!"

"Not that easy, baby." Dinatale's voice spoke like God on high through the helicopter intercom. "And Sugar-pop? Pray you die when you hit. 'Cause Gulab-Sha will be leading the rescue party."

"You hear that, Connie?" Bolan asked.

The pilot yanked on her collective, but nothing was happening. "Oh, I heard it!"

"So we kill them." Bolan caught Zanotto's gaze and held it. "We kill them all."

"You hear that, Dino? We are killing your ass!" Zanotto declared.

Dinatale sighed through the intercom. "Any last words, baby?"

"Yeah. You're the only short-dicked man I ever liked, and I don't like you anymore."

Dinatale snarled, "You goddamn—"

Bolan smiled as he watched Afghanistan hurtle up toward them. "Nice."

The Dauphin hit the side of the canyon like a car wreck. The rotors snapped off against the dust-colored stone and the aircraft immediately lost lift. The Halon fire extinguishers blasted into the cockpit and cabin as the fuselage rolled three times and hit the valley floor. It rolled again and came to rest in a shallow stream.

Bolan hung upside down in his seat for a moment as he got his bearings and then pawed off his headset. "You okay?"

Zanotto groaned. "We kill them." Her head had hit the cockpit door, and blood was leaking in a thin stream into her hairline. "We kill them all."

Bolan reached out a hand for the roof and clicked out of his harness, then slid down out of his seat. Smoke was filling the cockpit despite the fire-suppression system. He twisted upright and put an arm around the pilot as he clicked her out of her harness. "Connie, we're on fire."

"Gotta get my grab bag…." Zanotto twisted upright in the upside-down aircraft. "Get the door gun. It's stowed behind the last seat in the cabin."

Bolan crawled into the smoking and ticking cabin. He unclipped the PKM machine gun and took two 100-round canvas ammo bags. Zanotto crawled out of the cracked cockpit door, dragging a knapsack after her. Bolan went to the minifridge. The door was ajar and the contents were strewn all over. The beer was all smashed, but a bottle of champagne and two bottles of water were intact. Bolan scooped up the beverages, as well as a pair of mangled sandwiches and his own weapons and gear and got out of the burning aircraft. Zanotto knelt unsteadily but was instinctively checking the loads in her submachine gun. Bolan stuffed the supplies into his knapsack and then locked a belt of ammo onto his weapon.

"Connie, let me see your phone."

"Yeah…" She dazedly handed it over and Bolan crushed it beneath his heel. He was pretty sure there was a tracking device inside it. He reached down and pulled the pilot to her feet. "C'mon, we gotta move. We gotta move now."

"I know, we—"

Bolan looked up at the sound of rotors. "We're out of time."

"What do we do?"

Bolan glanced around. The Germans had only one transport back in the valley, but it could carry up to twenty armed men. They were in a canyon. There was no time to hike out of it, and Zanotto didn't look as if she could climb at the moment. Bolan took a long hard look at the smoldering fuselage of the Dauphin. It was a miracle the stricken aircraft hadn't burst into flames yet. "Start crawling."

"Crawl?"

"Yeah, crawl, and leave your weapon. You're a woman, and Dino wants his fun. There's a good chance they'll land and grab you rather than strafe you with the door guns."

Zanotto brought a hand to her head. "Great, and you?"

"I'm going back in the chopper."

"That thing is about to explode!"

Bolan pulled the white phosphorus rifle grenade from his pack. "Yeah."

Zanotto wiped away the blood that wouldn't stop running into her face. "I'm bait."

"Yeah."

She tossed aside her submachine gun and started crawling along the little stream away from the wreckage. Bolan clambered back into the Dauphin. Inside, smoke was filling the cabin with the stench of burning plastic. It was joined by the smell of aviation fuel.

The chopper was going to go up any second.

Bolan squinted through stinging eyes as the NH90 transport swooped over the canyon and dropped low. Both cabin doors were open and door gunners leaned out on their chicken straps behind MG-3 machine guns. The troop compartment was jammed with a mix of the remaining Gebirgsjaegers and Gulab-Sha's thugs. Bolan bided his time in the burning cabin.

He was going to have to let them get close.

Zanotto held up a hand against the rotor wash and collapsed onto her side, as helpless as a lamb. The chopper slid across the sky and did a short orbit over the wreck of the Dauphin. The crumpled fuselage shook with the thumping of the rotor blades above. The NH90 then moved back toward the more interesting target. Zanotto crawled, bleeding and helpless, as the helicopter dropped down over her like a giant spider intent on its prey. Germans and tribesmen leaned out of the cabin doors, their sadistic whoops and whistles audible over the sound of the rotors.

The savages in the chopper were going to have some fun.

The Executioner stepped out of the wreckage of the Dauphin.

The NH90's starboard door gunner gaped in shock and grabbed for his weapon's spade grips. The carbine kicked against Bolan's shoulder and the beer-can-sized grenade looped through the air and through the cabin door. The Executioner lowered his sights and rattled off a 5-round burst from his rifle. The door gunner sagged in his straps. Several men tried to aim their rifles out the door while others waved their arms, screaming, aware of the grenade in their midst.

Hell suddenly opened inside the NH90.

The white phosphorus grenade had a bursting radius of seventeen meters, and it violently expanded to fill every centimeter of the cockpit and cabin and geysered out the doors. The men within were occluded by superheated smoke and white phosphorus filler burning at 5,000 degrees Fahrenheit.

Bolan roared, "Connie! Run!"

The ex-fitness champion's feet flew as molten metal rained down in streamers like the Fourth of July. Burning and screaming men rained out of the sides of the chopper, as well. The chopper went into a crazy spin as the pilot and copilot flailed and screamed inside the burning cockpit. The rotor blades snapped off against the canyon wall, and the transport instantly lost lift. The burning helicopter dropped like a stone, trailing clouds of white smoke and burning yellow sparks.

Zanotto's eyes widened as she looked over Bolan's shoulder. "Coop! Down!"

Bolan heard the whoosh of the Dauphin igniting behind him. He took five running steps and dived into the stream. Zanotto hit the water a second later. It was barely six feet deep at its deepest, but Bolan crawled along the bottom and met Zanotto in the middle. The water around them thumped and hissed as bits of various burning helicopters landed sizzling against the surface. Chunks of burning phosphorus began floating downward, blinking and sputtering like fireflies. The grenade's filler would burn for sixty seconds, and only lack of oxygen would stop it. Even underwater, exposed flesh could be burned down to the bone. Bolan and Zanotto twisted like snakes beneath the water to avoid the burning metal element.

Bolan broke the surface as the last burning bits in the water around them sank bubbling into the mud. Zanotto breached a second later, and the two of them slogged back to the bank. The NH90 had slewed fortuitously about fifty yards away before it had fallen. Its fuel tanks had gone up, and it was burning out of control. No one had gotten out alive. Half a dozen men had dived out as the flames consumed them, and they had fallen to a more merciful death. The Dauphin was burning somewhat more sedately, but between them, the two wrecks were sending huge clouds of black-and-white smoke into the sky.

Bolan scooped up his weapons and gear and handed Zanotto her grab bag and weapon. "You okay?"

She nodded shakily. "Yeah."

"Good." Bolan stared at the mountains to the west. "We gotta do distance."

13

Dinatale looked long and hard at the smoke rising into the sky through his laser range-finding binoculars. Ulva and the German missile team stood with him. Dinatale spoke into his tactical. "Toe-jam, you seeing what I'm seeing?"

Stanislawski responded across the radio warily. "I see smoke, to the east."

"That's right, smoke, and I'd make that two plumes, wouldn't you?"

"Yes, Dino, I count two smoke plumes," he responded unhappily.

"Uh-huh." Dinatale had the disturbing tendency to be more quiet and conversational the angrier he got. "And that's a lot of white smoke in the northern plume, wouldn't you say?"

"Yes, much white smoke."

"So you tell me, big man, you know anything that would make that much white smoke?"

Stanislawski let out a long breath. "White phosphorus?"

"Yeah, I think that's a real good guess. White phosphorus. Now, I happen to know the German army uses red phosphorus in their incendiary-smoke grenades, and Shield hasn't issued any incendiaries at all to Sha or his goons."

The Pole didn't bother replying.

"Now," Dinatale continued. "I just ain't buying the idea that Connie is packing willie petes in any creative body cavities.

So that leaves Cooper. Where could Coop have gotten hold of incendiaries?"

"He must have—"

"I'll tell you where, Toe-jam. Coop and Dirk have been shop-lifting from our Shield stash again, and I believe that falls under your area of responsibility."

The big Pole took a deep breath before answering. "Yes, Dino. The responsibility is mine."

"Where is Dirk now?"

"Since morning, I have assigned Tomlinson and Garrett to keep casual watch on him. Both have closed-circuit tactical radios and are to alert me of anything suspicious."

"From your position can Dirk see the smoke?" Dinatale queried.

"Yes, Dino." Stanislawski cleared his throat. "Everyone is looking at it."

"Dob, I believe I'd like an update on the Dirk situation immediately."

There was a short pause before Stanislawski came back. "Mr. Dinatale, neither Tomlinson or Garrett are responding."

"Toe-jam…"

Stanislawski's voice panted from running. "I am now in tent of Dirk and Cooper."

"And?"

"Garrett is inside. He is dead. His trachea appears to be crushed. I have not located Tomlinson—"

"Forget Tomlinson. You're going to put together a strike team. Shield-led, some Germans for backup and get some of Sha's men that know the area and know how to track. I'll get hold of Fir and get you helicopter support ASAP. I want Connie's and Cooper's heads."

"Yes, Dino, but what about Dirk?"

"Dirk?" Dino lowered his binoculars. "He hasn't gone far. He's Delta. Outnumbered? Outgunned? Behind enemy lines? This is the bullshit his kind train all their lives for."

"What do you wish me to do?"

"I told you, I want you to go and get Cooper."

"But what about village?"

"Dirk wants to save the village? Let him try, but when he does?" A very ugly smile crawled across Dinatale's face. "Iron Klaus and Gulab-Sha are going to arrange—how shall we say?— a crisis of conscience for the good lieutenant."

"SO WHY DIDN'T Dino just shoot us in camp?"

Bolan finished bandaging Connie Zanotto's brow. "You've got family, friends and you're a decorated veteran. Me? Dino doesn't know what I represent, but the fact is you're a pilot whose job is flying missions over some very dangerous real estate. If you go down, it's got to be plausible. You and me? We just died in a tragic helicopter crash, and if anyone comes to investigate, all they're going to find is a burned-out hulk that will confirm the story."

"Yeah?" the pilot countered. "But now there are two burned-out hulks."

Bolan shrugged. "Tragic midair collision. It actually helps the story along."

"Well, you've just got it all figured out, don't you?"

"Yeah," Bolan agreed, "and if I can, so can Dino."

"Yeah."

"Connie, you flew us here. Where are we?"

"Kabul's about three hundred miles north. Kandahar's about the same, except south. The main highway between them is about fifty miles west, but with all the mountains between it and us, it might as well be on the moon." She lifted her chin eastward. "We're real close to the Pakistan border, but not any part you'd want to visit."

Bolan cracked the champagne. "Thirsty?"

Zanotto just stared. "Isn't that going to dehydrate us?"

"German wine is lower in alcohol than the French stuff. We cut it half and half with water, and we should be fine." Bolan pulled out one of the bottles of sparkling water. "Thirsty?"

"Jesus, we're about to die in Afghanistan and you're making spritzers."

"I read your file. You used to do some bartending. You mix 'em."

Zanotto took the bottle of sparkling wine and bubbly water and spun them in her hands the way she spun her revolvers and began mixing them in a canteen cup. "You got it." They both looked up at the sound of rotors in the distance. "Jesus, here they come."

Bolan crouched back behind the rocks. "Yup."

Zanotto frowned as she handed Bolan a beverage. "You don't seem very worried."

"Don't worry." Bolan took the cup. "I'm worried."

"You really think we can pull an escape and evade on an entire company of mountain troops? With gunships?"

"No, but if Captain Fir goes that route, we have a secret weapon."

"Oh? And what's that?"

Bolan drained the cup and handed it back. "You."

"You know, I already dropped and crawled for you. What's next on your little agenda? Me dropping my top?"

Bolan smiled tiredly. "Actually, yeah, something like that."

Zanotto simply stared.

Bolan shrugged. "That's one of the few advantages we have. Captain Fir is playing games with Gebirgsjaeger men and matériel, and he just lost a transport with all hands. Now, he can tell German coalition command he's got Taliban in the hills, he's lost a chopper, and bring in everything he's got, but I'm doubting that every man in Gebirgsjaeger E Company is in on this. Hell, when we took the valley, most of the Germans were sent back the same day while Shield operatives and Sha's men set up the business end of things. Fir has one or two picked squads of men who are in on this, tops, and maybe one or two pilots, and you?" Bolan grinned. "You're the hottest-looking helicopter pilot this side of the Caspian Sea."

Zanotto lifted her cup. "Gee, thanks. So?"

"And I'm betting a lot of the nice young German lads took

notice. Fir can't realistically tell his men to shoot any hot babe on sight, and if you step out from behind a rock naked and say 'I surrender,' or scream for help the jig is up. He can't have two Americans captured by anyone not in the loop."

"So I should be ready to drop my drawers at a moment's notice?"

"We'll keep that as Plan B, but I'm figuring they're reporting the helicopter as lost in an accident, and Fir and Dino are going to clean this up with the forces they have on hand. Right now, they're probably dropping a hunting party down at the crash site. Then the chopper will go high and act as a spotter."

"You know, I hate to be a downer, but I'd rather take my chances naked and surrounded by German mountain men. I don't know what you've heard about Dino, but whatever it is it's true. He's that damn good. If Deadshot Dave takes his rifle off the wall and comes a-hunting?" She shook her head bitterly. "We're dead, and I'm not dropping my pants for Gulab-Sha and his forty scumbags. Before it comes to that, I'm expecting you to put me down easy."

"I'll put us both down easy before it comes to that."

Zanotto fought back tears. "You don't get it. I've seen him shoot. Dino's one of the top ten riflemen on the goddamn planet."

Bolan nodded, and when he spoke there was no braggadocio in his voice. "So am I."

Zanotto looked Bolan up and down half in awe and half in disbelief. "Jesus, who the hell are you?"

Bolan took a long hard look at the stubby carbine in his hands. "I'm going to need a rifle. Something with some reach."

"Yeah? And where are you going to get one?"

"Oh, one should be coming along presently." Bolan took a long look at the PK machine gun. He was loath to abandon its firepower, but at almost twenty pounds it was going to weigh them down like an anchor. "You think you could hit something with this?"

"I've fired an M-60 door gun. Is it much different?"

Bolan picked up the machine gun and racked the action on a

live round. "Not enough to make a difference. Before we went down, I saw this canyon fork about a half klick from here. Here's what I want you to do."

"IT'S PRETTY DAMN SIMPLE," Dino explained softly to Stanislawski as he took his rife from its case at the crash site. With its dinged and stained wooden stock, a casual observer would have mistaken the Remington 700 for a beat-up old hunting rifle that had seen better days. It was indeed a hunting rifle, but one that had been built from the ground up to hunt human beings. At sniper school, the instructor had directed each applicant to give his weapon a woman's name and to be utterly faithful to it, because if he did the weapon would be faithful to him. Dinatale had gone to the armorer at the Marine Corps rifle team shop at Quantico and bribed him a case of whiskey to instruct him on how to glass-bed the barrel and tune the action himself. Among the Janes, Bobby-Sues and Helens, "Lightning Girl" had taken top honors during qualifications. During operations throughout Central America and the Middle East, she had reaped heads. Dinatale had spent untold hours loading his own ammo until he found the perfect combination of bullet weight and powder. In any condition, he knew exactly what the rifle could do and what it couldn't. One could argue calibers, actions and optics until hell froze over, but in a way, sniper rifles were like fighter planes. In the end, it wasn't the machine but the man behind it that told the tale in a dogfight. The 700 was an old dog, but she could still hunt.

Dinatale pushed rounds into the action as he addressed the big Pole. "The helicopter has been tasked for some other duties, and we just aren't admitting what happened here today and calling in for more support. So we are going to play this as a standard hunt and sweep. We track them. We drive them. Sooner or later, they're going to have to expose themselves and shoot. When they do, we take them."

Stanislawski hoisted his own Polish "Alex" sniper rifle. Its skeletonized plastic stock, fluted barrel and pistol grip made it look like a weapon right out of *Star Wars*. "We will lose men."

"That's right." Dinatale surveyed his hunting party. He had Ulva leading a four-man section of Gebirgsjaegers, six of Sha's men, and Poertner and Frame were both leading three-man fire teams of Shield operatives. "Now, Coop's got a carbine, he's got optics, but that Mini-Beryl is still a short-ranged proposition. He's also got a few rifle grenades." Stanislawski flinched as Dinatale regarded him critically. "That ain't good, but then again, max range is 200-250 meters. Connie's got that Polish squirt gun you gave her and her six-guns—we're talking fifty meters or less."

The Pole eyed the burning hulk of the Dauphin. "It is too hot to check, but I think we must be assuming that they have door gun."

"Well, now, that could make things interesting," Dinatale agreed, "but that's going to be hard to tote around. In the end, once they start shooting, we have them. We flank their position and drive them before us. Meanwhile, you and me are hanging back with our rifles looking for head shots. Unless, of course, the boys manage a rush and overwhelm them."

Stanislawski nodded. It was a hard plan to fault. Dinatale was a very dangerous man. "I understand."

"Good." Dinatale motioned to Ulva, and the three of them walked over to where a Shield contractor and an Afghan squatted in the dirt. "Sadiq, what've you got?"

Sadiq was a blade-thin bedouin and former Jordanian Special Forces Brigade who had graduated to Jordanian intelligence. Dinatale had met him during some very byzantine business in Iraq and had hired him on as his Arabic translator. It was Sadiq who did most of Shield's deal brokering, legitimate and otherwise, in Afghanistan. The Afghan was a tiny man, barely cracking five feet tall, but he was muscled like an ape, and he stabbed the tip of a huge, single-edged Khyber knife that was almost as big as he was into the dust and then pointed westward. Sadiq nodded. "Kaawa says he has two tracks, one large and one small, a man and a woman. They're heading west. He says they are moving very fast and the man is heavily laden."

Stanislawski grunted unhappily. "Door gun."

"Undoubtedly," Dinatale said. "Anything else?"

"Kaawa says he found significant blood traces behind the rocks near the Dauphin crash. One of them is hurt, but not so badly that they cannot run."

Ulva squinted into the swiftly rising sun. "Westward. They are trying for the Pakistan border."

Dino considered the mountains in the west. "Northern Pakistan is Taliban territory. It's terrorist central in those hills. Sadiq? I think we have a few friends in Kabul, who have a few friends in Islamabad, who have friends along the border, who might be very interested in getting their hands on an American secret agent and a female Ranger, don't we?"

Sadiq's lips twisted in a cruel smile. He'd been harboring fantasies of Connie Zanotto's violation for some time. "Yes, I believe we can arrange a very warm reception for Connie and her new friend on the border."

"Good. Get on the horn and make it happen."

Sadiq pulled out his satellite phone and started making calls.

Dinatale raised his voice. "All right. Listen up. I want a skirmish line going down this canyon. Sadiq and Kaawa will be tracking on point. Marko, you, Monahan, Kasper and the rest of the Afghans are backing them up. Ulva, you and your fire team are fifty yards back. The second Connie or Coop open up, I want your grenadiers to frag the shit out of them.

"Frame! I want you and Pascal hanging back as a reserve and ready to run to plug any gap or swing wide as needed. Toe-jam and I are going to pull a climb and crawl along opposite sides of the canyon and look for the shot. Any questions?"

Murmurs passed through the hunting party in various languages as the orders were disseminated.

Stanislawski scowled. "I believe some of the men realize they are cannon fodder."

Dinatale nodded and raised his voice again. "The men on point? It may get rough, so I'll make it simple. I'm paying a ten-thousand-dollar bonus to the man who kills Cooper and brings me his head. I'm paying ten thousand to the man who kills Connie and brings me her head. For that matter, hell, the man who brings Connie down alive gets first crack at her."

Seditious murmurs turned to laughs of ugly speculation, monetary and otherwise, among the men. Dinatale nodded to himself. His hunting party was salty and ready for violence. "We got about six hours of daylight, gentlemen." He flashed his most winning smile. "Let's go hunting!"

14

Sadiq tackled Kaawa as the machine gun opened up. Kaawa's cousin Emal came apart as the 10-round burst stitched him from his crotch to collarbone. Ali screamed as his legs were reaped from beneath him a second later. Kasper caught sight of the strobing muzzle-flash and raised his rifle. Kasper was Belgian, ex-Foreign Legion and had willingly sold his soul to Dino Dinatale after Operation Desert Storm. His soul shuffled off this mortal coil as a 5-round burst of Russian .30-caliber rifle rounds broke his chest open like a bamboo birdcage. A third Afghan fell, and the rest ran for cover in all directions.

"Grenades! Now!" Sadiq shouted at the top of his lungs.

Fifty yards back, Ulva's grenadiers fired their 40 mm grenade launchers in a salvo. There was no hiding the trip-hammer tearing of the machine gun nor its strobing muzzle-flash. The grenades landed throughout the rock formation and detonated, sending jagged bits of steel whizzing through the air in whipsaw clouds.

"Again," Dinatale shouted across the tactical link.

The mountain troopers loaded and fired again. Grenades looped through the air.

Dinatale's voice thundered across the radio. "Ulva! Burn them out with white phosphorus. Cover your advance."

Ulva snarled orders, and his men lobbed white phosphorus grenades into the rock formation. Streamers of burning metal and clouds of white smoke gouted up into the air as the area was blanketed.

Poertner yanked Kaawa up and screamed, kicked and cuffed his Afghans forward. "Go! Go! Go!"

Bolan watched the killers run past his position. He had told Zanotto to fire two bursts and then move. She'd apparently gotten excited and gone for four. He hoped she'd gotten away before the hail of grenades had reached the machine-gun hide, but there was no way and no time to check. Bolan was rifle shopping. He stayed low as Ulva and his four Germans trotted past in a skirmish line. Next to Dinatale's sniper rifle, the grenadiers were the most dangerous element of the hunting party. It was tempting to slaughter them now, but once he exposed his position, the crevice in the stone where Bolan hid would be his coffin. Bolan began climbing up the slot in the rock face as if he were scaling a chimney. He moved with the speed of a sloth, lifting one limb at a time and making no sound.

He froze at the pounding of boots above him.

The man atop the canyon wall wasn't particularly trying to be quiet. He was moving swiftly from one position to the next. Bolan waited until he passed and then continued climbing. He paused at the top. He didn't have a mirror or a pocket periscope. Bolan was just going to have to stick his head out.

He peered over the lip of the crevice.

Dobrus Stanislawski was ten yards away. His back was turned to Bolan, and he was crouching behind a formation of bladelike rocks and scanning the huge white clouds rising into the sky through the optics of a high-powered rifle. He clicked his tactical radio without taking his eyes off the target. "Dino, you got anything from your angle?"

Bolan emerged from the crevice in slow motion.

Dinatale's voice crackled back over the tactical radio. "Marko and Monahan are working their way back behind the smoke cloud now. I'm going to move fifty yards forward and see if they flush anybody out. Hold your position. Frame? Pascal? That goes for you, too."

"Understood."

Ulva spoke. "Be advised we have two Afghans killed and one wounded. Kasper's dead, too."

Bolan took a quick glance around. From his vantage, he could see the hunters moving forward on the canyon floor. However, he couldn't see Dinatale and he didn't know where Frame and Pascal were. He was going to have to make this fast. Bolan crept forward. He didn't have a silenced weapon and even the act of drawing his knife might be enough to alert the former GROM operator.

Bolan lunged.

He whipped the Mini-Beryl carbine over Stanislawski's head and yanked back. The big Pole's throat dovetailed brutally between the pistol grip and the magazine, and his windpipe closed as Bolan heaved. The Executioner didn't have the time to try to choke the former power lifter, and he knew he was dead if it turned into a wrestling match.

Bolan brutally twisted the assault carbine up and around as if it were a tire iron and the big Pole's neck were one big rusted bolt. The weapon torqued around, and Stanislawski's wedged head torqued with it. The Pole's cervical vertebrae snapped and popped like a burst from an AK-47. Bolan released his death grip, and the man sagged to the stones like a sack of potatoes. Bolan slung the carbine back across his chest and stripped the Pole of his rifle and ammo, his RAK machine pistol and its shoulder holster, as well as his tactical radio.

The radio crackled in Bolan's hand. "Dino, this is Monahan. We've found the machine gun. It's all torched to shit, but there's no sign of Cooper or Connie. Suggest you go ahead and have Sadiq send the trackers forward."

Bolan relieved Stanislawski of his canteen, a pair of protein bars and two hand grenades. One was purple smoke marking, and one was a frag.

Monahan's voice became a little urgent. "Dino, this is Monahan. Come back."

Bolan stashed his trophies, and suddenly his instincts

screamed a warning. He threw himself to one side, but the .308-caliber rifle bullet hit him in the chest with over a ton of muzzle energy. The rifle shot echoed off the canyon as Bolan fell backward. His chest felt like a closed fist, but he forced himself to roll. The second bullet impacted inches from his head and blasted chips of stone into his face. Bolan kept rolling and slumped behind the shelter of the rocks.

"Cooper!" Dinatale's voice called across the canyon, his voice a mocking singsong. "I see you!"

Bolan spent a moment just breathing. The bullet had hit the carbine. The stamped-steel receiver of the weapon was torn open, and the bullet had mushroomed against the bolt.

Dinatale's voice came across the radio. "All units, Cooper is on the eastern fork of the canyon, eastern wall. I have him pinned down. All units converge. Grenadiers, I will direct fire when you're in range." He paused for a sadistic moment. "Ulva, have your men load white phosphorus. Burn his ass."

Bolan groaned as he unslung his crushed carbine and threw it aside.

Dinatale called out across the canyon. "You got about fifteen seconds before you fry, Coop. So tell you what. You stick your head out, I'll take you clean."

Bolan managed to draw a breath. He was fairly sure no ribs were broken.

Dinatale spoke across the link. "Coop, I'm pretty sure you have Toe-jam's tactical, so listen up. I won't shit you about surrendering. You know what I'll let Gulab-Sha and Iron Klaus do to you. But the deal stands. Frankly, I want to take your goddamn head. It's a personal thing. So stick it out, and you go out like a light. You don't? You'd better pray you burn to death, because if you don't, you're going to burn to death anyway, Coop. Only it be from a blow torch that I'm holding in my hand." Dinatale's voice rose an unstable octave. "So stick your goddamn head out!"

Bolan clicked the radio. "No, I don't think so."

"Then fuck you, Cooper! I rain fire on you! I rain fire on you right now!"

"Dino?"

Dinatale regained some control and the sadism returned. "These are your last words, Cooper. Make 'em good."

"I'll see you around."

Bolan pulled the pin on the smoke grenade and tossed it back over the rock. Purple smoke bloomed and began expanding in all directions. Bolan waited. Dinatale's rifle began cracking in rapid fire from across the canyon. He was randomly shooting into the smoke, thinking Bolan was already up and running. Bolan counted shots and when the sniper hit five he rose and ran.

Dinatale was screaming across the link. "Grenadiers! Smoke cloud is your target. Fire at will."

Bolan ran along the plateau as the 40 mm projectiles thudded from the canyon floor. He threw himself into a crevice carved by the seasonal floods from the melting snows and landed on soft sand. Molten metal burned into the sky behind him. The white phosphorus and purple marking smoke melded to turn the world into a surrealistic hell lit from within.

Dinatale yelled in the distance. "You're dead, Cooper! You hear me? I'm talking to a fucking ghost! And I can't begin to tell you what I'm going to do to Connie!"

Bolan idly wondered how Dinatale had ever passed the psych exam at sniper school. He grimaced as he felt the pain of the bruise blossoming on his chest as he snaked his way along the narrow channel in the stone. Dinatale had almost nailed him off-hand at six hundred meters.

The drill instructors at Quantico could forgive a lot for that kind of shooting.

FRAME STARED INCREDULOUSLY at Stanislawski's corpse. It had been badly burned by the white phosphorus, but even burn damage could not explain the strange angle of his head. "Jesus Christ! He snapped Toe-jam's frickin' neck!"

Dinatale glared bloody murder at the scar-faced young paratrooper but kept his mind on business. "All right, same plan, we—"

"Same plan?" Frame was appalled. "Shit, Dino! We just got our asses handed to us. Dob is dead, and we lost Kasper and three of the Afghans. We need gunships, as well as—"

"One more word."

Frame froze as Dinatale's fighting knife hissed from its sheath and the point stopped just under a line of stitches below his left eye.

"One more word, Frame, and God as my witness I'm going to finish the job on your face."

"Goddamn, Dino!" Frame flinched. "Jesus, I'm just saying—"

"I know what you're saying, and you're wrong." Dinatale sheathed his knife. "The plan worked perfectly." He kicked the mangled carbine lying in the dirt. "By all rights, Coop should be dead and Connie should be giving us all lap dances right now. He got lucky. His luck just ran out. He also can't fire his rifle grenades anymore. So we run the plan again. We run them before us and run them down. We have four hours of daylight left. I want this shit over before dark."

Ulva stared long and hard at the charred Pole and exercised remarkable restraint. "You know you have my respect, Herr Dinatale."

"And I love you, too, Sergeant. What's on your mind?"

"This Cooper, he will have Stanislawski rifle, yes?"

"Yeah, he scampered off with it. What's your point?"

Ulva was a mountain trooper. All his training told him that a sniper in terrain like this was a worst-case scenario.

Dinatale's eyes went to slits. "You think he's better than me?"

Ulva shrugged mollifyingly. "Is anyone?"

"No, Ulva. No one is. Read the news and check my references. Plan remains the same. Coop gets one shot. Two at most. Then we have him."

Sadiq stepped forward and spoke diplomatically. "Frame's instincts are correct. Gunship support would be best, but Dino is right. We cannot afford the exposure. I agree with Dino. We run Cooper and Connie again. They get one or two shots at most, and I will ensure that—" Sadiq paused for effect "—our local allies will be in the best position to receive those shots. I will deploy them in tracking pairs. Cooper cannot allow two armed men who know this country to get behind him. Nor do I believe he will split away from Connie again. When he takes the shot, which sooner or later he must, we have him. He is running out of tricks."

Everyone nodded at Sadiq's wisdom save for the Afghans, who were still not entirely sure they were unexpendable.

Dinatale nodded. "Let's move out."

The hunting party spread back out into its arrow formation.

Dinatale smiled. "Oh, and Frame?"

"Yeah, boss?"

The butt of Dinatale's rifle snapped into Frame's eyebrow. Jimmy Frame's carbine dropped from his hands, and he fell to one knee and clutched at his crushed and torn stitches. Blood drooled between his fingers and across his eye. "Don't ever contradict me in front of the men. Don't ever contradict me again. Ever. You got me?"

Frame glared up at Dinatale through blood and his patchwork of stitches.

"Oh, you still salty, boy?" Dinatale smiled. "You want to go for two? Or maybe you and me should just lay down our rifles, go down into the canyon with what God gave us and see who climbs back up."

"No." Frame's glare turned to bitterness. "That's all right."

"Jimmy?" Dinatale inquired.

"What?"

"Who's the man?"

Frame's voice went dead as he looked up at the man he'd sold his soul to. "You're the man, Dino."

"Say it again. I like the sound of it."

Frame's voice faltered, and he couldn't meet Dinatale's eyes. "You're the man."

Dinatale nodded in satisfaction. "Pick up your rifle, Frame. Get your ass in line. As a matter of fact, get your ass up front and take Kasper's position." He watched Frame go with a sneer. He'd always hated Army Airborne, and Frame should've been dead anyway after the Ziaee job. Dinatale decided the young man would be dead after this one. That also gave him an idea. "Sadiq!"

The Jordanian turned from setting the Afghan trackers out in pairs. "Yes, Dino?"

"Get on the horn with HQ. Get hold of Jorn and Kurt. I got a job for them."

Wheels clearly turned in Sadiq's mind at the choice of personnel. "What do require of them?"

Dinatale rested his rifle on his hip as his hunting party spread out. "Just a little life insurance."

CONNIE ZANOTTO KNELT in the shadow of a cliff and peered westward over the sights of her submachine gun. Bolan spoke the password softly. "Honey, I'm home."

She lowered her submachine gun with a sigh as she turned to find Bolan standing behind her. "Did you bring the groceries?"

Bolan reached into his pack. "I brought you a protein bar."

Zanotto snatched it and ripped it open with her teeth.

"I also got a canteen, a radio, a rifle, a machine pistol, a set of night-vision goggles and a hand grenade."

"Well, hell, Coop, remind me to bring you next time I go shopping at the mall."

Bolan peeled open a protein bar and tore in. "How was your day, dear?"

Zanotto shoved a huge bite to one side of her mouth. Her hair was singed and frizzed, and her face was the light shade of pink of someone who had mostly managed to avoid flashburns. Every other square inch of her was covered with spent smoke particulate. "Me? I got nuked. The PKM is toast."

"Yeah." Bolan cracked open the canteen. "Dino shot my gun, too."

"I'm sure he was shooting for something else."

"He was, but some Polish steel got in the way. My carbine got wrecked." Bolan tapped the Alex rifle. "It was a fair trade."

"Speaking of Polacks." The pilot chewed and swallowed. "Did you see Dobrus?"

"I killed him."

Her eyes widened slightly. "Oh."

"Yeah, you got four, but the problem is Dino's hunting party is still at reinforced-squad strength, and those Gebirgsjaeger grenadiers are going to give me an ulcer."

Zanotto finished her food. "Well, the last plan worked out pretty good. You got another one?"

Bolan had been giving that some thought. "There're a couple things we can try. From what I was able to pick up, the Afghan trackers are being directed by a guy named Sadiq."

Zanotto's nose wrinkled. "That one's bad news. When people like Gulab-Sha aren't around to pound people with lumber, I've heard Sadiq does Dino's interrogations for him."

"Yeah, but the good news is he also sounds like the only one with any Afghan or Arabic, and you single-handedly wiped out a third of Dino's trackers. They can't be happy. We take out Sadiq, and command and control of the local contingent goes out the window."

"Sowing tension, apprehension and dissension." Zanotto nodded approvingly as she took the canteen. "I like it. Got anything else?"

"Yeah, besides Sadiq, there were five other Shield contractors. You whacked one named Kasper."

"Yeah." Her face fell. "I know."

"You knew him?"

"Yeah, I knew him. You might say he caught me on the rebound after Dino and I broke up." Zanotto shook her head slowly. "He still came to kill me anyway."

"Marko's out there along with two guys I never heard of named Monahan and Pascal."

"I've transported the last two a couple of times. Monahan's a Marine like Dino, and Pascal was an air commando, the sharp end of the search and rescue teams. Other than that, I don't know much about them." Zanotto cocked her head. "Wait, you said five more."

"Yeah, Frame's part of the hunting party."

She smiled slyly. "And…?"

Bolan unslung the Alex and judged the remaining light. "And I think it's time someone had a 'Come to Jesus' with that boy."

"Nice. What do you want me to do?"

Bolan began rummaging through his pack. "I have a couple of ideas."

15

Frame stared at the note in mounting horror. Dinatale had shoved him up front with the trackers. He had found a crumpled piece of paper as he moved through the maze of rocks and canyons. Frame was former Army Airborne. Besides jumping out of airplanes, he'd had significant training in sneaking around behind enemy lines, and he knew full well the author of the note was very close. Close enough to ensure that it was Frame who found it. The note was as terse and swiftly written as an old-style wire telegram.

> Frame, you are in my sights. Dino betrayed us at the Ziaee house. Sold family and us to the Taliban. Dobrus was the grenadier in the village. Dino and Fir's men are responsible for slaughter of Rangers in Jalkot Canyon. Dirk and I came to investigate. If you accept this, lower your weapon and nod your head.

Frame lowered his assault rifle and slowly nodded.

Bolan rose from the rocks directly in front of Frame. The RAK machine pistol was aimed at Frame's face. "Good lad."

"Aw, Jesus…" Frame sagged. "Listen, Coop, I—"

"We don't have much time." Bolan peered at Frame's resplit eyebrow. "What happened?"

"Dino buttstroked me when I questioned the plan."

"Nice boss you got there."

Frame sighed bitterly. "Yeah."

"You want a new job?"

Frame stared down the machine pistol. "And just what would that job entail?"

Bolan quoted the 101st Airborne Division. "A rendezvous with destiny?"

Frame sighed heavily. "I'm screwed."

"You in, Jimmy?"

Framed eyed the Polish steel in Bolan's hand. "I'm supposin' you'll kill me if I don't."

"Naw, but I can't have Airborne on my ass, either." Bolan lowered his aim. "So I'll just shoot you through both legs, and you can tell Dino any story you like." Bolan cocked his head at the sound of movement down the ravine. "Make up your mind. I'm on a tight schedule."

"Well, I guess I'm on Dino's shit list, anyway." Frame nodded. "And I guess I still owe you. I'm in."

"Good. Prove it."

"Prove it?" Frame's stitches bent quizzically. "How?"

"Who's the best tracker Dino's got?"

"Little guy named Kaawa, and he's good. Like bushman-of-the-Kalahari good."

"Call Sadiq and tell him to bring Kaawa. Tell him you found something."

"I found what?"

Bolan pulled a protein bar wrapper out of his pocket and dropped it to the dust. "That."

"Then what?"

Bolan pointed toward a mausoleum-sized rock behind Frame. "I'm going to be right here."

Frame frowned at the group of rocks in front of him from which Bolan had emerged. "Why aren't you going to be there?"

"'Cause I don't want to be back there. Neither do you."

"Aw, shit, man…"

"Just do it. And when they come, stay low. When the shit hits the fan, fire a couple of bursts into the air. Then say my shots came from the southeast."

Frame stared in confusion. "What?"

"Just do it."

"Now?"

"Yeah, now."

Frame clicked Send on his radio. "Sadiq, this is Frame. I think I found something. You better bring Kaawa up with you."

Sadiq came back instantly across the link. "We are coming."

Bolan walked back to the rock behind Frame. Zanotto knelt behind it. Her grab bag had contained a survival kit with fishing line. Bolan nodded as he assumed his position and she took up the loop of line he'd buried in the dirt.

Sadiq and Kaawa came running at the double. "Frame, what have you found?"

Frame squatted on his heels and pointed at the wrapper near the rocks. "I found that, and I don't think either Cooper or Connie are dumb enough to leave that lying around by accident."

"I agree." Sadiq clicked his radio. "Dino."

"What have you got?"

"I believe Frame may have found a booby trap."

"What kind?"

"I have not ascertained that yet. I will—"

Bolan tapped Zanotto on the shoulder and she ripped back on the fishing line. The line snapped up out of the sand, and the anti-tank rifle grenade behind the rocks detonated as its contact fuse armed, and fire and molten metal erupted upward along the canyon wall. Frame began firing his rifle at nothing in particular.

"What the hell is happening?" Dinatale roared across the link.

Bolan rose and fired the Alex at the back of Sadiq's head. The tracker's skull crumpled like an eggshell. The Executioner flicked the bolt of his rifle, and Kaawa spun just in time to take Bolan's second shot between his eyebrows. Zanotto plucked up the smoking spent shells and shoved them in her pack. She coiled up the fishing line and began running without being told.

Bolan grabbed the front of Frame's shirt and shook him. "Southeast! Tell Dino you saw the muzzle-flashes to the southeast." Bolan pointed at a rise. "Five hundred yards! In those foothills!"

"Yeah, but after that—"

"After that, I'll tell you right across the link what to do. If everything goes south, link up with Dirk and Babrak tonight. There's a rock formation and culvert leading away from it at the far end of the fields. That's where the villagers will be leaving them food."

"Babrak? I thought you…" Frame flinched from Bolan's look. "Sorry, shouldn't have doubted you."

"Forget it." Bolan released the paratrooper. "I gotta go."

Frame began shouting across the link. "Sadiq is down! Kaawa is down! Sadiq detonated an IED when we took sniper fire! Five hundred yards to the southeast…"

Bolan pounded down the trail after Zanotto. She ran with a fluid, ground-eating stride and called back over her shoulder, "So how did we do?"

Bolan caught up and matched her pace. "Tension, apprehension and dissension have begun."

"GODDAMN IT…" Dave Dinatale was no longer in his usual quiet, conversational rage mode. As the CEO of Shield looked at Sadiq's and Kaawa's staved-in skulls, his face purpled as if he were going to boil over. "Goddamn it…"

Jimmy Frame was pretty sure this was his last moment on Earth. "The shots came out of those foothills. I saw the second muzzle-flash and returned fire. The IED was the bait to get us milling around and set us up for the shot."

"No shit, Sherlock!" Dinatale snarled. "Ulva, get those ragheads tracking."

Ulva's own rage was bubbling to the surface. "And how do you expect me to do that? I do not speak Pashto. Nor do I speak Arabic."

"Do you happen to know any of their goddamn names? You recruited them. Let's start with that."

Ulva's normally florid face went white with rage. He stabbed a finger at one of a trio of Afghans kneeling over Kaawa's faceless corpse. "That one. He is named Jamshid."

Dinatale pushed past the German. "You! Jam-shit!"

Startled, Jamshid glanced up as the American advanced on him.

"Yeah! I'm talking to you!" Dinatale stabbed two fingers at his own eyes and then pointed to the foothills. "Get tracking!"

Jamshid shook his head and pointed northeast.

"Yo, asshole!" Dinatale rammed his finger towards the hills. "I'm not going to ask you twice!"

"He does not understand what you are saying," Ulva scoffed.

Dinatale considered shooting Jamshid and then the German. "He understands goddamn good and well what I'm saying. The gutless wonder just doesn't want to do it."

Frame began ad-libbing. "Maybe he's trying to say there're two tracks?"

Marko Poertner spoke a second before Dinatale detonated. "Would they split again? Sadiq thought they would not."

"Sadiq's dead. Shows what he knows." Dinatale regained a measure of his composure. "Connie couldn't make two head shots at five hundred yards. That means Coop is in the hills. If they split, we go for Coop while there's still light. Without Coop backing her up, flygirl doesn't stand a chance." Dinatale nodded at Jamshid and pointed northeast. "The woman? The woman went that way?"

Jamshid blinked.

"The woman!" Dinatale's voice rose again. He cupped his hands in front of his chest as if he were holding a pair of 36 double-Ds and then pointed north. "She went that way?"

Jamshid leaped to his feet in rage clutching his weapon. His two confederates grabbed him and dragged him back as he hurled invectives in Pashto. Ulva's voice dripped in scorn. "I believe he thinks you have called him a woman because he wants to go to the northeast."

Dinatale considered killing everybody. "Marko."

The German contractor snapped to attention. "Yes, Dino!"

"Get the Afghans moving. Charades, blowjobs, hundred-dollar bills, I don't give a shit, but get them motivated and moving up into those hills. Everyone else, same formation."

Poertner began pantomiming a man with a rifle and pointing up in the hills. The Afghans watched the performance sternly and then began moving, grumbling and shaking their heads. Dinatale watched as the hunting party moved out and then broke left and pulled the big fade into the rocks.

Cooper's next shot would be his last.

ZANOTTO WENT PRONE next to Bolan. "They fell for it?"

Bolan gazed unblinkingly through the Polish 10x optic as the hunting party headed into the foothills. "Oh, yeah."

"So what do we do now?"

"Is that a pair of laser range-finding binoculars in your knapsack, or are you just happy to see me?"

"Both?" she suggested.

Bolan smiled without taking his eyes off his targets. Dinatale was nowhere in sight. "The Germans. Range me."

Zanotto pulled out her binoculars and swept them across the hunting party. Marko Poertner and Monahan were in front with the Afghans. The Germans were behind, ready to charge forward and launch a salvo of grenades. Frame and Pascal were bringing up the rear. She brought her optics back on the grenadiers. She pressed the button on the laser range finder, and the binoculars sent out a laser beam invisible to the human eye. The microcomputer inside calculated the distance at which the beam stopped when it hit a German's back. "Six hundred and fifty meters."

It was fairly long range, particularly with a rifle Bolan was unfamiliar with, but he trusted Stanislawski's attachment to weapons, and Polish steel in general. Bolan waited for one of them to stop moving.

"Six hundred and seventy-five."

Bolan waited.

"Six hundred and eighty-five."

One of the Germans stopped for a moment and removed his helmet.

"Seven hundred meters."

Bolan's eyes slitted as Sergeant Ull Ulva pulled a camouflage bandanna out of his thigh pocket and mopped his brow. The blond head was tempting, but seven hundred was starting to get long. Ulva was wearing a vest, and German armor was as good as American or British kit. The question of the day was whether Ulva had worn his ceramic back plate to go hunting in the hills. Bolan let out half a breath and slowly took up slack on the trigger as the rifleman's mantra silently ran though his mind. "Don't pull the trigger, squeeze…squeeze…squeeze…."

Dust flew from Ulva's clothes, and he pitched forward into the rock in front of him. Bolan didn't wait. He swung his optics onto the man next to him. The man threw himself down, and Bolan took the wing-shot. The man's arm flapped wildly, and then he disappeared behind the rocks. Zanotto plucked up the spent shells and scooted down the slope. Bolan slung his rifle and slid down after her. Behind him, rifle fire crackled and a pair of grenade launchers thumped dully, but they were far out of range. It was Dinatale Bolan was worried about. He didn't know where the Marine was or at what range. Bolan waited for the bullet to hit him between the shoulder blades as he ran, but the crack of the high-powered rifle never came.

Bolan hit the rocks running and moved for his next firing position.

DINATALE BREATHED. Long ago, his sniper instructor at Quantico had noticed that Dinatale, though a dead shot and beloved by his messmates for his easy charm and quick wit, had some serious anger issues bubbling below the surface. The instructor had taken him aside and taught him a Buddhist breathing technique he had picked up from a monk during his second tour in Vietnam. It was a trick that had served the sniper well in Central America. He used it now to center himself, breathing to fill his belly from the bottom up and then his rib cage in the same manner. The breath was a four count in and then an eight count out. The instructor had given Dino the mantra *"Sa Ta Na Ma"* to silently repeat during the counts. It meant "Truth is Oneness." Dinatale had replaced the Sanskrit words with "Kill Kill Kill Kill," four times in and eight times out.

Marko Poertner was screaming across the link. "Dino!"

Dinatale opened his eyes. He was pretty far from his happy place, but he was focused. He clicked his radio. He knew Cooper would be listening, but he had a good idea where Cooper's shots had come from and he didn't want to reveal his position. He personally wouldn't have taken the second shot, but he had to admit Cooper was in something of a dilemma. "Marko, report."

"Ulva's dead. Dittmer has lost his left arm at the elbow. Two of the Afghans, Jamshid and I think Haroon, have gone AWOL into the hills."

Dinatale did a mental head count. He had ten men, three of them Afghans who could no longer be considered reliable. "How are the remaining Germans?"

"They're pissed and want some payback."

"Good. Hold position."

Cooper spoke across the link. "You're having a hard day there, Deadshot."

Dinatale's knuckles went white around his rifle but said nothing.

"Well, the good news is the day is almost over. Of course, I have Dob's night-vision gear. When night falls, we're going to have some real fun. We've already seen who the better sniper is. Let's see how you and your little buddies do against a knife in the dark."

Through a titanic effort of will Dinatale restrained himself and clicked over to a private frequency. "Fir."

Captain Fir came back immediately. "What is your situation, Dino?"

"I want a chopper. ASAP."

Fir paused. "I thought we agreed risking another chopper was unwise save for insertion and extraction. You were going to take care of this."

"Ulva's dead, and I'm down to ten men. The situation has changed. I need air support. I need it now. While there's still light."

"I do not doubt you, my friend, and I have two gunships in E Kamp at present. Unfortunately, I am not sure either pilot can reliably be exposed to our…activities, if you take my meaning."

"What about transports?"

"Florian is still here. He is the same man who inserted you this morning. He is flying the NH90."

"Good, send him."

"Do you wish me to fit the helicopter with rocket and gun pods?"

"No time, just send it." Dinatale resisted the desire to taunt Cooper back. This wasn't a pissing contest. It was a killing contest, and one the sniper intended to win. "Tell Florian this is what I want him to do."

16

Bolan and Zanotto ran for their lives. They weren't going to make it. They couldn't outrun a helicopter. Tracers streamed down from the starboard door gun. Bolan dropped to one knee and snapped up his rifle. The Alex rifle rammed back against his shoulder in recoil, and the NH90 veered away sharply as the bullet ricocheted off its nose. It was the only advantage they had, and it was almost purely psychological. The pilot knew Bolan had already shot down one helicopter that day, and he was paranoid of being number two. However, Bolan had no way to launch his remaining rifle grenades, and unless the German was stupid enough to stop and hover for him, a kill shot through the windscreen would be pure dumb luck. Putting the twin-engine aircraft out of commission with a bolt-action rifle would be next to impossible.

They were being herded. Inexorably, they were being driven back toward the valley. Dinatale and his hunting party were hard on their heels, and the chopper above betrayed Bolan's and Zanotto's every move.

All they could do was run, and soon running wouldn't be an option, either. Zanotto's head wound wasn't serious, but she had lost a lot of blood, and the former fitness champion's superhuman aerobic capacity was starting to fail. Bolan himself was bone tired. Very soon, the only option left would be to turn and fight, and when that happened they were dead. The minute they stopped to engage the hunting party, the door gunners would take him, a salvo of grenades would rain down on them or a bullet from Dinatale's rifle would come out of nowhere.

Zanotto stumbled to a halt beneath an overhang and steadied herself against the rock face of the arroyo. The chopper pilot's voice shouted across the link in a heavy German accent. "Targets beneath cliff, five hundred yards from your position."

Bolan stopped and trained his rifle upward. The helicopter was close and orbiting somewhere just out of sight. In a moment, it would rise up for altitude to spot them. That's when he would take his shot. "You all right?"

Zanotto doubled over and threw up.

Bolan nodded to himself grimly. This was it. They made their stand here. He held out the remaining canteen. "Wash out your mouth, wait a few seconds and then drink a little."

Zanotto took the canteen with a shaking hand. "I'm sorry, I should've—"

"Don't sweat it." Bolan loosened the RAK machine pistol in its holster.

Zanotto handed back the nearly empty canteen and squared her shoulders. "How do we play it?"

Bolan looked around. There were several large boulders beneath the overhang. "The cliff above will make it hard for the grenadiers to lob anything in on us. That and the rocks will make it hard for Dino to get a straight shot. The only way the chopper can get at us is to hover low over the lip of the arroyo and give me a good shot at him. It's not a bad strong point. They're going to have to come in and dig us out." Bolan patted the rock wall behind them affectionately. "Right here, this is where we make our stand."

Bolan emptied his backpack. He had five rounds left in the magazine of the Alex and two more 10-round magazines remaining. His MAG pistol was full. He palmed the one frag he'd taken from Stanislawski and set it on a rock for easy access. Bolan drew the last rifle grenade. He had no way to launch it and no time to improvise an IED with it. He set it down next to the frag. It was still a foot and half long with a lobe of high explosive and fragmentation rings on one end. If all else failed, he could beat someone to death with it.

It just might come to that before the end came.

"Sandwich?"

Zanotto laid a revolver within easy reach. "No, I'm not hungry."

Bolan pulled out the half empty bottle of wine. "Champagne?"

Zanotto snatched the bottle. "You've been holding out on me."

They passed the bottle back and forth and waited for death to come knocking.

Dinatale rang the doorbell as his voice came across the link. "Hey, Coop. My eye in the sky says he thinks you're hiding under that overhang? You hiding under that overhang?"

Bolan ignored the voice on the radio. "Connie, they're coming. It'll probably be a pincer movement."

"Yeah. I know." She chewed her lower lip as she scanned back and forth down both sides of the arroyo. "Where's the chopper?"

"If I were Dino," Bolan said, "I'd dismount the copilot, as well as one door gunner and his weapon to reinforce the ground force. They only need one pilot to spot and one gunner to rain on us."

"Great."

Automatic weapons tore down into the arroyo from above. Grenade launchers began thudding from out of sight above the lip of the little canyon. The Germans were firing at a very high arc, looping their munitions nearly straight up, and long seconds passed before the grenades hit the sand. Bolan and Zanotto hunkered down behind the rocks as the weapons detonated and shrapnel spun and sparked off the stones above and behind them. Bolan laid down his sniper rifle and drew his RAK. He snapped down the folding foregrip, deployed the folding stock and chambered a round. "Here they come."

Men came pounding down both sides of the arroyo.

A German took point on each section, depending on his armor to protect him. The Polish buzz gun in Bolan's hands stood no chance against Kevlar and ceramic. Bolan lowered his sights and the RAK tore into life, and the Gebirgsjaeger screamed and fell as Bolan's burst tore away both of his knees. The unarmored Afghan behind him took Bolan's next burst in the chest and fell, spitting blood on top of the howling German. Bolan's weapon racked back on a smoking empty chamber.

Zanotto fired in the other direction, but Poertner was leading the charge. He took the hits on his armor and charged forward, firing as he came. Zanotto ducked down as bullets smashed against the lip of her cover.

Bolan pulled the pin on the frag and hurled it at Poertner and his section. The grenade snapped like a giant firecracker, and jagged metal whipsawed in all directions. Poertner was in the lethal blast radius, and blood misted the air around him as his arms, legs, groin and every other part of his body not covered by armor was rent and torn. The Afghan behind him was miraculously untouched and came forward spraying his AK-47.

Bolan dropped to reload his RAK as the man came on. The killer's weapon clacked open, and he drew his huge Khyber knife without pausing and lunged over Bolan's rock like an Olympic triple-jumper.

Bolan caught the flying bandit in midflight and slammed him to the sand. He seized the Afghan's wrist as the man tried to jam the massive dagger up into Bolan's throat with both hands. Bolan used his size and weight to lean in and stop the steel's advance toward his trachea. His free hand snaked out for the rifle grenade. His fingers closed around the launch tube and he raised it like a truncheon. The beer-can-sized warhead slammed down into the Afghan's skull in brutal finality.

"I'm out!" Zanotto snarled.

Bolan slammed his last mag into the RAK and tossed it to her as he drew his MAG pistol. "You owe me!"

Pascal and a German came forward at a trot, firing their weapons from the shoulder. Zanotto sprayed a burst into Pascal but he kept coming, and she yelped and dropped as she took his return fire. Bolan spun the launch tube and fin assembly away from the base of the grenade and fired his pistol through the bullet trap in the base. Without the fire-through launch assembly, the rifle grenade couldn't fly, but the fuse armed. Fire squirted out of the base and seared Bolan's left hand as he hurled the fusing grenade. Pascal and the Gebirgsjaeger were almost on top of them. The grenade hit the sand nose first and blew. Pascal fell to his knees, and the German staggered. Bolan rose and shot Pascal twice in the face. The German sprayed in return but his face was a mask of blood, and his blind fire scored the rock face behind Bolan. The Executioner shoved his pistol forward like a fencer and squeezed the trigger three times. The hollow of the German's throat erupted like a rose of blood. The second shot rammed his front teeth into his esophagus, and the third took him in the left eye.

A machine gun opened up from the left, and Bolan knew the door gun had been dismounted. Men would be advancing under its covering fire. He shoved the MAG up over the boulder and squeezed the trigger in rapid semiauto. Random luck rewarded him with a shriek of agony. The pistol snapped open on empty.

Bolan sagged behind the rocks. "Connie."

Zanotto was on hands and knees clutching her face. Blood dripped between her fingers. "Yeah...I'm okay."

Bolan lifted her chin. A bullet had scored her left brow and drawn a furrow down past her ear. She was bleeding like a stuck pig, but Bolan couldn't see bone. "You're okay."

Zanotto stared at Bolan's left hand. "And you?"

He examined his hand. The palm was blackened, but that was mostly superficial powder burns from the fuse rather than searing. He gritted his teeth and made a fist. It hurt like hell, but Bolan's hand obeyed his will. "I'm okay."

Bolan took a deep breath. He was burning with thirst, but he ignored the rawness in his throat. Thirst was the last thing he was going to die of. "There were too many Afghans. I think Jamshid and Haroon came back because they had nowhere else to go."

Zanotto nodded wearily. "Okay."

"So I think Dino still has Monahan, one German up to speed, one with only one arm, the copilot and the door gunner."

"And the chopper above."

"And the chopper above," Bolan agreed.

She gave Bolan an exhausted smirk. "And Frame."

"Yeah, and Frame. So Dino's got six men."

"Sounds about right." Zanotto's face was pale as she pushed herself up onto her knees. She drew her spare .38 and handed it to Bolan. "You got six. Make them count."

Bolan took the revolver and cocked it. "I'm thinking the door gunner is going to start spraying in a second, and then the German is going to sneak forward under his fire and lob a grenade into us."

"Sounds about right."

Bolan popped up.

There was a gooseneck at the northern end of the arroyo. Bolan had time to snap off one shot as the machine gunner threw himself and his weapon prone, and then the MG43 machine gun opened up. Zanotto cringed as rounds hammered against the rocks and full-metal-jacket bullets spanged and spalled off the rocks all around them. Bolan hit the sand prone and snaked his arm around his cover and exposed enough of his head to take a look. Two men were running forward under the covering fire. One was the German grenadier but he wasn't firing grenades. He held his assault rifle at his shoulder and instantly swung it on Bolan. The second man was Monahan, and the Shield contractor carried a satchel charge. Bolan ignored the German and shot Monahan. The contractor's armor took the two hits, and he pulled the fuse on the explosive package.

Bolan raised his aim for the head shot but Monahan was already weaving. The German fired a burst and stone chips exploded into Bolan's face like shrapnel as bullets ricocheted off the rock by his head. Bolan was nearly blind, but he kept squeezing his trigger until it was dry. He rolled back behind cover blinking blood and grabbed for the little automatic pistol on his ankle. "Connie! Shoot!"

Zanotto shoved her pistol over the top of the rock. Bolan rose with the pocket pistol in both hands and they commenced firing.

A war cry shook the shallow walls of the arroyo. *"Allah Akhbar!"*

A pair of AK-47s ripped into action at the southern bend of the arroyo. Babrak and Noorzay charged forward firing their weapons in wild bursts. Dirk came out from the bend behind them. A rifle grenade was fixed to the end of his weapon, and it thudded off the muzzle and looped straight for the door gunner at the north end. Dust flew from Noorzay's vest, and he spun and dropped as a bullet took him from the high ground. Monahan twisted and fell as he took multiple hits from all directions, and the satchel charge fell to the ground. The German stooped to grab the fallen explosive. Bolan emptied his pistol into the German's chest, but he wasn't stopping.

Monahan's satchel charge detonated, and the arroyo erupted like a volcano of sand and smoke.

Bolan winced against the hot wind and the blast of dirt and gravel and then leaped from behind his cover. Dirk and Babrak were up and dragging Noorzay. Monahan and the German were gone. At the north end, the machine gunner lay across his weapon bleeding like a sieve. Bolan scanned the high ground through the smoke and dust as Dirk and his rebels ran behind cover. Bolan moved back beneath the overhang. He didn't know where Dinatale was, and he couldn't afford to give him the first shot. Bolan clicked his radio. "How you doing, Dino?"

Silence answered.

Bolan spoke conversationally. "Dino? As I see it, you've got a one-armed Gebirgsjaeger and a copilot who's shitting his pants right about now. Oh, and there's you and your rifle, but you two have been failing all day."

"Cooper." Dinatale's voice was shaking. "I'm gonna—"

"I got a Delta Force commando, your girlfriend and a nice

young man from the village with a great big knife who is eager to make your acquaintance."

"I am gonna rip you a new rectum, little man. You and me are—"

"Why don't you and me do it right? We both have rifles. We both have knives and night vision. It's almost dark. Let's do it. Just you and me, the old-fashioned way, and see who's still alive come sunrise."

"You son of a—"

"I saw you hit Noorzay. By the angle, I'm thinking you're about four hundred yards due east of here up in the cliffs. Maybe Dirk and I should just take you down now." Bolan could hear the helicopter dropping down out of the sky. By the rotor noise he made it about three or four hundred yards east. "You disappoint me, Dino, but don't worry about it. Sometime soon, maybe in Kabul, maybe in Baghdad, maybe at Shield HQ Houston or that beach house of yours in the Florida Channel Islands, but I will find you, old man, and your shriveled ass will be mine." Bolan let his voice go ugly. "Oh, and tell that turncoat Frame he made his choice, and I'll be looking him up real soon."

Dinatale didn't reply. Neither did Frame, but Bolan was pretty sure the paratrooper understood the message. The only answer was the sound of rotors hammering the sky for altitude echoing in the arroyo.

Dirk grinned. "Dude! You intimidated the Deadshot! You made him your bitch!"

"I doubt it." Bolan knelt by Noorzay. "And if I did, it won't last long. He still has Shield and Fir on his side, and we're on foot God only knows where."

Dirk shook his head. "I know exactly where we are."

Bolan probed Noorzay's wound. Dinatale's bullet had punched through his shoulder, and it would have been clean save that Noorzay's clavicle had gotten in the way and about two centimeters of bone had been pulverized. Bolan let out a breath and glanced at Dirk's pack. "You got morphine?"

"Shield don't stint on nothing, man. I took a full field med-kit on my way out of town."

"Good. We've got to bind him up, and then he's going to have to walk."

"Okay." Dirk pulled his med-kit. "Where we walking? Kabul?"

"We'll never make it." Bolan took a field dressing and started attending to Zanotto's wounds. She smiled up at him through a mask of blood.

"I'm fine."

Bolan applied antibiotic to the bloody furrow along her temple. "You know something?"

"What's that?"

"Bullets, helicopters falling out of the sky?"

"Yeah?"

"You have to quit trying to stop them with your head," Bolan suggested.

She smiled wanly. "You should see yourself, crater face."

Bolan brought a hand to his face, and it came away sticky and red. He'd eaten some rock chips.

Dirk rigged a sling around Noorzay. "So, Pakistan?"

"No, if Dino were trying to stop us from crossing the border he would have leapfrogged ahead of us. Nothing good is waiting for us there."

"So where do we go?"

Bolan raised a bloody, knowing eyebrow.

Dirk sighed. "We're heading back to the village?"

Bolan looked at Babrak. "I promised him his village would be free."

17

Bolan scanned the village through Zanotto's binoculars. They'd made a forced march through the night to try to get back by dawn, but despite their best effort it was midday and they were exhausted. No one was working the poppy fields. Only a few of Gulab-Sha's men were lurking by the sides of buildings and in alleyways, watching all approaches to the village.

"He's waiting for us," Bolan stated.

Dirk watched the ghost village. "You don't think Dino bought your 'some day, some way' speech?"

Bolan trained his scope from house to house. "Maybe, but he's still turned the village into a death trap in case we come back anyway."

"Yeah, while he puts his feet up in Kabul and drinks a cool one."

"No." Bolan could feel the sniper's presence like the shadow of death hanging over the valley. "He's here, probably not in the village, but someplace in the surrounding hillsides, waiting with that rifle of his."

"Yeah, someplace with a real sweet vantage on the village. He's just waiting for us to start sniping or grenading. Once that begins, he starts picking us off."

Bolan nodded. "And I'm thinking he's done playing around. If we attack, Gulab-Sha and his men will kill every last man, woman and child in the village and then pull a scorched-earth routine and disappear."

"And blame it on the Taliban." Dirk spit. "So how do you want to play it?"

"We took out eight of Sha's men up in the hills. I figure he's got about thirty-two men left. Iron Klaus is wandering around someplace with a couple of Toni's goons. I'm thinking there're at least two to four Shield contractors."

Dirk took a sip from his canteen. "Then there's us."

Bolan looked at his team. Zanotto was done in. Babrak was burning anger for fuel. Noorzay sat stoically holding a German pistol in his hand. They had run out of morphine hours ago, but he had trudged along despite what had to have been agonizing pain. The fact was most Afghan villagers were no strangers to privation and pain. Bolan turned his attention back to the village. "Well, look at this."

Frame walked across the square and leaned up against the mosque. Through the scope, the paratrooper appeared to be looking straight at Bolan.

Dirk smiled. "He knows this is where we'll be observing from."

Frame lit a cigarette and then put a hand over his left eye and rubbed it. He casually stuck his thumb against the wall behind him and tapped it twice.

"That beautiful scar-faced son of a bitch!" Dirk nodded. "One-eyed Sha and his men are in the mosque!"

That was the way Bolan read it, too. Frame scratched his chest and for a second let his hand hang there. He made a hard fist and then opened his thumb and first two fingers in a vague *K* shape. He yawned and looked up toward the top of the hill most of the village perched upon.

Bolan smiled. "Iron Klaus is up in Babrak's house."

Babrak almost lurched to his feet. "The German! With my mother and sisters!"

Bolan put a steadying hand on his shoulder. "Just be glad it's him rather than Sha."

Frame pushed away from the mosque and made a 360-degree show of scanning the rim of the valley. He turned back in Bolan's direction and rolled his eyes. Bolan sighed as he received confirmation. "Dino's somewhere out here with us, and Frame doesn't know where."

Dirk grimaced. "Damn."

There were three things that struck fear in any soldier. One was the word *incoming!* Two was the word *tanks!* But the most dreaded warning a soldier could hear in battle was the word *sniper!* Deadshot Dave Dinatale was the Angel of Death with a Remington 700 for a scythe, and he was waiting.

Bolan gave it a fifty-fifty chance that Dinatale had seen Frame's performance and interpreted it. He waited a moment for Frame to fall with a bullet through his brain, but if the sniper had seen it he was too smart to reveal his position. "All right. A night infiltration is our only shot. We rest here while Dino and his boys sweat out the day. If Frame survives the day, he's our Trojan horse. I'm going to insert through the fields. Dirk, you make your way around the valley rim and come down toward Babrak's house."

Zanotto frowned. "What about me?"

"You've taken two head shots in twenty-four hours. I suggest you get some beauty sleep. If we don't make it, you and Noorzay have a hell of a long hike to Kabul."

The pilot reached into her bailout bag and pulled out a thick, folded square of black cloth. She shook it out to reveal a burka. "Standard bailout gear for any female operator in the Middle East. You get me in the village, and I can go anywhere and contact anybody."

Bolan smiled tiredly. "You're in. You insert with Dirk."

Zanotto waggled her eyebrows. "You know, I've heard stories about Dirk's insertions…."

Everyone burst out laughing except Noorzay, and when Babrak explained it to him he grinned despite his shattered shoulder. Bolan nodded inwardly. The most likely outcome was that they would all be dead by dawn, but his team was salty and ready to try. "We sleep in shifts until midnight. Then we make our move. Babrak, you're with me."

Noorzay looked unhappily at the 9 mm Heckler & Koch he held in his hand. "And what of me, Mr. Cooper?"

Bolan looked the young villager up and down. By himself, the hike to Kabul would most likely kill him. "We can't insert you in your condition, so you have a choice. You can sleep, eat and then begin walking out of here. I'll give you contact numbers to the American military, and if you can make your way to a city you can tell people what happened here."

The look on Noorzay's face showed Bolan that the idea of walking out of here, much less abandoning his village, was too painful for the young man to contemplate. "Or?"

Bolan shrugged. "Or once the shooting starts, you can walk to the village and do whatever damage you can."

"I will see you tomorrow morning, then, Mr. Cooper." Noorzay raised his pistol awkwardly in his left hand. "In my village. Or in Paradise."

BOLAN CRAWLED through the darkness.

Babrak followed him as they made their way slowly and painstakingly through the poppies on elbows and knees. Bolan was sure Dinatale had night-vision goggles, but if he was using them through the scope of his rifle his field of view would be narrow, and he had the whole valley to cover. Bolan had smeared all of his garments and face with mud and leaves. The poppies were blooming. In about a week, the beautiful flowers would drop their petals to reveal the capsule within containing opium gum that would be harvested and turned into heroin for the European and American markets. The plants were growing in closely spaced, orderly rows supported by trellises made of sticks and twine. If it weren't for the flowers, the field would have looked like a vineyard. The plants had grown a yard high, and it would take a discerning eye to spot Bolan on his belly in the acres of blooming flowers. Unfortunately, Uncle Sam had spent a great deal of time and effort making sure Dino Dinatale had one of the most discerning eyes on Earth. Bolan awaited the bullet with every move he made. He and Babrak made it to the edge of the field unscathed.

The one advantage they had was that Dinatale and his men probably didn't know about the culvert at the far edge of the poppy fields. It was shallow and snaking, and unless one actually walked its length, it was impossible to detect among the rock formations and overgrown gorse. The culvert led right to the edge of the valley. The most probable infiltration point would be the foothills that descended on the village like craggy steps. That was the path that Dirk had taken. That was where Dinatale would most likely be doing his hunting.

Bolan watched the sentry standing just ten yards away. It was one of Toni Von Bach's men. The German was nominally dressed as an Afghan tribesman, but he wore an armored vest over his tunic and carried an Uzi. He had night-vision goggles, but they were pushed up onto his forehead so that he could smoke a cigarette without the glowing end lighting up his lenses like a flare.

Bolan moved, Noorzay's Khyber knife clutched in his hand. The blade was as wide as a vegetable cleaver at the base and then tapered sharply to a wicked point. The edge was razor thin but thickened into a T-shaped rib along the spine. The design was thousands of years old and had been made with penetrating armor in mind.

The German jerked and gagged as Bolan's left hand cupped over his mouth and slammed the lit cigarette down his throat. He went as stiff as a board with shock as Bolan plunged the needle point of the blade through the thin back armor of the vest and found his kidney. The Executioner yanked the blade free of the German's back and drew the shaving-sharp edge across the killer's throat.

Bolan caught the man as he fell and dragged him back into the poppy field. The Executioner appropriated his armored vest, goggles, wool cap and shawl and gave them to Babrak. He pulled the goggles down over the young man's eyes and tucked the shawl high up on his chin. "Stay here for now."

Babrak tensed. "But I wish to fight!"

"You'll have plenty of opportunity. Wait for the signal."

"What shall this signal be, Cooper?"

"All hell breaking loose. Now, light a cigarette, stand around nd look bored and pretend to be a sentry."

Babrak spoke softly. "I see." He walked out of the field and t a cigarette. It was a thin ruse, at best, but Babrak was not hailed ver the tactical radio and no bullet came.

Bolan waited five minutes and then left the field, moving om rock to rock back up to the village. The rugged hill left early every house built on a different level, creating winding and oping alleyways between each dwelling. It was ideal for infil- ation. He made his way upward toward the headman's house. olan crept along the back of the mosque. There was noise in- de, but no one was praying. It was the coarse laughter of bru- l men. Bolan spoke little Arabic and less Pashto, but he knew xactly what was going on within.

Gulab-Sha and his men were about to be let off the leash. Dino inatale was preparing to cry havoc and let slip the dogs of war. ave that in this case they were wolves, and the men, women and hildren living in this valley were the sheep to be shorn and aughtered.

Bolan froze as the door to the mosque flew open. Light ooded out from the interior as two men emerged. One man car- ed a bastinado like Sha's across his shoulder and the other was Shield contractor who carried a cocked MAG pistol. Each cked on a large bottle of German beer. They staggered slightly ut walked uphill toward the headman's house with purpose and ere followed by shouts of encouragement from the barbarians ithin.

Babrak had two sisters.

Sha and his men were hungry for the fun to begin and wanted appetizer.

Bolan shadowed the two men up to the headman's house. The hield man with the pistol kicked open the door, and the action was met by shouts and screams of alarm. The two raiders entered and more screams and shouts were quickly followed by the sounds of blows. Women within began wailing in despair. The two men came out, dragging two girls in thin cotton nightdresses by their hair. Babrak's father, Behroz, crawled across the lintel of his house, dragging his pulped feet behind him as he begged for the honor of his daughters.

The two men brutally put their boots to the old man.

Back in the house Bolan recognized the sick laughter of Klaus Kleelander.

Bolan slid the Khyber knife from its sheath. A woman in a burka came out of the alley next to the headman's house wailing and waving her arms in supplication. The two men ceased stomping the old man and turned toward their new quarry. The man with the pistol holstered it and backhanded the woman to her knees. He seized her hair through the hood and dragged her along as they moved downhill toward the mosque. Bolan followed, a shadow moving through darkness.

In the inky darkness between the blacksmith's stall and the house of the rug weaver, the woman in the burka rammed a U.S. aircrew survival knife edge up into the bladder of the Shield contractor holding her and ripped it upward until the steel met his sternum. He sighed and fell to his knees, and his intestines uncoiled out of him like gray lengths of rope.

The man with the club released his captive but took a shocked split second too long to unlimber his weapon. The black-shrouded woman snap-kicked him in the groin. The man bent double and fell to his knees. The woman hitched up her burka and spun with the confidence of someone with an advanced teaching certificate in cardio kickboxing and unhinged his jaw with her heel. Teeth flew, and the man fell backward to the dust. A quick swipe of the short, black aircrew blade across his carotids ended his life of sin. Behroz's daughters shuddered and wept and clutched each other.

Bolan spoke quietly. "Connie Z."

Zanotto whirled and then lowered her knife. "Coop."

Bolan stepped into the thin strip of starlight between the huddled houses. "Where's Dirk?"

"Don't know. Lurking. He told me to infiltrate and then broke off into the shadows to do his Delta thing."

"All right, we—"

Bolan and Zanotto leveled their weapons at the same as time the door to the blacksmith's house opened. Bolan had noted the man before. His name was Dastgir, and he was small, slight and almost sparrowlike. He might have been confused more for a florist than a blacksmith save that he had forearms like bowling pins, and he had been glaring pure hatred at the Germans and Gulab-Sha's men since the occupation had begun. Loosely in his hand he held a hammer with a two-inch iron ball bearing welded to the striking end. He stared at the headman's daughters, Zanotto in her burka, the two dead men in the street and then Bolan with a neutral look on his face.

Bolan lowered his blade. "Connie, how's your Arabic?"

"Remedial."

"Do what you can. Tell him to take the daughters of Behroz Daoud into his house and give them sanctuary. Tell him we free the village tonight."

The pilot spoke in halting Arabic. The blacksmith answered back in a flurry. Zanotto pulled the burka's hood back and shook her head. "I couldn't get it all, but basically he's saying we came with the unbelievers. I fly for them. You killed Babrak and Noorzay. He saw the ears. He doesn't trust us."

Bolan unslung his Uzi and spoke directly to the blacksmith. "This belonged to the man guarding the poppy fields. Tell him Babrak lives and waits in the field for the signal to attack. Noorzay is injured, but alive. We free the village tonight."

Zanotto stuttered out a few sentences and rolled her eyes in frustration. "I can't translate all that."

Bolan held out the Uzi to the blacksmith. "Tell him those were the ears of Changaze's men. Tell him if he doesn't trust me, kill me now."

Zanotto's jaw dropped for a half a second, and then she translated.

The blacksmith took the Uzi and spoke very quietly. Zanotto's eyebrows rose. "He wants to know what you want him to do."

Bolan knelt and took the two dead men's pistols and added them to knapsack of weapons on his back. "Are all of Sha's men in the mosque?"

"He says not all but most."

Bolan rose and handed the two pistols to Dastgir and looked to the house across the tiny lane. "Will the weaver fight?"

Zanotto nodded as the grim-faced ironworker answered. "He says all the men of the village will fight. But they don't have enough guns."

"Ask him if the weapons of the villagers and Changaze's men are still in the hidden cave."

Zanotto spoke quickly. "He says yes."

"We kill the men of Gulab-Sha. We kill the Germans. We kill the men of Shield." Bolan drew his borrowed Khyber knife and held up the bloody blade. "We kill them until there are none left."

18

t took ten minutes to sow the seeds of rebellion. The villagers had had enough. They were used to the abuses of warlords, but Gulab-Sha was not their local warlord, and when Western, infidel invaders began dragging men's daughters out into the streets at night all bets were off. The word spread from house to house and hut to hut.

Bolan had dispensed his knapsack of fallen pistols taken from the battle out in the canyons. Most of the men of the village had never fired a handgun. Nearly every man over the age of twelve had fired an AK-47. The plan was simple. Shoot the sentries, take their weapons and then free up the ordnance in the cave. The men without guns drew the huge knife that every Afghan highlander owned. Women from the age of eight to eighty held curved daggers or knives taken from the kitchen and sat in their parlors as still and unblinking as serpents.

There would be no mercy in the village this night, and God help any of the invaders who were left alive when the battle was over. "It won't be long before Sha and the boys wonder where their buddies are. It's time."

Zanotto stood and checked the load in her revolver. "How do we play it?"

"First we go to the headman's house and kill Kleelander. Then we come back and take the mosque."

"I've heard some rumblings about that. The men are willing to go into the mosque and drag Sha out, but they're not willing to burn it."

The problem had occurred to Bolan. The holy place had already been defiled, and torching the building and shooting Sha's men as they came out would save the lives of many villagers. However, what was defiled could be cleansed, and the mosque was the social and spiritual center of these villagers' lives.

"Then we go in and take Sha out. Hand to hand if we have to. Tell them," Bolan directed.

"Jesus." Zanotto spoke to the blacksmith, the weaver and the small assemblage of village elders who had sneaked into Dastgir's forge. They nodded in understanding. "So how are you going to take the headman's house? Behroz's daughters say Iron Klaus is in there, holding court with a Gebirgsjaeger and three of Fat Toni's muscle."

"Ask Babrak's daughters if they are willing to return to their father's house."

Zanotto spoke slowly to the two young women. The daughters of Behroz had a whispered conference with the women of the blacksmith's house and nodded their willingness. "They'll go."

Everyone tensed at the sound of a quiet knock on the door. Dastgir's son, Kastagir, spoke a little English. Bolan had sent him to find "the scar-faced one."

The door to the forge swung open, and Jimmy Frame grinned through his stitches and scabs. "Hey, man, where's the party?"

"Up at Iron Klaus's crib." Bolan tilted his head toward the headman's house. "You want to go?"

"Oh, I brought our invitations." Frame reached into his pack and pulled out two of the same diminutive Polish pocket pistols Bolan and Dirk had, but these had stubby black sound-suppressor tubes screwed onto the muzzle. "I decided to raid Dobrus' stash since he was dead."

Bolan took one and checked the loads. "We're going to drag Babrak's sisters and Connie back up the hill and take the house. Connie's our ticket in. Frame, you lead the way. We need to know where Dino is."

"Got it."

Bolan took Frame's kaffiyeh and wound the cloth around his head until only his eyes showed. They moved back up the hill, and once they got to the little village square they made no pretense of concealment. Bolan and Frame dragged the weeping women back up to the house of their father.

Frame pounded on the door. "Klaus! It's Frame!"

A German mountain trooper answered the door. "What is it?"

Frame ripped Zanotto's veil away and brutally flung her to her hands and knees. "Look what I found."

The Germans were reclining on cushions, drinking beer and smoking from the family water pipe. Behroz sat in a corner clutching his bloody feet and rocking in shame as his wife and youngest daughter served the invaders like honored guests while his elder daughters were undoubtedly being raped below.

Kleelander and his men rose. Zanotto cringed as the Germans leered down at her. Frame stepped in and slung Behroz's daughters by the hair on top of Zanotto in a pile of weeping femininity. "Connie infiltrated the village yesterday. The girls didn't want to be raped, so they gave her up. I figured you might want to debrief them before I throw them back to Gulab-Sha and his boys."

"Good. Very good." Kleelander put his hands on his knees and looked at Zanotto in ugly appraisal. "You and me. I have been waiting."

Frame took a step forward. "Dino said ten grand to the man who brought Connie in, and first crack at that fine behind. You can take a number like everyone else."

Two of Von Bach's men's hands went to their pistols. Kleelander's eyes slitted dangerously, but everyone had heard Dinatale proclaim the bounty. He waved off his men.

Frame ignored the two gangland enforcers. "Where's Dino?"

"He is…around," Kleelander answered.

"Yeah? Like where? If Connie got into the village undetected, then God only knows were Dirk and Cooper are."

"The situation is in hand, Mr. Frame. I will report your find to Dino." Kleelander took out his radio. The Gebirgsjaeger held his short assault rifle and was giving Bolan the evil eye. "Frame, who is this one?"

Frame shrugged. "You know him, he's—"

Bolan snapped the silenced little pistol up under the German's jaw and pulled the trigger twice. Frame yanked out his own gun and shot one of Von Bach's men. Bolan shot another three times in the face, and Frame sent the fourth fountaining with arterial spray to the floor. Bolan whipped his gun for Kleelander, but Zanotto had lunged up and her knife arced for Kleelander's throat. The German was a lot faster than the aura of relaxed violence he exuded let on. He caught Zanotto's wrist and twirled her with the aplomb of a tango dancer and reeled her into his embrace. He knew he would never be able to bring his slung Uzi to bear in time. Instead an Italian stiletto clicked open against Connie's throat, and she gasped as he pressed it hard enough to part skin. Kleelander tucked his head low behind Connie's and grinned. "Pistols. Drop them."

Bolan and Frame pointed their silent pistols, but Kleelander was neither afraid nor backing down. "Pistols! Or I cut her! *Schnell!*"

Bolan's weapon never wavered. "Klaus, did you bar the windows in the room behind you?"

Kleelander scoffed. "I will not fall for—" The man had not risen to the number-two position in a German drug syndicate without having honed his survival instincts. He whirled as he perceived the presence behind him, but he was drug muscle rather than Delta Force, and he was far too slow. Dirk flowed from the shadows and threw a straight right, and he held his Afro pick in his right hand like a push dagger. The fan of stainless spines punched into the big German's neck. The first six slid into his throat and stoppered his scream. The remaining three on either side punctured his carotid arteries and carotid nerve bundles. Kleelander spasmed as his body locked up, choked out and strangled. Zanotto ripped out of his embrace as he collapsed to the floor. Kleelander shuddered and died as the African-American grooming implement interfered with three of his vital bodily functions all at the same time.

"Have to get me one of those," Bolan said.

Dirk knelt, yanked the pick from Kleelander's trachea and wiped it on the dead man's clothes. "You'll need to get yourself one messed-up perm first, or no one's gonna buy it." He replaced the pick in the back of his coiffure and nodded at Frame. "Good to see you on the winning team, Jimmy."

"Good to be on the winning team, Dirk."

Dirk rose. "So, we take the mosque now?"

Bolan nodded. "Yeah, we take it, but I really wish we had a read on Dino's whereabouts first."

"Yeah," the black commando agreed. "I got a bad feeling."

"Let's get on that laptop and get a message out to the cavalry."

Dirk shook his head. "I checked that. Phone line's been cut, somewhere outside the village."

Bolan had a bad feeling, too. "We need to get the confiscated weapons out of the cave and into the hands of the villagers. Particularly, any machine guns or light support weapons. We have to assume there may be an attempt to retake the village before we can get the word out about what's happening. Dirk, I need you to take out the two guards by the cave."

"Man…" Dirk feigned insult. "Where do you think I been?"

"You have any kind of inventory on the weapons?"

"At a quick glance, there was at least three RPGs, couple of light machine guns, one heavy and a truckload of AKs."

"Let's get the villagers armed up." Bolan liberated the dead Gebirgsjaeger's weapon, web gear and armor. "Frame, me, you and Connie are going to pull the same trick to open the door to the mosque and then the villagers pour in after us."

"You got it, boss."

Bolan checked the load in the rifle and fixed its bayonet. He stared a full circle around the room as if he could see through the walls. It wasn't the Executioner's eyes that were searching, but his instincts.

Where the hell was Deadshot Dinatale?

BOLAN AND FRAME DRAGGED Zanotto between them toward the mosque. Several of Sha's men were milling around outside gripping their weapons, clearly wondering where their comrades had gone. Frame waved, and Zanotto let out a moan. The bandits grinned, and one pounded on the mosque door. Light flooded out as it opened. Gulab-Sha himself filled the door frame, holding his bastinado in one hand and a Stechkin machine pistol in the other. His one, beer-reddened eye glared down at Frame as he rumbled in broken English. "I send Mukhtar, Shield man, for daughters of Behroz!" He thrust his hideous face almost nose to nose with Frame. "Where?"

Frame shrugged. "Behroz's daughters are both virgins. Klaus and his boys decided to take first crack at them."

Gulab-Sha rose to his full height like a storm cloud of imminent violence.

Frame wrenched away Zanotto's veil. "Her, on the other hand? Mr. Dinatale wants her…punished. Figured he'd give you first crack at her. Figured you and your men might have some…ideas."

Sha literally licked his lips. "I have ideas." Zanotto yelped as he seized her by the arm and bodily flung her into the mosque. The men within roared.

Frame grinned. "Mind if we watch?"

Sha spit but jerked his head in invitation. "Perhaps you learn something."

Bolan lowered his carbine and put a burst through the backs of Sha's legs. The circle of men surrounding Zanotto jerked around at the gunshots. Zanotto produced her revolvers from beneath her burka. The pistols rolled in her hands in rapid-fire as she reaped would-be rapists like wheat. There were no innocents in the mosque. The holy place had been turned into a beer hall and bandit lair. Dozens of sandals slapped in the streets outside as the waiting villagers charged. Half of the bandits didn't even have their weapons in hand, and Bolan and Frame concentrated on the men who did. Half of Sha's men ran screaming in all directions, interfering with those ready to fight. There was nowhere to go. Muslims knelt during their devotions. There were no pews to hide between, no cover save for the minibar in the back, and there was only one door leading in and out of the mosque's single large room.

Gulab-Sha and his men were bandits in a barrel.

Bolan dropped his smoking empty rifle and filled his hands with pistols. Both he and Frame stepped to either side of the door as villagers began streaming in. Dastgir the blacksmith led the charge. He fired his Uzi dry, then his pistol and then began going to work on the fallen with the heavy iron sphere of his rising hammer. Bolan and Frame had to stop shooting as the battle devolved into a brawl. Sha's men were drunk and had been caught with their pants down. Surprise was total. They were shot down, dragged down and finished off without mercy.

Bolan considered mercy as he watched Gulab-Sha drag himself out the door on his elbows. The smoking MAG pistol rose in his hand. Dastgir held out his hammer and shook his head. The message was clear. There would be no mercy shot for Gulab-Sha.

The women of the village burst forth from every household brandishing blades that curved in every direction. Over the past few days Bolan had heard far too much of the traditional wail of despair. Now they shrieked in celebration. A blind man familiar with the region might have thought the wedding of a young couple was being celebrated. What was being celebrated was *badal,* revenge.

Gulab-Sha screamed like an animal as the women of the village fell upon him and began carving him like a calf.

Bolan turned away. No one was being castrated in the mosque, but the carnage wasn't much better. He reloaded his pistols, scooped up his carbine and slapped in a fresh magazine. Zanotto had stripped away her burka and taken up a rifle and ammo from one of the fallen. She winced as she took in the atrocity going on outside. Sha was still screaming, but his broken-slate baritone had gone up several octaves. "Jesus!" She turned to Bolan. "Aren't you going to do something?"

"You're a woman, Connie. They might let you join in." Bolan shook his head slowly. "But I wouldn't step out there to stop it if I were you."

"Jesus..."

Dirk entered the mosque. "I'd listen to the man. All most of these villagers know is that we came with the invaders, fought for them and for some reason turned against them. These people want revenge, they want it by the boatload, and it won't take much of a misunderstanding for them to turn on us."

Bolan glanced out across the square. "Dirk, what's the situation in the rest of the village?"

"I passed pistols from window to window. Once the shooting started, those who weren't tasked with taking the mosque took the sentries. As it stands, all hostiles are down, and I've got four armed men at each corner of the village. I've got ten villagers bringing the rest of the weapons down from the cave."

"Good enough. Get Behroz down here, get someone to carry him if you have to, but I want him to give a liberation-how-wonderful-we-are speech to his people."

"I'll bring him myself. That's—"

Dino Dinatale's voice came across the tactical radio. "That was some sick shit, Coop."

Bolan clicked his transmitter. "Why don't you come on down, Dino? I know some ladies who would love to meet you."

"Think I'll take a pass, but I'll give you credit. I didn't detect jack shit until you stormed the mosque."

"You remember what I said about finding you wherever you go, Dino? You run to whatever stinking hole you think you might have friends, but your kind of friends will turn on you for the money I'm going to put up, and I have resources you wouldn't believe. So you go ahead and run, but you'll just die tired. You give up now, and it's prison, and you pay for dishonoring the Medal of Honor. You make me chase you, you're living like an animal for the rest of your short life until I end you. If I catch you here in Afghanistan, I stake you out for the ladies. Give it up now, last chance."

"That's awfully bold talk, Cooper."

"I've got a hundred armed villagers who know these mountains like the back of their hands and a Polish sniper rifle. The hunting party heads out in ten minutes. What've you got, Deadshot?"

Bolan could hear Dinatale smiling across the tactical link as he spoke. "I've got gunships."

The next thing Bolan heard was the sound of rotors.

19

The rockets screamed down out of the sky. The few electric lights in the village went out as the power cut. Tracers streaked like lasers out of the night, tore up geysers of dust along the narrow village lanes and shredded men. The villagers ran stumbling and screaming in the starlight, while the assassins above killed with the precision of night-adapted predators.

Bolan pulled his goggles down over his eyes and peered upward. The two German NH90s had door gunners on both sides of the cabin, and the add-on pylons were studded with weapon pods. The cabins were full of armed men.

Dirk jogged up with Behroz riding him piggyback. "Too late for the Gettysburg Address?"

"No!" The mosque crumbled in fire and smoke as the salvo of 2.5-inch rockets hit it like a swarm of meteors. "Now's the time!"

"Um…okay!" Dirk shrugged the human load on his shoulders. "What do you want him to say?"

"Those are NH90s! They're transports, not gunships. Tell his people to stand and fight. Tell them to stand and shoot. Tell them to bring the choppers down or die."

Dirk craned his head around and spoke in halting Arabic to the old man. Bolan pulled a rifle grenade from his commandeered German equipment. He clicked the illumination round over the muzzle, shouldered his rifle and sent the grenade skyward. The grenade hurtled up and detonated into incandescence like a small sun. The two helicopters were suddenly illuminated as they circled the village like a pair of sharks. Bolan stood lit up in the middle of the square. He swung his rifle on the closer chopper and held down his trigger. Sparks shrieked across the canopy and the nose of the chopper began to turn toward him accusingly.

Dirk shoved his hands under Behroz's haunches and military-pressed the old man overhead like a human pulpit. Behroz's voice rose in a high-pitched alto that cut across the sound of gunfire. The old man was the one who climbed the mosque's tiny minaret and sent his voice echoing across the valley to call the faithful to prayer. Now his voice rang out and called the faithful to war. He pointed at Bolan in example as the Executioner stood his ground and fired, and the old man's voice rose higher still.

Every villager with a weapon turned from their flight and began firing. Firing at gunships was nothing new to Afghans. For most, it had just been a while. The old veterans turned first. *"Allah Akhbar!"* roared from their lips as they emptied their rifles.

Bolan dropped his empty magazine and slapped in a fresh one. He grabbed another rifle grenade and clicked it onto the muzzle. He would have killed for an antiarmor round, but a frag would have to do. The carbine bucked against his shoulder and the grenade sailed up to slam into the side of the helicopter's fuselage. It did little damage, but one of the troopers firing his rifle out the cabin door clutched his face, screamed and fell to the smoking ruins of the mosque beneath him. The villagers screamed at the victory and continued firing. Bolan held down his trigger and burned another magazine into the helicopter.

Frame ran up with one of the PK machine guns they'd taken from Changaze's men days earlier. He slammed it down across a crumbling wall and sent a hail of lead into the side of the other helicopter. The door gunner sagged in his straps, and two of the men within shuddered and fell out. The chopper dipped its nose and sped out of range. Dirk and Behroz stood in the middle of the square shouting encouragement for all to see in the slowly falling light of the flare. The first helicopter spun sixty degrees, and the 27 mm Mauser cannon pod it carried sledgehammered into life in automatic fire.

Bolan shouted but was already too late. "Dirk!"

Dirk and Behroz came apart like rags in the high-explosive onslaught.

The villagers were not deterred as their headman and the hero who had started their revolution died. The men were instant martyrs, and the villagers howled with renewed rage and continued firing. A girl of no more than twelve ran forward through the firefight clutching an RPG-7 bigger than she was and delivered it to Zanotto. The pilot shouldered the weapon, and the rocket roared from its tube and smashed into the belly of the murder machine circling above. Flame burst out from both sides of the cabin, and men screamed as they were fried and fire ripped up between the rotor blades. The tail of the helicopter dipped like a crippled fish. The thunder of one engine died, and components within the second clanked brokenly. The remaining engine screamed as it pushed for altitude, but it was clearly losing power. The pilot dipped the nose and tried to get his aircraft out of the killzone.

Bolan's voice rose to iron-lunged decibels. Only a few of the villagers had any English, but his words needed no translation as he reloaded and fired into the stricken aircraft. "Bring it down! Bring it down! Bring it down!"

Every man standing fired his weapon into the burning NH90. Bolan dropped his spent rifle and drew his pistols. The 9 mm popguns were nothing more than fleabites to the huge helicopter save that it had been cracked open from cabin to engine compartment and every piece of lead ricocheting around in the fuselage helped the process along. Zanotto dropped her rifle and fired her revolvers dry. The NH90's fuselage sparked as if it were wrapped in firecrackers as every weapon in the village was brought to bear upon it. The NH90's remaining engine spewed smoke and went silent. The chopper spun into autorotation, and the screams of the men within were plain for all to hear. The chopper collided into Behroz Daoud's house. Snapped rotor blades flew, and secondary explosions lit the night as the rockets remaining in the pods detonated.

There were no survivors.

The flare settled to the dust of the village square and sputtered and died. The burning helicopter was throwing flames thirty feet into the air and shed plenty of light. Bolan picked up his carbine and reloaded. Villagers dragged their dead and wounded off the streets and into the houses that were still standing. Zanotto had found another rocket and came forward with the RPG perched across her shoulders. Frame carried his machine gun against his hip. "Where's Dirk?"

Bolan gazed at the pattern of shell craters where Dirk and Behroz had stood and the bloody rags of two men intermingled among them. "He's gone." He turned his gaze away from the fire and lowered his night-vision goggles over his eyes as he stared out across the valley. The other chopper was hovering far out of rifle range over the poppy fields. Bolan clicked his radio. "Hey, Deadshot, how many choppers of yours have I shot down now?"

The radio crackled but was silent.

"You're gonna pay for Dirk, Dino."

Dinatale's voice dripped venom. "The Delta prick should have known his place."

Bolan's knuckles creaked around the grips of his spent pistols, but his voice remained level. "You got one chopper left. It's your only ride home. You bring it on—we bring it down. You'd best go play hide and go screw yourself while you can. I'll be along presently."

Dinatale snarled wordlessly and cut transmission. The helicopter settled down in the poppy fields, and Bolan could see Dinatale loping down the eastern hillside.

"He's getting away," Frame growled.

Bolan squinted through his lenses. "Maybe…"

A figure had risen by the western edge of the poppy field. It aimed a weapon, and a grenade launcher thudded toward the chopper. The projectile landed squarely in the cabin. The grenade lit up the troop compartment in a yellow flash. The man was already charging forward firing his rifle from the hip. The pilot rammed his throttles forward to take off when another man rose up from the poppies a few yards away. He clambered awkwardly into the open cabin using only one arm and stepped over the dead and dying gunmen within. The pilots thrashed about in their seats, unlocking their harnesses and grabbing for weapons. A second later the cockpit was lit by a pair of short, sharp flashes from a handgun, and the pilot and copilot slumped forward onto their controls.

Dinatale was already scampering back up the rocky hillside like a mountain goat.

Bolan shrugged. "Maybe not."

Babrak's voice shouted happily across the radio. "Cooper!"

"This is Cooper."

"Noorzay and I have captured a helicopter!"

"Any survivors?"

"None!"

"Good work. Get up here on the double. I need you."

"Yes, Cooper!"

There would be time later to tell the young man his father was dead. "Connie, you think you can fly an NH90?"

"Never have, but it can't be too much different than a Black Hawk."

"How many passengers can it hold?"

The pilot's nose wrinkled in thought. "Twenty, I think."

"Take a few men and get down there. Make sure it's still airworthy. Frame, I need you to round up about sixteen men who are still willing to fight. Babrak and Noorzay both speak English. Have them help you." Bolan gazed out across the valley. Dinatale had already disappeared. "I want to be in the air within thirty minutes."

THEY WERE AIRBORNE in forty-five. One of the NH90's engines kept making odd noises and triggering blinking red lights on Zanotto's controls until she turned the engine off. The remaining engine strained and roared in emergency war power, but

Bolan already knew he was too late. He sat in the copilot seat and spoke to Aaron Kurtzman over the radio. "Are you sure?"

"Sure enough, Striker. We've been watching Gebirgsjaeger E Kamp on satellite since your last transmission. Twenty minutes ago a helicopter took off. Ten minutes ago it landed outside the valley and took off again immediately. NSA is sifting through radio chatter, but I'm betting Dino called in for extraction."

Bolan didn't need to bet. He was sure of it. The sixteen villagers behind him in the battered troop compartment were angry and willing, but there was no way they could take E Kamp. Captain Fir would blow them out of the air and figure out how to explain it later. "How soon until the chopper reaches E Kamp?"

"They already passed it, Striker. By our vector they're heading straight for Kabul."

"Anything you can do about it?"

"Striker, all we have is your word Dino Dinatale has done anything wrong, and we're in Afghanistan. We can ask the capital city police for help, but Dinatale is well loved in town, and this is going to take months of investigation. A couple of bribes in the right place, and he will be at large in the world before we can act. The Germans are going to be another matter entirely. Accusing Captain Fir of anything is going to blow up in our faces. Hell, even if the German army investigates and finds out about what he's been up to and can link him to Toner Von Bach, it's likely to cause such a stink the Germans might withdraw from Afghanistan entirely."

These were all things Bolan had considered. This had all started as a renegade mission and it would have to end the same way. "Then I need two things."

Bolan could almost hear Kurtzman girding himself to do the impossible. "Shoot."

"There's a good chance Fir may call in a massive strike on the village. Gunships, napalm, scorched earth and then try to explain it all away later. I need American troops on the ground, in the village, ASAP, and the Germans need to know they're there."

"I think I might know a Delta Force troop that would be willing to go in right now."

"I was hoping you'd say that."

"What else do you need?"

"I need clearance for a flight plan into Kabul."

"Striker…"

"Dino is heading back to Shield headquarters. His cash money is there. His drugs are there, and one whole hell of a lot of incriminating evidence is there. It'll be our last chance to stop him before he bugs out."

"Shield HQ Kabul is a fortress, Striker. You're going to assault it by yourself?"

"I have a team."

Kurtzman was quiet for an incredulous moment. "You have a helicopter full of tribesmen."

Bolan glanced back at the grim-faced men filling the troop compartment. Half of them were clearly airsick, and all clutched their weapons as the helicopter screamed across the sky in a white-knuckle ride.

"Maybe so," Bolan acknowledged. "But they want payback. I'm heading to Kabul, Bear. I'm landing on Dino's roof and assaulting. Clear me a path."

20

Shield Headquarters, Kabul

"Blow it!" Bolan shouted. The door to the rooftop was security steel embedded in a low trapezoid of concrete. Zanotto dipped the nose of the chopper and released a three-rocket salvo into the stairway door, and it disappeared in black smoke and fire with the remnants flying down the stairwell. "And the chopper!"

She swung the nose of the NH90 toward the German army aviation MBB 105. "That chopper belongs to the Bundeswehr."

Bolan nodded. "So does this one!"

Zanotto accepted the logic and sent a trio of rockets into the hapless helicopter sitting on the pad. The chopper cracked open like an egg giving birth to fire as the rockets smashed through the cockpit glass and detonated within. Bolan rose from the copilot's seat. "How many we expecting?"

"If he's here, Fat Toni never goes anywhere without at least four bodyguards. Captain Fir came here in a chopper that holds four passengers plus the pilot and copilot. Dino usually has six security men on the premises at all times. They're locals, but loyal. They'll be ex-Afghan army or Northern Coalition militia and willing to help him with after-hours dirty work. As for Shield faithful, I think you ventilated most of them, but there may be one or two I don't know about."

Bolan nodded. Eighteen to twenty men, almost even odds except that most of Dinatale's men were soldiers and entrenched in a fortified building while most of Bolan's fighters were exhausted, abused, airsick tribesmen. Then again, Bolan had a gunship and payback on his side.

"Get me into Dino's office, then land the team on the roof and assault."

Zanotto stared at Shield headquarters and then at Bolan. "You think I have the key or something?"

"What about that Mauser automatic cannon under your pylon?" Bolan countered.

The pilot grinned ferociously and swung the helicopter out over the street and aimed the Mauser automatic cannon at the black polarized glass of Dinatale's office. The helicopter shook as the cannon spit out ten rounds in the blink of an eye, and the bulletproof window glass and three feet of surrounding wall were chewed away in an instant. Bolan strode back through the troop cabin and hooked a rapelling rope into a cleat in the door frame. He drew the Stechkin machine pistol he'd liberated from Gulab-Sha and stepped out onto a smoking rocket pod.

"Go!"

Bolan stepped into space. Zanotto brought the nose of the chopper over the roof of the building, and Bolan swung through the smoking hole in the side of the building. Bolan's boots crunched on glass, and he filled his other hand with the RAK he'd taken from Stanislawski. The room was full of acrid black smoke, and most of the lights had been smashed out. The fire-suppression sprinklers rained down and hissed and spit on burning and smoldering wreckage. Banded stacks of dollars and euros were scattered around Dinatale's shattered desk. Two kilos of heroin lay on the floor. One was torn and spilling its powdered misery into the carpet. The other had drops of fresh blood on it. More tellingly, Dinatale's beloved Model 700 lay with its action hanging out of its cracked stock, and the optics were blown out and bent. Bolan's eyes narrowed. The panel to the private gun room was open, and the light was still on. Several racks were empty and several ammo and accessory lockers were open.

Deadshot Dave Dinatale was with Polish steel and still on the premises.

Bolan could hear gunfire erupting on the roof. Whatever Dinatale and his pals had been expecting, it had not been half a platoon of enraged villagers launching an airborne assault. "Connie, what have you got?"

Zanotto's voice came across the link over the sound of rotors and gunfire. "Assault team is deployed. I am orbiting. A couple of assholes stuck their heads out the stairs a few seconds ago and got 'em shot off by Frame and the boys. Expect hostiles coming your way."

"Copy that, Connie. Stay in orbit, and stop anyone or any vehicle coming out of the building. Give them one across the bow in warning, and if they don't stop, light 'em up."

"Copy that, Coop. Be advised, local fire and police, military and coalition are blowing up the radio."

"Keep me advised."

Bolan strode through the building with a machine pistol in each hand. Armed men spilled out of the stairwell. Bolan recognized two of Von Bach's bodyguards, and the weapons blazed in the Executioner's hands. Blood blossomed in wet stains on the fronts of their suits, and they fell without getting off a shot. The man behind still wore the battle tunic of the Gebirgsjaegers, and he tossed a grenade at the big American. Bolan put a burst into the mountain trooper's face before he could duck back into the stairwell. The barrel-shaped grenade rolled clattering down the hallway.

Bolan put his shoulder into the door to the copy room and dived to one side as six thousand steel ball bearings blasted out in all directions and filled the hall with death. The Executioner was up in an instant. He reached into the gas-mask bag slung over his shoulder and pulled a grenade of his own. He pulled the pin, and the cotter lever pinged away as feet pounded in the hallway. Men shouted in alarm as he lobbed the German grenade out of the copy-room door and then screamed as the weapon detonated and spewed its lethal cloud of steel. Bolan stepped back into the hall with his machine pistols spraying.

Another bodyguard and a Gebirgsjaeger were down. One of Von Bach's goons in a suit was still standing, but a pair of bursts put him down. Bolan's pistols clacked open on empty. The fat man himself was still standing, as well. Hundreds of bright red pinpricks of blood were appearing all over his white silk suit as if the giant German gangster had been mauled by a pack of sewing machines. His face was miraculously untouched, but his hands dripped blood, and his pistol fell from his fingers. None of the 2 mm ball bearings had managed to pierce deeply enough into Von Bach's substantial bulk to affect anything vital. He stared at Bolan a moment, and then a high-pitched scream tore out of his throat. His sausage-sized fingers curled into claws, and his vast mass burst into a remarkably fast charge. Bolan sidestepped the lumbering attack and snapped his left hand out in a backfist strike. He still held his empty machine pistol in his hand, and a pound of Russian steel cracked into Fat Toni Von Bach's temple. Teeth flew as Bolan's weapon unhinged the German's jaw and punched him to his knees. Bone crunched as Bolan drove the butt of his pistol into the back of Von Bach's skull as if he were driving a nail.

Dead, the German drug dealer fell face-first to the floor.

Bolan tossed away the empty, bloodstained machine pistols and unslung the carbine from around his back. Frame shouted from the stairwell. "Coop!"

"This floor is clear."

Frame came into the hallway followed by Babrak and a dozen villagers. Bolan did a quick head count. "You're missing a few."

"A few of the boys got a little too jihad happy and charged the gunmen in the doorway upstairs. Two went down, and I left two more to keep an eye on them. Neither wound is fatal, but they need a medic and the quicker the better."

"You seen Dino?"

"No, but I saw Captain Fir heading down the stairs. I suspect he is dug in on the ground floor like a tick. At least two of his men have squad automatic weapons. Whoever steps out of the stairwell or is in the elevator car when it opens is going to get cut to pieces."

That was the way Bolan saw it, as well. "How many grenades you got?"

Frame patted down his web gear. "Four."

"Give me three and keep one for yourself, just in case."

"I don't think a couple of grenades are going to—"

Bolan held out his hand. "I'll show you a trick about the German DM 51."

Frame began handing over DM 51 grenades. Bolan took one and unscrewed the fragmentation jacket containing the ball-bearing fragmentation projectiles to reveal the hexagonal inner grenade containing the high explosive. He did the same to the next two and unscrewed and discarded their fuses, as well. Bolan screwed the grenade cores together in series like the stages of a rocket.

"Cluster charge!" Frame grinned. "Gotta love that German engineering!"

"There's an old saying in Europe." Bolan took his own three remaining grenades and relieved them of their fragmentation sheaths. "Germans make three things better than anybody."

The stitches crisscrossing Frame's face arranged themselves quizzically. "And what are those?"

"War, weapons—" Bolan linked the three grenades together to produce a second Bangalore torpedo and handed the weapon to Frame "—and mistakes."

Frame stared at Bolan seriously. "You're like, smart 'n' stuff."

Bolan went to the elevator and opened up the elevator car's ceiling access hatch. "I'm going to send the elevator down. I want simultaneous detonations, if possible. So toss yours down the stairwell when I say go."

Frame positioned himself by the stairs. "Got it."

Bolan flicked the switch on the shaft door and then punched

the button in the car for the ground floor. He pulled the pin on the cluster charge and watched as the car descended the dark shaft. The open access hatch in its roof was a yellow rectangle of light. The car came to a stop and its doors opened. The rip-saw sound of machine-gun fire instantly echoed in the shaft as the gunners below cut loose.

"Now!" Bolan opened his hand and the cotter pin pinged away. The three linked grenades fell down the shaft and through the access hatch in the roof of the elevator car.

Bolan prudently stepped back.

One hundred eighty grams of plasticized nitropenta detonated. Without eighteen thousand steel ball bearings to slow it down, the high-explosive blast wave expanded out of the elevator car like a superheated hurricane. A tongue of orange fire and smoke blasted up out of the access hatch like a geyser. A half second later, Frame's charge hit the floor of the stairwell and blew.

"Go! Go! Go!" Bolan roared.

Frame and his personal village militia thundered down the stairs while Bolan grabbed one of the dangling elevator cables. He wedged the greasy cable between his boots and slid down the shaft. Smoke oozed up from the mangled hatch, and the roof of the car was bubbled and bulged as Bolan's boots hit it. He dropped down through the hatch and strode into the lobby with his G36 carbine leveled.

Four men lay dead in the lobby, two by the stairs and two at Bolan's feet. One of each pair wore German uniforms and had a machine gun near them. The other two were locals wearing Shield logo polo shirts with armored vests hastily pulled on over them. All four men leaked blood from their ears, noses and the corners of their eyes from the blast overpressure. Dino Dinatale and Captain Fir were still at large.

"Connie, anyone go out the front or back door?"

"Nope, but you have police, fire and military units including armor converging on the building. I'm—" Zanotto suddenly broke off.

"Connie!" Silence crackled across the link. "Connie!"

Zanotto came back. "Coop, I've got a pair of British Apache gunships telling me to land on the roof and stand down."

"Do it."

"Coop, I—"

"Do it."

"All right, Z Flight standing down."

Frame and his little army spilled into the lobby. The paratrooper grinned at the two fallen machine-gun sections. "Damn, you're good."

Bolan took one of the fallen MG3 machine guns and loaded a fresh 100-round belt. "Dino and Fir have to be at basement level."

"Nothing down there but the firing range and the parking garage, and only one way out."

Bolan moved to the stairs. "Let's finish this." He took the stairs four at a time as he heard the sounds of engines revving in the parking garage. Bolan kicked open the door only to find a pair of Shield VIP armored Chevy Suburbans burning rubber for the exit ramp. Bolan dropped to one knee and burned one hundred rounds into the black-tinted armor glass of the tailgate, but the bullets sparked and whined away. Bolan dropped his smoking weapon and clicked his link. "Connie! Are you still airborne? I've got two vehicles coming out the garage."

"Negative, Coop. But I don't think you're going to have to worry about them getting away."

The sound of automatic cannon fire confirmed Zanotto's report. Both Suburbans came squealing down the ramp in Reverse. The cannon sound came again, and the truck closer to the exit flew apart from bumper to bumper in a series of explosions that sent rended metal flying in all directions. The second Suburban screamed around in a reverse bootlegger's turn and came straight at Bolan.

Frame handed Bolan three linked DH 51 grenades. "I passed around the hat, and the boys got you a present."

Several of the tribesmen behind Frame nodded happily. Bolan pulled the pin. "Tell the boys to get back in the stairs." He released the safety lever and counted to two and hurled the grenade at the Chevy's windshield. Bolan dived for the stairs and slammed the door behind him. The steel security door buckled inward slightly from the blast. Bolan ripped it open and drew his pistol.

The Suburban had slammed into the wall. The engine compartment of the SUV was gone, and the armor glass of the windshield shattered and sagged inward. Rather remarkably, one of the back passenger doors opened and Captain Fir fell out choking to the pavement.

Bolan strode up and peered inside the smoke-filled vehicle. Everyone else was dead or unconscious, and Deadshot Dinatale wasn't inside. Bolan considered the captain as he pushed himself to his hands and knees, and decided the man should live at least long enough to give a complete list of the traitors in the Bundeswehr. Fir got an unsteady knee under himself, and his hand fumbled toward his holstered pistol.

The Executioner yanked the German to his feet and hit him with a short, hard right. Fir rubbernecked and fell back against the SUV. Bolan hit him a second, third and fourth time, flesh tearing and bones breaking beneath his fist. Fir's eyes rolled, and he sagged down the side of the Suburban and sat unconscious, drooling blood. Bolan glanced up as a British Scimitar armored reconnaissance vehicle rumbled through the smoke at the top of the rank. It ran over the wreckage of the first smoking SUV and crushed the remains of the Suburban like a tin can. The turret of the little wedge-shaped tank traversed for the second and pointed accusingly at Bolan.

The big American put up his hands.

The hatch flew open and Colour Sergeant Bourne grinned at Bolan through raccooned eyes and the bandage covering his broken nose. "Well, hullo, Yank!"

Bolan lowered his hands. "Colour Sergeant."

"Brigadier Toler heard a rumor you were headed into town and guessed where you were headed. Figured there might be a bit of a dustup, figured the Royal Marines might lend a hand."

"Very timely."

"The brigadier sends his regards, by the way." Bourne gazed about at the burning wreckage. "It all seems fairly well in hand. Anything else I can do?"

Bolan turned toward the steel door between the garage and the indoor range. "That door is annoying me, and I'm all out of grenades."

"Right!" The Scimitar's turret turned. "I'd cover my ears if I were you."

Bolan covered his ears, and the 30 mm Rarden cannon fired three quick shots that resounded in the garage like thunderbolts from Zeus. Very little remained of the door to speak of.

Bourne hopped down off his vehicle and clicked open the stock of a Sterling submachine gun. "Private! No one gets out of the garage without my express orders."

A voice shouted back up the hatch. "Right, Sergeant!"

Bourne shrugged. "Shall we have a look, then?"

Bolan, Bourne and Frame walked to the shattered entrance while a dozen villagers fanned out behind them. Bolan took point and went through the door with his pistol ready. The range lights were on, but no one appeared to be home. He moved down the range to the target area.

Frame held up his hands back at the firing line. "We got nothing!"

Bolan stared down at a manhole. The cover had not been replaced. He stared down into the darkness, and the smell rising from below told him it went down into the Kabul city sewers.

Frame came downrange. "You got anything?"

"No." Bolan shook his head. He shone his tactical light down, but there was nothing but a pair of dead rats. "Dino's gone." Bolan stared hard at the rats' twisted little bodies, and his instincts spoke to him.

One of the villagers shouted and leaped down the hole with knife and pistol in hand. *"Allah Akhbar!"*

"Wait!" Bolan roared, and he had to tackle Babrak as the young man tried to follow. Bolan rose while still restraining him as the villagers surged forward howling for blood.

Bourne shouted in alarm. "Bloody hell!" He fired a burst into the ceiling. "Back! Back! Back!"

Bolan released Babrak and looked down the hole knowing what he would find. The villager below twisted, foamed and convulsed as he died. No one was going to be following Dinatale through the sewers tonight.

Bourne was appalled. "Bleeding nerve gas! That's bleeding nerve gas!"

Bolan nodded. It was nerve gas, and the last piece of the puzzle had just fallen into place.

21

El Paraiso, Honduras

Cristobal and Enrique Chimeltenago were dead. Dino Dinatale stared at the two corpses. Each man had a hole in his head. The two Mayan brothers were murderers and torturers extraordinaire, but what the two brothers truly excelled at was tracking. Dinatale had used both men and the full gamut of their skills extensively during forays across the border into Nicaragua. They were also the caretakers of Dinatale's house in the highlands.

Dinatale scanned the surrounding hillsides from his front yard.

Only a dirt road led to the house, and the surrounding landscape was almost vertical and thickly forested with only a few navigable trails. Dinatale was intimately familiar with every one of them. He had personally gone out that morning and checked his telltales and booby traps. He had everything from motion sensors and magnetometers to trip-wired grenades and concealed pits full of bamboo stakes smeared with unmentionable filth. Not a leaf had been disturbed. There wasn't a single footprint to be found save his own and those of the brothers, but Deadshot Dinatale could feel it in his bones.

He was here.

The local police had tipped him off that a beautiful helicopter pilot and a very dangerous-looking gringo had landed at Tegucigalpa International Airport a week ago, and then disappeared. Dinatale had sent murder teams throughout the city and set spies on the U.S. Embassy. He had called in every favor he knew with the darker elements of Honduran internal security, but all had come up empty. He had set fresh traps and baited them by letting himself be seen in the district capital, and then he had waited.

Now Cristobal and Enrique were as dead as doornails.

Dinatale glanced around the hills and tried to judge the shot. The sniper had him dead to rights if he was still out there. The question was, why hadn't he? Something might have made him move, or perhaps one of the more primitive, nonalarmed booby traps had taken him, but Dinatale wasn't buying it.

The bastard was out there.

Dinatale smiled to himself. He could feel the asshole watching him right now. He'd bragged about being a better sniper and challenged him to come out and play back in Afghanistan. Dinatale hefted his Blaser 93 tactical rifle. The German weapon was all black plastic and rakish, futuristic angles rather than the warm wood and classic lines of his beloved old Remington, but it was chambered in .300 Winchester Magnum, and he could make thousand-yard shots with it. If Dinatale could get back to the tree line, then the mother of all sniper duels was about to occur, and Dinatale had the home-field advantage. His plan formed. He would head for the Nicaraguan border. Cooper couldn't afford to let him get out of the country, and he'd be forced to follow. Dinatale's mind worked the strategy. He would drag the son of a bitch through the line of his booby traps, and if he evaded those the duel would end when—

Dino Dinatale flinched as a small object fell out of the sky in front of him.

He stared down incredulously at the object stuck in the soft earth. It had fallen points-first and stood up from the soil on its twelve steel spines. The plastic handle of the Afro pick was molded in the form of the Black Power fist.

The bastard was right behind him.

"Hello, Dino."

Dinatale cringed inwardly but kept his voice neutral. "Coop."

"Turn around. Real slow."

Dinatale turned very slowly to find himself staring down the barrels of a .50-caliber Desert Eagle pistol and a Beretta 93-R.

Mack Bolan stared at his opponent. Dino Dinatale was unshaved, unbathed and had dark circles under his eyes, but he was far from defeated and he was clearly vibrating with the need to try to bring his big sniper rifle to bear and blow off Bolan's head.

Dinatale eyed Bolan's pistols. "How'd you find me?"

"You deleted your computer files and fried your hard drive on your way out, but my cybernetic people are better than yours. We retrieved a lot of data, and a lot of your off-the-books money ed here."

Dinatale's eyes flicked around the hills. "So how did you sneak past my safeguards, past the Chimeltanago brothers— ell, how did you sneak past me?"

"I didn't. I parachuted in."

Dinatale blinked. "I paid goddamn good money to be made aware of any overflights of any kind."

Bolan nodded. "You know? I love Honduras, but their air defense radar net just isn't up to B-2 Stealth bombers."

Dinatale simply stared. "You dropped in out of the belly of a stealth?"

"I told you I had access to assets you couldn't dream of, but you didn't listen. But you did listen when I told you I was the better sniper. That got all under your skin, and it itched. And when you heard Connie and I were in-country, you got yourself all excited and cowboyed up to play the sniper game, just like I knew you would. The problem is that I don't play games." Bolan shrugged but his pistols didn't move. "You're problem is that you got played."

Dinatale's knuckles creaked around his rifle.

Bolan read the sniper his rap sheet. "You set up your own Shield contractors to be killed. Poor sons of bitches who worshiped the ground you walked on. You killed your own clients. You killed United States Army Rangers. You trafficked in heroin, human lives, nerve gas and your own kind." Bolan's arctic-blue eyes were as cold as tombstones as they flicked to the pick sticking up in the dirt. "And you killed a friend of mine."

"Fuck him, and fuck you." Dinatale sneered. "What are you my judge and jury?"

"I'm not your judge, and I'm not your jury." The Executioner left the third option unspoken between them.

Dinatale snorted in contempt. "So why am I still breathing?"

"Because the President of the United States asked me to give you one chance to come in."

Dinatale blinked again. "Come in?"

"You served your country, Dino. You can still serve it now. You're famous, a genuine American hero. You can come in, plead guilty, tell everything you know and then go to Leavenworth and show the world that no one is above the law. You won the Congressional Medal of Honor. No U.S. court will give you the death penalty."

Dinatale bared his teeth in an ugly smile. "So, I do the honorable thing and get to rot in a cell for the rest of my life? Nice."

Bolan wasn't smiling. "You can rot right here in the dirt if you prefer."

"Great, so—"

Dinatale moved.

The sniper was snake-strike fast. He tossed the eleven-pound rifle at the muzzles of Bolan's guns and slapped leather for the .45 holstered at his hip.

Bolan fired. A double-tap from the big Desert Eagle and a pair of bursts from the Beretta spun the flying rifle away in a shower of sparks. Dinatale had just cleared leather when Bolan gave him a dose of the same. He fired and kept firing until his pistols ran dry, Dinatale's pistol fell from his fingers and the sniper himself fell to the dirt.

The Executioner let out a long breath and reloaded his pistols. He'd wanted Dinatale alive. But Bolan had given Dinatale his choice.